BLAIR DENHOLM

# DROP SHOT

HARLAN COBEN

# DROP
# SHOT

vinci
BOOKS

## By Blair Denholm

The Fighting Detective

*Fighting Dirty*
*Kill Shot*
*Shot Clock*
*Trick Shot*
*Shot to the Heart*
*Drop Shot*
*Point Blank*
*Moving Target*
*Cold Shot*

Vinci Books

vinci-books.com

Published by Vinci Books Ltd in 2026

1

Copyright © Blair Denholm 2022

The author has asserted their moral right to be identified as the author of this work in accordance with the Copyright, Designs and Patents Act 1988. This work is a work of fiction. Names, characters, places and incidents are the product of the author's imagination or are used fictitiously. Any resemblance to actual persons, living or dead, places and incidents is entirely coincidental.

All rights reserved. No part of this publication may be copied, reproduced, distributed, stored in any retrieval system, or transmitted in any form or by any means, including photocopying, recording, or other electronic or mechanical methods, nor used as a source for any form of machine learning including AI datasets, without the prior written permission of the publisher.

The publisher and the author have made every effort to obtain permissions for any third party material used in this book and to comply with copyright law. Any queries in this respect should be brought to the attention of the publisher and any omissions will be corrected in future editions.

A CIP catalogue record for this book is available from the British Library.
Paperback ISBN: 9781036708276

The EU GPSR authorised representative is Logos Europe, 9 rue Nicolas Poussion, 17000 La Rochelle, France
contact@logoseurope.eu

## Chapter One

THE LATE AFTERNOON sun shimmered like an incandescent disc against a vast lapis canvas. It beat down with a ferocity to match the efforts of the two players, who sizzled tennis balls across the net while the spectators in the stands struggled to raise a cold drink to their lips. The punishing heat, even with nightfall less than half an hour away, helped to create patches of sweat that bloomed on the athletes' clothing. The men had needed to change their sopping shirts and socks at the end of the first set. As a man who grew up in the cooler climes of Great Britain, ex-pat Detective Sergeant Jack Lisbon of the Queensland Police Service was able to sympathise with them. The conditions on court were almost unbearable.

He tugged the brim of his baseball cap lower over his eyes as the sun invaded his line of sight. Jack had almost declined the invitation to attend the tournament, but for a sports fan the opportunity to see a top-ten ranked player in action proved irresistible. Worth putting up with a few hours of outdoor discomfort. His boss, Inspector Joe Batista, had been comped two tickets for him and his wife but, thankfully, they had other plans. The chief passed them on to Jack who gleefully accepted the gift.

As the serving player double faulted and the crowd groaned in sympathy, Jack sensed his partner Detective Constable Claudia Taylor leaning across and into him. It was counterintuitive to back off; her presence usually demanded closer proximity. But the heat was too intense to be rubbing up to another human being, no matter how much you were attracted to them.

The next point was over in a flash. From the left-hand side of the court, the favourite returned serve with a flick of the wrist, the ball scorching past his opponent's desperate outstretched racquet. A ball-boy arched his back to avoid being tagged by the little green missile, which thundered into an advertising sign. The crowd clapped in appreciation of the master's supreme skill. The enthusiasm behind the applause had waned over the course of the match, which, in Jack's opinion, was the most one-sided contest he'd seen since Manny Pacquiao knocked the bejesus out of Ricky Hatton in 2009. Still, the punters had paid their entrance fees and would watch the slaughter to the bitter end. The slack-jawed umpire drawled out the call. *Game McAdam. He leads five games to love, second set.* The players crossed paths at the net post as they headed for their seats before changing ends. The challenger's head hung low and his feet dragged, the champion bouncing and grinning from ear to ear. The world number ten, cocky local lad Roderick McAdam prone to volatile temper tantrums, had only dropped two points in the match. Win the next game – on his own serve – and the match was his. He was in a class of his own against the poor opponent, Sean Depp, a non-ranked player from Perth.

'A closed-roof stadium with air-conditioning is what's

required for this climate,' bemoaned Jack. He used the sleeve of his already drenched t-shirt to mop up droplets of perspiration from the skin between his nose and upper lip. A wasted effort, since new sweat beaded to replace that which had been wiped away. 'This damn humidity's giving me a headache.' He grabbed a bottle of purple Powerade from under his flip-down plastic seat and guzzled the contents like his life depended on it. 'This is the bleedin' tropics. You'd think they'd schedule play for night time, innit?'

'And you'd think a smart bloke like you would know plain old water is better for quenching your thirst than that gimmicky rubbish.'

'Each to their own, Claudia.' He pointed at tiny writing on the label. 'This stuff's got extra vitamins and minerals in it. Replenishes lost energy.'

'Whatever,' she chuckled.

'Give me some ice, will ya.'

Taylor pulled a blue foam cooler box out from under her seat and opened the lid. Jack reached in and took out a handful of ice cubes, rubbed them over his face and dropped a couple of them down the back of his neck and the front of his shirt. He closed his eyes tight as the cubes worked their cooling magic.

Taylor observed his antics goggle-eyed. 'If it's too much for you, just say the word. We can go somewhere else and watch it on TV. From the inside of a pub.'

'Don't be daft.' He waved his hand around. 'Look at all the people here enduring it. Lots of them are old-age pensioners. If they can handle it, so can I.'

Jack took the opportunity of the short break to flick through a program he'd purchased. The tournament, The Pilmer Challenge, was the brainchild of local billionaire sugar magnate Clyde Pilmer. It was a bizarre competition, billed as the tennis equivalent of the old boxing tents, where unknowns could slug it out with travelling professional boxers for a bag full of money. In this case, Pilmer was offering a winner-take-all first prize of five million dollars, dwarfing the money up for grabs at the Australian Open, due to start in two weeks. Only sixteen players – unranked amateurs hand-picked by Pilmer from club competitions around the nation – were admitted to the tournament, with the notable exception of local boy Roderick McAdam, at just 19 years-old already number 10 in the world. McAdam could claim the coveted number one spot in two weeks' time by winning the Australian Open, with the proviso that a couple of top seeds crashed out early. Pilmer had paid all the competitors' travel and accommodation expenses – including for McAdam, the only one who could actually pay his own way. Unheard-of bonus incentives were the bait for the journeymen: $500,000 to take a set off McAdam and $250,000 just to break his serve. McAdam was the lion, the challengers – the lambs to the slaughter.

Jack folded the program and put it back in his pocket. With only four players left in the tournament, so far Pilmer hadn't had to shell out a penny in prize money. In fact, he was raking in the dollars from pay TV deals he'd made with the world's biggest broadcasters. The event was so bizarre it had generated massive interest. Jack understood why. It was like the macabre enjoyment people get from watching a car crash. In any case, it was shaping up as a huge payday for McAdam with the pretenders – barring a miracle – destined to go home empty-handed apart from their fifteen minutes of fame.

The umpire gave a time warning, as the players took every second of their allotted break to sit under broad umbrellas and pour liquids into their dehydrating bodies.

Depp's head disappeared into a water-soaked towel, while McAdam pulled a brand new racquet out of a bag, peeled off the plastic cover and tapped the strings against the palm of his hand. Jack thought it was ridiculous the bloke needed a new weapon to dispatch his teetering foe – he could almost deliver the final knock-out with a ping pong paddle. Young Depp probably couldn't afford to use more than one racquet per match. The umpire called the men back out onto the court in his flat-voweled Aussie drawl.

Jack glanced at his watch. 6:54pm. The sun had just dipped under the horizon, but it would still be light for another hour or so. This was the last match scheduled for the day, and thank God for that. He prayed McAdam would quickly and humanely finish off his victim so everyone could go home. Four aces in a row would be good. He felt the urge to have a wager with Taylor.

'I reckon Depp won't lay a racquet on the ball,' said Jack, waving a twenty-dollar bill in her face. 'And if he does, it's straight into the net or out.'

'Last of the big-time gamblers, huh? OK. You're on, Lisbon. I reckon he can at least win a point.'

*Quiet please*, said the umpire from his little crow's nest. The crowd of a thousand or so spectators at the Yorkville Tennis Centre went silent as one, waiting to see the end to the challenger's abject humiliation in front of a global audience of millions.

Jack focused his eyes on the receiver. He'd been watching Depp more than McAdam for the majority of the match. Most would be looking at McAdam as he prepared to serve, Jack knew that, but this public thrashing interested Jack much more as a psychological study of the inevitable loser.

Depp had started the first game of the match with poise,

immediately wrangling two points off McAdam's opening service game to be up 0–30. Spectators oohed and aahed, anticipating a boilover and the no-name player scoring a massive prize.

But it wasn't to be. Staring at the prospect of a $250,000 payday, Depp either choked or McAdam decided to stop toying with his prey and step on his opponent's throat. McAdam reeled in the points. Bang, bang, bang, game. And with that, Depp was a lame duck with every bit of confidence gone.

A quick glance to the left confirmed that McAdam had finished his five-bounce settling routine. Then Jack shifted his gaze back to Depp. For the first time in the short and brutal match, there was a glimmer of something positive in the unranked player's expression, a spark of determination. Jaw set firmly, feet planted wide, body low and swaying. The guy had made up his mind – he was utterly destroyed but he'd go out swinging. In his peripherals Jack observed the high ball toss, the blur of the racquet as McAdam bent his back and swung up to meet the ball. The *ping* of the ball connecting with the fresh strings of the new implement was like a gunshot. Depp took a wild swing as the ball homed in on his racquet's sweet spot and the ball whistled back low over the net well out of the reach of McAdam, rooted to the spot.

0–15.

A repeat of the oohs and aahs from the first game of the first set. Was there something special about to happen?

Jack heard a soft cough to his left. Taylor, grinning, held out her hand and Jack dropped a twenty note in her palm. She winked a *thank you* and they both looked back to the court.

McAdam flicked his fingers at a ball boy standing

ramrod straight behind the baseline. The kid understood the signal and bounced a ball to the server. McAdam swatted the ball away contemptuously and nodded for another. This one seemed to be to his liking. He took a deep breath and again went through his routine. Five bounces, a flick of sweat from his brow. Jack again fixed his attention on the receiver. More motion in his sway, Depp stood in line with the doubles lane. Whack. Depp had guessed wrong. The ball flew down the centre of the court like a rocket, landing just inside the service box. Depp didn't even try to reach this one.

15–15.

The crowd seemed to lose its hope like a balloon leaking air. The next two points came in the form of a pair of blistering aces.

40–15 and match point. The end would surely come with the next serve. McAdam had found his groove again. Still, Jack observed the receiver.

*Fault*, called the chair umpire.

Depp bounced up and down on his toes again. Jack wasn't sure, but he thought he detected a snarl on the challenger's face, as if he was saying to McAdam, *Bring it, arsehole!*

The second serve dipped over the net with a wicked curl, but swung wide, landing six inches outside the service line. *Double fault*. 40–30. Still match point. This time Jack switched his gaze to McAdam. What was going on?

The champion bounced the ball ten times instead of the trademark five, tossed the ball high, but then backed away at the last second, waving a hand in front of his face. 'These bloody flies!' he yelled. The crowd chuckled. After a shrug of the shoulders and a wipe of his face with a tiny towel tucked in the back of his shorts, he sent down another thunderbolt. Jack's eyes darted to the other side of the net. The ball was an Exocet missile, all Depp could do was desperately block it with the racquet held firmly in front of his face, eyes shut tight. The ball ricocheted off the strings, lobbed high into the air, and then gently plopped over McAdam's head after he'd followed through on his serve all the way to the net. The ball landed a foot inside the line.

*Deuce.*

Now the crowd was wriggling like one big agitated mass of worms. The champ had not had to face a score like this in the first two elimination matches. Spectators were gibbering so loudly the ump had to call for silence again.

*Fault!* The first serve was way long, landing almost at Depp's feet.

Jack wondered what was going through McAdam's brain.

*Double fault!* This one sailed into the net, halfway up.

*Advantage Depp.*

The crowd were on their feet, whistling, stomping and cheering. McAdam bent double, racquet planted handle-end onto the blue surface of the Rebound Ace court, hands on the racquet head and chin resting on the back of his hands. He held the pose for twenty seconds before straightening. At the other end, Depp was hopping up and down like he was walking on a bed of hot coals.

McAdam took a couple of deep breaths, performed the standard routine. The serve took Depp by surprise – half strength and with a vicious swing to the left. Depp scrambled, returned with a weak sliced backhand that clipped the top of the net before landing half-way down the court, sitting up nicely for McAdam to destroy any way he chose. McAdam uncoiled his body and let rip with a scorching forehand cross-court passing shot.

## Drop Shot

*Deuce,* said the umpire.

A roar went up from the crowd. Jack and Taylor were screaming too, but not in appreciation of McAdam's skill. The ball was clearly out, everyone could see it – except for the lineswoman and the chair umpire. The game – and $250,000 – was rightfully Depp's.

Jack turned to Taylor. 'Did you see that? Six inches out!'

Taylor didn't reply as she screwed up her eyes, focussing on the reaction of the wronged player. Jack watched Depp, too. The man wasn't going to take this travesty of justice lying down. Instead of approaching the umpire to complain, Depp threw his racquet to one side, marched to the net, clasped both hands together imploringly. The crowd went silent, eager to hear the exchange.

'What the hell are you playing at?' said Depp. Courtside microphones picked up the chat and delivered it to the spectators over loudspeakers.

'I'm playing by the rules.' McAdam wore an affronted expression. 'Now, go back and prepare to receive so I can finish you off.'

'C'mon, Rod, I won the game. Don't do this, mate!' Depp was a lightly built man who looked far from intimidating, but one could imagine smoke pouring from his ears.

'Do what?' McAdam stared at his fingernails.

'Be a man and concede the point to me. Everyone saw the ball was a mile out.' Depp looked up at the mass of people in the stand opposite the umpire, cupped his hands to his mouth. 'Didn't you?' he hollered.

'YES!' came the almost unanimous reply.

McAdam shook his head. 'Mate, I didn't see it. I have to trust the officials, there's no challenge procedure in place, no hawk-eye technology. We all knew that when we signed up.' He shrugged. 'The officials are paid good money to make the calls, not me.'

The remark about the money seemed a deliberate provocation. Depp had just been deprived of the equivalent of a lottery win to your average Joe. A life-changing event for a man who was no more than a very good pennant-level tennis player.

'You're a dirty cheat, McAdam. An arrogant son of a bitch!' He pointed an accusing forefinger at the trembling lineswoman, 'You!', and then at the chair umpire, who's face was granite-calm despite the unfolding melodrama... 'and you! You two are a fucking disgrace. Paid off by Pilmer to make sure that bastard wins everything!'

A large section of the crowd cheered approvingly. The world number ten enjoyed a reputation as one of the tennis tour's bad boys, a modern-day John McEnroe for whom winning meant everything. McAdam decided to rub salt into the wound. 'Nobody cares about your opinion, whatever your name is.'

The same section of the audience that cheered Depp now booed McAdam, who had far fewer fans in the stands now that he'd decided to play hardball with the underdog. But he wasn't about to change tack to placate his detractors, no matter how loud and numerous. 'You're cooked, son. I won the point fair and square. But hang in there, it's back to deuce. You'll just have to try harder to earn that cash for breaking my serve. How much was it again? Oh yeah, a quarter of a million dollars.' McAdam tilted his head back and roared with laughter.

In the blink of an eye, Depp had jumped the net and was right up in McAdam's grill. Their heated conversation was white-noise, each screaming obscenities at the other, noses inches apart. Within fifteen seconds, four men in black shirts had raced onto the court, two quickly restrained Depp as he cocked his right arm ready to throw a punch. They pulled him away as the two other goons stood like bodyguards in front of the millionaire sports star, arms folded across their chests.

'Holy hell,' said Taylor. 'If this weird-arse tournament on its own doesn't get Yorkville on the world map, that scuffle certainly will.' She pointed at the prostrate figure of Depp the aggressor, restrained by two bald gorillas from Pilmer's security team.

'You're not wrong,' Jack laughed. 'This is better than pro wrestling. But I feel sorry for the lad.'

'Robbed blind, I'd say. But we've certainly got our money's worth.' Taylor held her phone aloft, as did a large percentage of the crowd. It reminded Jack of fans at rock concerts, more concerned with getting a memento than actually enjoying the show.

Jack slugged more Powerade, gestured towards Taylor's mobile. 'You getting a video for Facebook?'

'No. Evidence. In case it gets really nasty and someone gets hurt.'

Jack had to call bullshit on that one. 'Rubbish. There's TV cameras everywhere getting it all on tape. The hired muscle seem to have it under control.'

'Actually, you *were* right,' she grinned, caught out on her little fib. 'Almost. It's for Instagram. Facebook is so yesterday.'

'Is it now?' Jack's relationship with social media was like the one he had with his ex-wife. Infrequent and troublesome.

All eyes and ears were fixated on the running scrum at the eastern end of centre court. The security detail escorted a wriggling and screaming Depp off centre stage, through a dark tunnel and, presumably, into the dressing room. Just before disappearing, Depp managed to turn around and offer a parting word, clearly audible to everyone. 'You're fucked, McAdam!' He tried to yell out something else but one of the security men wrapped a hand around Depp's mouth and muffled the words.

The umpire waited for the excited crowd to pipe down, which took a good five minutes. Once he'd obviously decided full silence was not returning, he ploughed on through the hubbub, thanked all the on-court officials, players and ball boys and girls, and especially the sponsor, Pilmer Enterprises. All the while, McAdam sat motionless in his plastic chair, head covered by a lime-green towel, as his coach massaged his shoulders.

Pilmer would be rubbing his hands with glee, thought Jack. Outstanding publicity. A packed auditorium and off-the-charts TV ratings would be guaranteed for tomorrow's final against…Jack had to consult the program again…a Tasmanian left-hander called Hugh Marshall.

A reporter from a major network tried to interview McAdam. She only got two questions into it before she had to abandon the attempt. The aggravated crowd's renewed jeering was too much. Microphone by her side, she headed for the safety of the exit.

Bag slung over his shoulder, McAdam smiled and waved triumphantly even as the spectators saw him off with another barrage of whistles, boos and insults under a shower of food and drink containers.

In the blink of an eye, Australia's misunderstood golden boy had become its most hated athlete.

## Chapter Two

'DID you enjoy the tennis last night, DS Lisbon?' asked Yorkville Police Station's lanky boss, Inspector Joe Batista. 'I heard there was a huge drama at the end of the match.'

Jack took a sip of his take-away double-espresso, set the paper cup back on his desk and started rolling up his shirt-sleeves. 'That's an understatement, guv. I've never seen anything like it. You don't happen to have any tickets for the final tonight, do you?' The final, as opposed to the daytime preliminary matches, was scheduled for 8:00pm, under lights. On his drive in to work Jack heard over the radio that McAdam had demanded the organisers switch the time or else he'd walk and the event wouldn't go any further. Despite three easy victories – the last one via Depp's disqualification for unsportsmanlike behaviour – he claimed his body was beginning to wilt in the lead up to the Australian Open, something he couldn't tolerate further despite the enormous prize money on offer. He had the world number one ranking in his sights, after all.

The chief shook his head. 'Sadly, no, DS Lisbon. But

why would you want to watch a repeat of that fiasco? To be honest, the whole concept doesn't sit right with me. It's like a public execution.'

'I don't know,' said Taylor hopefully. 'With the entire country behind him, the Tassie kid might actually have a chance. He slaughtered his three opponents on the other side of the draw.'

Jack tapped a couple of keys on his work computer to log in. 'And who were they, Claudia? Worthy adversaries or third-rate wannabes like poor old Sean Depp.'

She raised her shoulders in a mini shrug. 'I don't know.'

'I'll tell you in a minute.' Jack picked up a copy of *The Yorkville Times*, licked his finger and flicked to the sports section. 'Looks like Pilmer's been sourcing his victims from far and wide. Facing off against McAdam in the final is Hugh Marshall. Top-ranked amateur in Tasmania.' He leaned back in his swivel chair and cracked a couple of knuckles before resuming his perusal of the paper. His hands ached slightly from an overly enthusiastic session with the heavy bag after his morning jog. 'And Claudia, you're dead right. Marshall flogged the three blokes on the other side of the draw as easily as McAdam beat his opponents. He's booted out, lemme see, Charles Jalin from Melbourne, Quinn Chapman from Sydney and Craig Young from Adelaide. Score lines of 6–0, 6–0, same as McAdam.'

'Doesn't mean this Marshall has a hope against McAdam, though,' said Taylor. 'The difference in ability is like chalk and cheese.'

'True.' Jack nodded. 'Plus there's the fact McAdam is a full-time pro while the other blokes are part-timers.' He took another sip of coffee. 'But even so, it looks like whoever organised the draw wanted the strongest of the also-rans safe from McAdam so the amateur could at least have a chance in the final. Might even get that $250,000 Depp missed out on.'

'Let's see how much of a chance this guy is.' Taylor clicked on her mouse, adjusted her glasses and peered intently at the screen. Jack could see the list of search engine results reflected in Taylor's glasses. She clicked the second link in the list. 'It says here Marshall was a hot prospect as a junior, but he was hit by tragedy and dropped out of the tennis scene for a number of years.'

'What happened?' said Constable Ben Wilson from his desk on the other side of the office. 'The story's ringing bells.'

'Oh my God!' cried Taylor.

'What?' Wilson again.

'His mother and father were murdered in their beds seven years ago. Poor kid.' She took a sip of tea before fixing her attention back on the computer. 'The culprit was never caught. Marshall himself was a suspect at the beginning.'

'Incredible.' Jack sat up straight.

'Hang on, here's a link to an interview he gave after he was asked to play in the Pilmer Challenge. Marshall was seventeen when his mum and dad were killed. He had a complete mental breakdown. Hobart detectives had him under a microscope for two years before they finally cut him loose as a suspect. There was incriminating DNA evidence at the scene, but there was also other DNA that couldn't be identified. Plus it was impossible to find a motive; the parents died penniless and there was no inheritance. After the murder he moved in with an auntie. Four years of therapy and serious medication. One day he decided enough was enough, applied for university and earned himself a science degree. He's currently working as a marine biologist in Hobart, Tasmania.'

'Anything more about the murder investigation?' said Jack eagerly.

'Not in this article. The questions in the second half of the piece are about him rebuilding his life.' Her lips moved as she read in silence. Then she concluded, 'He went back to tennis to keep fit, the early natural talent returned and he soared to the top of the amateur ranks in Tasmania.'

Batista coughed into his fist. 'Ah, as much as I find this whole soap opera fascinating, don't we have some important police work to do?'

Taylor removed her reading glasses, tied her dark hair back with a yellow scrunchie and smiled at the chief. 'Indeed we have, sir. A big drugs case, as it happens.'

'Operation Antarctic Freeze,' said Batista. 'It's up before the magistrate today, right?'

'Correct,' Taylor nodded. 'Jack and I have to give evidence and Constable Wilson here's assisting. We're about to put our lippy on and head over to the courthouse in...' she glanced at her watch... 'two minutes.'

'Good luck with the testimony,' Batista smiled encouragingly. 'I understand you've drawn Nunez as the magistrate. She's a hard nut to crack when it comes to punishing street crime.' The chief stroked his wedge of a chin.

'Yeah, it's old Barbara,' said Jack. 'But no need for luck, guv. We've got enough evidence to put away an entire government. Even Nunez won't be able to ignore it.' He shut down his computer, gathered together an unruly pile of manila folders. 'By the way, DC Taylor, what colour lipstick would you suggest for me?' said Jack.

'Black, to match your soul.'

'Very droll. But since we're prosecuting a bunch of Goths, I guess it might be appropriate.'

'Emos,' said Taylor, picking up a set of keys and her mobile phone.

'Yes, I've read the emails,' replied Jack with mock tetchiness. 'We're all set to go.'

She spun around, hands on hips. 'Seriously, DS Lisbon. Is my Australian accent still causing you problems?'

'Nah,' he winked. 'I know what emos are. And all the other subcultures. Hipsters, skinheads, stoners. What I wanna know is this: where have all the punks gone?' He bent over to retrieve a Spirax notepad from his top drawer, kept prattling on. 'I was a punk with a razorblade for an earring once upon a time, can you believe it?'

'Gimme a break, Jack.'

'It's true. I was in this gang of punks who...' He stood to continue the tale but found himself talking to the empty space Taylor once occupied – she was already at the exit clutching a shiny black briefcase, shoulder to shoulder with Constable Wilson, making for the car park.

---

TODAY, the accused six men and one woman would front the magistrate's court to learn whether there was a case to answer. Did the evidence stack up and would the matter proceed to trial in the supreme court? Would they be granted bail or remanded in custody? And, most importantly for Jack, could the beak wrap it up quickly so he could make his lunch date with gym queen Marietta Szabo? She'd given him another chance after he made a right cock-up of things last time and he was determined to make amends. Marietta wasn't his first pick for a girlfriend – he had a massive crush on Taylor but every time he thought he might summon the courage to do something about it, he put his foot in his mouth or did something stupid. He sensed the attraction was mutual, she gave off signals, but often they were of the "mixed" variety. *One day, Jack. One day.*

But for now, it was all about the arraignment.

Jack exchanged a smile with Taylor to his left and Wilson to his right. Their confidence was sky-high. The team for the state's prosecution were about to present wheelbarrow loads of proof at this summary hearing, both material and witness statements, so much, in fact, that Jack wondered why the defense lawyers had even bothered to put together a counter strategy. However, before proceeding to a full trial, there was the theatrical charade of the magistrate's court to get through.

The petite and bespectacled magistrate, Barbara Nunez, who, if one were to go by her frizzy grey hair and abundant wrinkles, should have retired more than five years ago, summarised the formalities of procedure, mainly for the benefit of the accused. Jack had been through this so many times he didn't even listen – like when the safety drill gets performed on an airplane.

Due to the seriousness of the crimes committed by the accused, the police expected every single one them would be held in remand until a full trial could be conducted. Knowing the magistrate's liberal reputation, though, all were prepared for leniency. Nunez concluded the warm-up routine and called upon the police to present their evidence.

Jack stood and opened a manila folder. 'Your Honour, if I may beg the court's indulgence for a moment.'

Nunez rolled her eyes. 'Please be relevant, DS Lisbon. Without your usual rambling. I've got a number of other matters to get through.'

Jack coughed. 'Of course, your Honour. No extraneous details. Even though this is *by far* the most important case you'll be presiding over today, or perhaps this year.' He smiled, picked up a piece of paper, and wasted no time before Nunez could respond to his remark. 'North Queensland's drug trade has been dealt a rather disruptive blow following our arrest – in conjunction with the Cairns Drug Squad – of seven people on almost 40 charges.' He paused and glanced at the assemblage of dark-clothed men and one woman behind the defense tables – some stared at their hands, others off into the distance, one blinked like a mole emerging into the sunshine. Their pale faces contrasted with their black attire and eye make-up. A couple of years inside would deprive these vampires of even more hateful sunlight; they might view a stretch in jail as a not entirely bad thing. Until they were inevitably made somebody's bitch, that was.

'Our investigations into the supply chain have uncovered storefront establishments across Far North Queensland that were used to launder money from the sale of class A drugs. We allege the group's directors, who those accused today are refusing to name but who we hope to also arrest before the end of the month, used the people before the court to launder in excess of $1.5 million dollars.

'Detectives seized 1kg of crystal methamphetamine with a street value of $1,000,000 and ecstasy tablets worth $500,000. A sophisticated lab was discovered at 98 Voss Street, Thurston, from which all equipment and materials for the production of ice have been confiscated.'

Jack sat and Taylor took over. She described the role each of the accused played in the activities of the syndicate. Then, she asked a court official to show a half-hour video of body-cam footage from the dawn raids. The magistrate watched with interest, wide eyes glued to the TV monitor.

The vision began with blue-gloved officers swinging a battering ram to bash down the front door of the Voss Street house, the serving of a search warrant on the sleepy-eyed accused, and the discovery of evidence. She and Wilson took turns clarifying what the footage from the raids showed in relation to the narcotics themselves, large bundles of cash, paraphernalia for making, weighing and bagging drugs, passports and firearms.

Having listened to everything Jack and his team had to say, then mitigating statements from the accused's representative, Barbara Nunez declared she would now make her ruling.

'The accused are not king-pins, but misguided pawns drawn in by the lure of quick money,' Nunez pronounced, her soft voice like a feather floating on a gentle breeze. 'They were sucked into a dangerous game, having been chronically unemployed and, let's be frank, coming from disadvantaged backgrounds. However, due to the serious nature of the charges and their unwillingness to name their controllers, I hereby order all of the defendants to be remanded in custody until a time for trial can be set.' Her words made Jack catch his breath, stunned the small gallery, press contingent and the defence lawyers into silence and made the accused burst into tears.

Conferring in a café after the hearing, the cops knew there was still a lot more work to do. The pack-mule Emos may have been taken care of, however the ringleaders still seemed untouchable. The level of threat was so great, not a single one of the accused was brave enough to point the finger.

'I'm not phased by their unwillingness to rat out their bosses.' Jack reached for a buttered date scone. 'We know who they are and we've got plenty of witnesses lined up from the Cairns station's detectives. I wouldn't be surprised if–'

He didn't get a chance to finish speaking his thoughts as Taylor returned from the service counter, cup of cappuccino wobbling in one hand, phone pressed to her ear with the other. 'What the...?' she exclaimed, placing the cup on the table with a rattle of spoon against china. Jack and Wilson jumped back in their seats to avoid getting splashed. 'Yes, of course, sir. We'll be there right away.'

Jack shot her an earnest frown. 'Wassup, Claudia? Have the Emos rolled over and spilled their guts?'

'That was Batista. Nothing to do with Operation Antarctic Freeze. You aren't going to believe this, guys.'

'What?' said Wilson, eyes bugging out like a demented insect.

'Looks like Roderick McAdam's not going to be playing tonight.'

'Come again?' said Jack. 'I've got five-hundred dollars riding on him winning the Aussie Open. And another five on him becoming World No.1.'

'You've done your money, Jack. He's dead.'

## Chapter Three

JACK MASHED spicy cinnamon-flavoured gum to help him concentrate on his driving as he sped across town to the Gasnier Hotel. Or the Hotel Gasnier. The sign above the front door simply said "Gasnier". Locals were divided on exactly what to call the place with opinion leaning slightly towards the latter. Most gave it the succinct epithet – The Gaz.

    Jack swore softly under his breath as traffic lights changed to red 50 metres ahead. He pushed in the clutch and flick-finger shifted down until the zippy Kia Stinger slowed to a halt. A check of the luminous dash clock – traffic was light this time of day and they should arrive at the crime scene in less than 15 minutes. The pub-slash-doss house was located near an industrial estate on the edge of the city limits. The Hotel Gasnier had a reputation as one of Yorkville's seediest accommodation establishments. Jack remembered three knifings and two bashings were reported there mid last year. Thankfully no one was killed. The Gaz was known as a hot-sheet joint, with rooms rented out by the hour to local prostitutes and their johns in the afternoons. When the sun went down it transformed into a hive for similar activities but with guests paying the full rate for an overnight stay. The hotel sat on the main highway north to Cairns, with clients often out-of-town truck drivers and other itinerant types as well as randy locals looking for a place to cheat on their spouse.

'Who found him?' Jack asked Taylor. 'Did Batista say?'

'The housekeeper. Apparently she dropped her bucket and mop and screamed the place down when she opened the door and saw McAdam on the bed. The hotel manager telephoned the station immediately after he confirmed the death with his own eyes.'

'This is the biggest thing ever to happen in Yorkville,' said Constable Wilson from the back seat. His eyes shone like stars in the rear vision mirror. 'Did Batista tell you anything else?'

'No,' said Taylor. 'Just to get our arses over there, pronto.'

'We'd better do as the boss says, then,' said Jack as he popped the clutch. Tyres squealed on hot tarmac as the car rocketed off to an appointment with a corpse.

---

JACK PULLED up at the corner of Crilly and Dauth Streets, so wide you could land large aircraft on them if not for the jumble of power lines spanning the tarmac, and yanked on the handbrake. The three officers clambered out of the airconditioned vehicle only to be assaulted by the ever-present blistering heat. Bright and strong and vicious, the sun tossed down scorching laser beams. They wasted no time hustling inside the grand old dame of a hotel. The high ceilings and slowly rotating fans brought some relief from the sticky heat, but not much.

The manager, a thickset middle-aged man in high-waisted shorts, checked collared shirt and sandals with long socks undoubtedly held up with elastic bands, greeted them at reception. He extended a hand to Jack, then Taylor. Wilson stood back, allowing the senior officers to do the talking. 'I'm the owner, Rudy Greer. Thank God you're here,' he said breathlessly. Sweat beaded on a heavily lined forehead. Jack quickly detected the unmistakable odour of freshly consumed overproof Bundaberg rum and cigarettes on his breath and body stink from his armpits. 'This is a terrible tragedy. I hope you can get to the bottom of it quickly. I can't afford the bad publicity.'

Jack locked eyes with the owner to further gauge his disposition. 'I'm afraid we're going to have to declare the entire hotel a crime scene.'

Greer looked away from Jack. 'Not the whole place, surely? What about the guests already here?'

'How many are there?' said Taylor.

'Well…ah…none at the moment. We're waiting for the…ah.'

'I know what you're waiting for,' Jack scoffed. 'The lunchtime hookers. I know this hotel's reputation for dodgy dealings and…' Jack paused '…violence.'

'Sure, we've had some unsavoury incidents over the years, but no murders. For heaven's sake, what do you—'

'We haven't got all day,' interrupted Jack, holding up his badge wallet. Taylor did the same. Wilson did nothing – his uniform was his ID. 'Where's the body?'

'Room 201. Please, follow me,' Greer beckoned with a

sideways nod. 'It's not far.' His voice betrayed a fatalistic attitude to the inevitable downturn in trade, the duration of which would be anyone's guess.

The officers followed the owner's awkward, shuffling gait up a set of richly carpeted stairs flanked by ornately carved balustrades. The building was a classic example of colonial Queenslander architecture, a thing of beauty in stark contrast to the ugly trade carried out within her walls. Twenty metres down a long and broad corridor, Greer extracted a key on a string from his shorts pocket and went to open the door. 'Wait, there's a key already in there. That'll save me the bother.' He tucked what was clearly a universal key to all the rooms back into his pants. 'He's... ah...in there. Shall I come in, too?'

'No.'

Greer sighed with relief.

'Wait downstairs and send the forensics team up here when they arrive.' Jack cast a glance at his watch. 'Which shouldn't be too long now.'

The man touched a forefinger, yellow-tan from years of nicotine addiction, to the side of his nose. 'Will do, Detective.' He turned and shuffled away, shoulders slumped. As he reached for the handrail at the top of the stairs, Jack yelled out. 'And tell the housekeeper to hang around, we'll be needing her statement.'

Greer turned and offered Jack a guilty frown. 'Oh dear. She was so shook up I sent the woman home.'

'Bad move. You should've kept her here.' Jack rubbed the bridge of his nose. Years of sin and debauchery had created a musky stink that had leached into the woodwork and the carpets and right now was making his sinuses throb. 'Ring her and tell her not to venture off anywhere and to expect a visit from us. We'll be needing her address.' The owner stood still, as if he'd turned to granite. Jack gave him a flick of a wave. 'Go on then!' Jack watched the man's head disappear as he descended the stairs. 'I'll be down to get a proper statement from you when we're done here. Don't leave the premises.'

The DS gathered his thoughts, then gestured for Taylor to enter the room. 'Ladies first.'

'Thanks,' she replied, with not a trace of gratitude. 'But I'd like to invoke the Queensland Police Service secret protocol.'

'And what's that?'

'Age before beauty.' Taylor took a step backwards, treading on Wilson's foot and drawing an oath from the unfortunate constable.

Jack tut-tutted and shook his head in bewilderment at a senior officer so squeamish she'd resort to such inane tactics. Inside, he was laughing his head off.

---

THE TENNIS STAR'S still body lay sprawled across the bed, lying on his right side, naked apart from a pair of dark blue boxer shorts. A small pile of vomit pooled next to his mouth and more puke encrusted his puffed-up lips. A wet patch marked his underwear at the front and about a quarter of the off-white bedsheet where he'd lost control of his bladder. This was by no means a bloody execution – there were just a few faint red dots lining the sheet next to McAdam's neck. Two flat, manky pillows were propped under his feet and the bedspread lay crumpled like an afterthought on the floor by the entrance to the bathroom. A ceiling fan whirred softly overhead like the beating of a hummingbird's wings. An old, wall-mounted Mitsubishi air-conditioner, flecked with mould around the vent, groaned but failed to cool the room as its manufacturer intended. In other words, the joint was as hot as an oven.

Jack's nose twitched. The room smacked of vodka and cannabis. The sources of the odours sat on a dresser table – a half-empty bottle of Smirnoff, two shot glasses, one rimmed with red lipstick, and an ashtray with two crushed-out roaches. The oddest thing about the crime scene, though, was the unnatural way the victim had been trussed up. Taylor let out a gasp.

And if a moment before Jack had been laughing on the inside, now he was in a mild state of shock. It was such a bizarre way to kill a person. He'd seen plenty of brutally slain human beings, but this origami-murder was a first.

'Holy shit,' he muttered under his breath. 'This looks ritualistic. Maybe satanic.'

'Bloody hell,' said Wilson, his broad shoulders spanning the doorway two metres behind his superiors. 'Like something out of a horror movie.' It was obvious he was itching to eyeball the victim from closer up. Since they'd got the call he'd barely paused to stop rambling about the drama the crime was going to create in the city, the country, the world! The lad would have to wait his turn to get his fix of the macabre.

Jack started thinking how this case would be presented to the outside world. All hell would break loose once word got out. He sensed a series of migraines was also inevitable.

'What on Earth happened here?' said Taylor, absently fiddling with her scrunchie. 'I...geez...' Her legs buckled slightly at the knees.

Jack noted a pallor spreading in his partner's cheeks, her chest heaving. He grabbed her by the forearm, tried to guide her towards a heavily stained fabric armchair. She pushed his arms away in protest. 'No need, Jack. I'm OK. It's just…I've never seen anything like this.'

He let go, left her standing next to the closed and curtained window, and stood door-side of the queen size bed. Jack leaned over the bed for a closer look at the victim, Taylor remained about a foot from the edge of the bed, only her eyes moving left and right. After a few moments she said, 'Don't touch anything, will you Jack. The ambulance hasn't even arrived to confirm he's actually dead.'

Jack's gnarled forefinger pointed at the deceased's dark blue lips and protruding tongue, then to the bulging eyes almost sticking out on their optic stalks. 'The maid could see he was dead. So could the owner.' He turned and beckoned for Wilson to come closer, eliciting an excited hop and skip from the constable. 'What do you reckon, sunshine?'

'Dead for sure.' The grotesqueness of the corpse's face dented the constable's initial enthusiasm. He briskly retreated to his guard position.

'And for your benefit, Claudia, I'll check myself to confirm.' Jack held a hand over McAdam's nose and mouth, bent his ear to the same area. 'Not a puff of breath.' He donned a pair of rubber gloves, gently took the victim's wrist. 'No pulse. I'm no doctor, but—'

'OK, OK.' Taylor abandoned her position and slumped in the chair she'd just declined. 'Enough, I get it.'

'Sorry about that,' said Jack. 'Might have gone a bit too far there.'

'No need to apologise.' Taylor shook her head. 'I'm used to your lame sarcasm.'

Jack pressed on with his examination of the freakish scene, paying particular attention to the elaborate way the man had been hogtied. He extracted his mobile and took photos from various angles. The victim, the surrounds, the vodka and reefers, under the bed, the empty bathroom and the inside of a small mirrored wall cabinet. Proper pictures would be taken when the forensics photographer arrived, but the DS liked to have his own set of crime scene snaps for reference.

Phone tucked away in his pocket again, Jack stood back a metre and took it all in. A piece of greyish cloth – on close inspection a towelling face washer – lay a few inches from the victim's mouth. Black fishnet tights were the apparent tool of execution. It looked like three pairs tied together; they stretched from McAdam's bound ankles and along the length of his obscenely arched back. Thence the stockings ran between bound wrists, finally forming a loop around the neck.

Jack recalled reading about a similar case back in the UK. An Eastern European sex worker had been murdered with her own lingerie in Soho fifteen years ago and the killer was never found. From memory, it was deemed by investigators that the victim's legs became exhausted as she tried to maintain the pose that prevented the nylon pulley system from engaging. The poor girl had ostensibly killed herself when her strength packed it in, her legs retracted and she choked to death. There may be another cause of death in this instance, but that would be up to Dr Margaret Procter and her forensics team to determine. The puke around his mouth hinted at a potential drug overdose. However at first glance, Jack would stake his beloved Toyota Hilux on this being the same MO as the Soho case. The booze and drugs would most likely have been an ice-breaker to relax the victim, put him off his guard. One question hung in the air for Jack.

'Why was McAdam even at this shithole the day before the final of the Pilmer Challenge?'

'No idea.' said Taylor. 'I've got another question. Where the hell are his clothes?'

'Good point,' Jack noted. 'There seems to be no belongings – no clothes at all that I can see apart from the boxer shorts he's got on, no mobile phone, wallet, nothing. The perp's carted all his stuff away and disposed of it, I'd say. Burned or buried the clothes and ditched the mobile in the sea somewhere would be my guess.'

'That's going to make things tough.' Taylor paused for a moment. 'I can't believe forensics haven't arrived yet.' She stared at one of half a dozen initials and obscenities scribbled on the wall a metre above the bedhead. 'What the hell's holding them up?'

'Want me to call in and see what's happening?' said Wilson. 'They should've arrived by now.'

As if on cue, the clunking of closing car doors echoed up from the street.

Margaret Proctor soon appeared, leather bag in hand. 'Someone order a pathologist?' The chief scientist's voice was deep, to match her tall and robust frame. A slight dip of the head as she greeted the officers. Proctor favoured light-green makeup to enhance her sparkling grey eyes but shunned all other forms of cosmetics. Once she'd informed Jack that women can consume a lot of lipstick over a lifetime, up to 3 kg every 10 years. She gave a rumbling harrumph as she elbowed her way past Wilson and lumbered into the room. A much shorter assistant scampered in close behind, kitted out like Proctor in a disposable white jumpsuit, blue rubber gloves and shoe covers. Proctor shot Jack her no-nonsense glare. 'It's mighty crowded in here, chaps. Let's have a quick heads up on initial impressions of the scene and then I'd request the three of you wait downstairs for a bit. I want to minimise contamination by you guys. You've probably buggered things up already.'

'Do me a favour, will ya Margaret?' said Jack. 'We're not bumbling amateur sleuths. We've kept well clear of the victim and been careful not to touch anything. Much.' He held up his gloved hand to drive home the point. 'I only checked his pulse – or should I say lack of pulse – to prove to Claudia that Mr. McAdam was dead.'

'Right,' said Proctor. 'It's immediately obvious that this is no run-of-the-mill murder. And we're not dealing with some average Joe here, either. This is a high-profile victim.'

'What are you implying, Margaret?' said Taylor. 'Dead celebrities require more thorough investigation than "average Joes" as you put it?'

Jack coughed into his fist. 'Claudia's right. Yorkville Police don't play favourites. If this was a tramp lying here, we'd be just as focused on getting a result.'

'That may be true,' agreed Proctor. 'I probably didn't express myself properly. But there's no getting around the enormous interest this is going to create.' She looked alternately at Jack and Taylor. 'You two are going to face intense media questioning. The town will be crawling with interstate press, foreign journalists. Plus the Internet's going to explode.'

'Well,' said Jack, stuffing a pellet of gum in his mouth and giving it a couple of chews. 'We can always second officers from elsewhere in the state if we have to in order to get this murder solved.'

Jack then briefed Proctor on what they'd learned so far, which wasn't much, apart from the fact Roderick McAdam was definitely *not* going to be claiming the world number one tennis ranking. 'Now it's up to you to work your magic, Margaret.'

'Thank you for the vote of confidence, DS Lisbon.' Proctor placed her leather kitbag on the floor next to the entrance to the bathroom. She bent over, unzipped the bag and with her head tilted said, 'I'd appreciate you officers giving me and Carla some space now so we can give the scene a thorough examination and gather evidence while it's still warm, so to speak.' She donned a disposable facemask and stood up to her full imposing height. Her assistant, newbie Carla Littlejohn, gave a nervous smile and also masked up. Proctor said, 'Give us an hour or two and we should be done.'

'Can you at least give us an approximate time of death before we leave?' said Jack. 'That knowledge can be mighty useful when questioning suspects.'

'You are an impatient man, aren't you?' The chief scientist walked around the body, touched the forehead. 'I'd say he's been dead for less than twelve hours. I can't be more precise than that without a proper examination of the victim. Back at the lab I'll be using a novel methodology where I can get you a time to within 45 minutes.'

'Impressive,' said Taylor. 'That will really help us to compare the TOD with suspects' alibis.'

'I hadn't thought of that, but yes, good point,' agreed Proctor. 'A team of Dutch scientists recently conducted a study and found that measuring potassium in the eye and analysing proteins in tissue can give a much more accurate result than standard temperature, rigor mortis and lividity parameters.'

Jack, dizzy from Proctor's geek speak, thanked her and agreed to meet back at the mortuary where he and Taylor would next be viewing McAdam – on the slab. Apparently the victim's parents were in town for the tournament, so they'd be called upon to officially identify the body at some stage.

'Never a pleasant duty for relatives,' said Proctor. She then turned to Constable Wilson and handed him a roll of yellow crime scene tape. She said to Jack, 'Alright if he hangs about after he's strung this up? To keep sticky beaks away.'

'Good idea.'

Jack instructed Wilson to run the tape across the doorway to the room and the front entrance to the hotel, where he was to stand guard until further notice. He then rang Batista to inform the chief that Proctor was on hand and the scene had been secured. He also suggested a call be made to the Pilmer Challenge organisers to let them know their star attraction wouldn't be fronting and to contact all ticket holders to let them know the tournament was off.

'I'm not telling anyone about McAdam's death until the parents have formally identified the body,' said Batista. 'Only then will we alert the press as per usual. And any other interested parties. I've already had the Assistant Commissioner on the phone. She's offered us every assistance in getting this solved.'

'Good news, sir.' As much as Jack enjoyed the glory of cracking cases with the support of his own team, the reality was, this time they'd need help.

'Follow protocol precisely,' Batista continued. 'Do everything by the book. All eyes will be on us. You hear me, Lisbon? No unorthodox nonsense from you or we all suffer the consequences.'

'Gottcha.' Jack had never heard Batista so rattled. His performance as head of Yorkville Police was exemplary, earning him a string of commendations since his move from Brisbane in the late 1990s. A man with a cool head for a crisis. Or so Jack thought. There had been an upturn in murder cases in the last couple of years, and the chief had handled each with poise. But this murder would test him like no other before. Was the Inspector about to crack? Jack knew he had to try and curb his own tendencies to ignore the rules. Easier said than done. 'You can count on me and Claudia, sir.' He ended the call and drew a deep breath.

## Chapter Four

THE STOCKINGS CAUGHT on his two-day-old stubble as he dragged them slowly across his face. He pressed his nose to the material and inhaled deeply, savouring the just-out-of-the-packet freshness. He wouldn't sniff used ones. He wasn't a weirdo or anything like that. They were a beige pair this time. Just cheap tights from the bargain bin, $1.50. He used cash, just like for the other pairs he'd picked up at the same store. You can't be too careful.

He held the new stockings at arms length, gave them a good stretch. Then he wrapped them around his hands until he'd fashioned a soft garotte. Another tug or two and the material stretched taut. Not as effective as a proper wire garotte with dowel sticks on each end, like the ones spies use in the movies, but it'd do in a pinch if you had to assassinate an enemy. Not that he'd actually strangle anyone with his own hands. That was out of the question. These cheapie nylons were intended for another purpose. A more mundane one. They were rather drab compared to the fishnet black numbers that did in Roderick McAdam. To be fair, though, it was technically a suicide. If he'd really wanted to live he'd have made sure he kept those athletic legs nice and bent at the knees. But no, maintaining an unbearable pose for three hours had proved too hard. Even McAdam's superior fitness couldn't save him.

It was an ingenious method. A bit of searching online for macabre ways to kill turned up this beauty. Complete with a diagram. But not so surprising, when you consider the web hosts instructions for creating all kinds of deadly devices, and no one does a thing to stop it.

But seeing the theory turn into practice, now that was something to behold. He'd watched the man gradually weaken until, just before dawn, the muscles could no longer do their job. Slowly, ever so slowly, they relaxed, until the ligature began to tighten around his neck. McAdam gurgled and blinked hard as he made valiant attempts to tuck his lower legs back under his thighs and thus prevent the asphyxia, but in the end, it was futile.

What a cry-baby McAdam had turned out to be when the realisation hit home. That he was going to die and his privilege and fame and money wouldn't save him. The tough guy who threatened opponents, officials, and even ball kids and spectators, turned into a blubbering tied-up pile of jelly when the penny dropped. Shameful, but that was the way with big-mouths like McAdam. You don't have to scratch too deep to discover what cowards they are.

And how easy it had been to lure him to the execution spot! The idiot suspected nothing. Nothing but hero-worshipping that is, a couple of willing girls to do his bidding. But he soon got a surprise, didn't he?

A knock at the door.

He uncurled the stockings and plopped them in a plastic shopping bag. He got up to answer the knock, whistling a cheery tune. He opened the door to see his neighbour, dear old Mrs Sullivan.

'Hi, Lily. Nice day, yeah?'

'I don't know about that. This heat's knocking me about.'

'Seriously, how long have you lived in Yorkville?'

She offered a wry smile. 'All my life.'

'Then I reckon you've probably acclimatised by now, hey?' The lovely old duck must be at least eighty. But she was fitter than many people half her age.

'I reckon you're probably right.' She held out a five-dollar note. 'Did you get the bread and milk for me? And the stockings?'

'I sure did.' He handed over the bag but waved away the money. 'Don't be silly. Just give me a couple of tomatoes from the plant we're going to stake up with those tights.'

A look of relief washed over her face as she tucked the note back into a small blue purse. 'You can be sure of that. And maybe a jar of chutney?'

How could he refuse it? Although he could afford to pay her now, she'd probably take offence. 'You are a love. I'll pop over later today to help you with the tomato plant.' He leaned forward, gave her a hug, savoured her comforting "nanna" smell that reminded him of the grandma who raised him while his parents worked their guts out trying to keep a roof over the family's head. A peck on the cheek and she was on her way.

## Chapter Five

THE DETECTIVES SHOULD HAVE CONFIRMED where Greer would be waiting, but the embossed brass "Boss" sign to the left of the reception at the bottom of the staircase gave it away. From behind a dark green door came the muffled sounds of an excited radio commentator calling a horse race together with Greer's coughing and swearing. Jack pounded his fist on the door.

'Yes? Who is it?' The radio clicked and went silent.

'Detectives Lisbon and Taylor.' Jack gave the bottom of the door a solid poke with his boot for emphasis.

'Come in, I–'

The DS had already barged inside, Taylor a stride behind. 'Let's not waste any time.' Jack grabbed a wooden chair, spun it around and sat on it backwards. He gestured for Taylor to join him across the desk from the owner. Whisps of acrid smoke from a just-finished cigarette hovered about Greer's head. She did as requested, but sat on it in the traditional way, crossed her legs and held her notepad and mobile phone in her lap. 'First of all,' said Jack. 'We need a copy of your CCTV footage from last night.'

'There isn't any.'

'Excuse me?' Jack frowned and squinted at the same time.

'I don't allow spy cameras in the hotel rooms. Discretion is the main reason for…'

'No, you misunderstand. I know there aren't cameras in the rooms. If there were, I'd be charging you for being a disgusting pervert. In fact I still might. I meant cameras for the public bar, car park and the main entrance, as required under the Liquor Act 1992 and the Liquor Regulation 2002.'

Greer drank from a cracked coffee mug. His sharp intake of breath told the detectives it was strong spirits inside. 'I shoulda been more pacific. There isn't any, full stop.' The fumes on his breath wafted across the desk.

'It's a requirement for licensed venues…'

'…that trade beyond 1:00am,' Greer interrupted. 'We close at 10:00pm, so there's no requirement.'

'Bullshit. I know the bar often stays open well past that. I attended a brawl here last year and the joint was rocking after midnight.'

'Sometimes I make an exception.' An oily grin was followed by a noisy slurp of rum. The thin fingers gripping the cup's handle betrayed thousands of smoked cigarettes. An overflowing ashtray smouldered next to a desk phone connected to an antiquated fax-copier machine. 'Must have been a special occasion. But anyway, what can I say? There's no security cameras anywhere on the premises. Don't need 'em. My pub, my rules.'

Jack rubbed his moist forehead. The anticipated migraine was already asking for admission into his brain. 'I'm going to double-check the liquor licencing laws. Something tells me you're skating on thin ice.'

'I checked already.' Taylor laid her smartphone on the desk. She'd pulled up the appropriate legislation. 'He's off the hook. Unless there's a specific condition on the licence, he doesn't have to have it installed.'

Jack swore under his breath. 'Is it a requirement of your licence? If you lie to me…'

'No, it isn't.' Greer crossed the room to a small steel file cabinet, rattled open a drawer, pulled out a document in a plastic cover and handed it to Jack. 'Be my guest. If you can find where it says I need those bloody intrusive things, point it out and I'll have the problem rectified.' He flashed uneven, mustard-coloured teeth. 'And I'll throw in a complimentary night in our Erotica Suite for both of youse lovebirds.'

With his eyes locked on Greer Jack passed the document to Taylor. The DS fought the temptation to pulverise the man's leering face into next week. Instead he said, 'Please remember, a man has passed away on your premises in horrible circumstances. A little decorum wouldn't go astray.' Jack paused before adding, 'Unless, of course, you'd like regular visits from the police. Just to make sure you aren't breaching more public health and safety regs than I suspect you already are. This whole place feels like a festering petri-dish.'

Greer held his hands up in mock surrender. 'Hey, I was only joking, officer.'

'No one's laughing, mate.' Jack remembered the Inspector's order to keep things on the down-low for the moment. 'I hope you haven't been blabbing to anyone about what's happened here. It could compromise our enquiries if you have. You're already in my bad books.'

'Of course not! All I done is rung Joanna and told her not to come in today due to unforeseen whatsanames. And I told Mercy to keep quiet, too, if she wanted to keep her job. She's into all kinds of mystical shit, voodoo and whatnot. Mumbling about curses as she got into the cab. She won't be advertising the matter, don't worry. If it were up to me, no one would find out. This'll be the bloody ruin of me! The hotel barely pays its way as it is. Why d'ya think I'm pinning my hopes on the gee-gees?' He pointed at a pile of torn up betting slips.

'Ah, 'cos you're an idiot?' Jack shook his head.

Taylor coughed to stop Jack going further with the insults. She held up the publican's liquor licence. 'He's telling the truth. No requirement for CCTV stipulated anywhere in the document.'

'Why the hell don't you have it, though?' said Jack. 'In this day and age you'd be mad not to. You could get sued for negligence.' A thought struck him. 'And you know what, sunshine? I reckon Roderick McAdam's parents might do exactly that when they find out about the shoddy operation you're running here. You'll become famous.'

The colour drained from Greer's face. 'Look, maybe I should have had security cameras put in, but it's too time consuming, costs money I can't afford to spend… But like I said, privacy is my main concern. It's no secret the Gasnier is a place where folks like to hook up on the quiet. I'm providing a community service here. If there's any aggro, I've got two sons who're quite capable of sorting out trouble.'

Jack needed to make more headway, fast. 'Right. No

CCTV. Bad, but all's not lost. Who was working here last night?'

'The regular crew. Joanna was working the reception, Ken and Andy were behind the bar across the hallway. The three of them have worked for me for years and I trust 'em like they was family.'

'That's it? What about those sons of yours?'

'Garth and Derrick. Yeah, they were here I think.'

'And yourself?'

'Nope. I was at home with the wife. I can't handle being around the place after sunset.'

'Why not?'

'To be honest, I'm kind of over the joint, know what I mean? I'm thinking of selling up.'

Jack sniffed and exchanged a look of understanding with Taylor. 'Right, I'll be having everyone's contact details – phone numbers, emails, addresses.'

Greer shrugged. 'Sure. Anything to help.'

'Do you have a register?' Taylor asked hopefully.

'What kind of register?'

'A bleedin' guest register, you pillock!' Jack's face reddened.

'Jack!' Taylor interjected. 'There's no need for rudeness. Poor Mr…ah…'

'Greer,' prompted the owner.

'Thanks. He's in shock, DS Lisbon, just like the rest of us.'

'I apologise,' said Jack, not sounding the least bit sorry. 'It's been a rough day.'

'Yeah, I guess it has. Come with me.' The detectives followed Greer into the adjoining cramped reception area. He reached under the counter and pulled out a hardcover notebook, placed it on the benchtop and opened it to yesterday's date, marked with a stitched-in red ribbon. Inside were the handwritten names of guests who checked in. But something wasn't right.

'What the hell?' said Jack, pointing at the entries at the start of the book. 'Check it out DC Taylor. Looks like more violations.'

'Waddaya mean?' Greer looked askance. 'All guests have to sign in when they arrive. What are you talking about, officer?'

'Supply of fraudulent information.' Jack's tone was flat.

Taylor shook her head slowly. 'Seems you've had some famous visitors already this year, and it's only January 7. Goodness me, on New Year's Eve you hosted Donald Trump, Boris Johnson and Justin Bieber. Impressive.'

The owner gave a guilty grin. 'Like I said. It's all about discretion. If these are the names they give, who are we to judge?'

'You're supposed to ask for proper ID.' Jack tapped a fingernail on the open ledger.

'No one told me that was the law. Is it the law?'

Jack and Taylor had to admit ignorance on the matter. Right now it was a moot point – this owner wasn't bothering about it. Combined with the lack of security cameras, Jack foresaw a tough road ahead.

'Well then?' Greer wriggled about in his chair like he had an itchy backside. 'What's the problem?'

'We need to know who was staying here if we're to have any chance of finding the guilty party. What about payment for the rooms?'

'Cash.'

'Always?'

'Well, most of the time. Of course we *do* accept cards if the guests insist on paying that way.' He pointed to an unplugged EFTPOS machine covered in dust. 'However the men who meet their girlfriends here don't want to leave a paper trail. So it's pretty much always cash.'

'*Girlfriends?*' said Jack with a throaty chuckle. 'That's a good one. And I bet you don't declare all those cash payments to the tax department, do you?'

Greer's unruly brows wedged into a steep V. 'Sorry, I thought you were investigating a murder, not financial matters.'

This bloke was begging for a thumping. Jack counted to ten in his head, skipping the even numbers to reach the destination faster, then exhaled slowly. 'Fair call, sunshine. Now, can we see a record of payments for yesterday's guests.'

Greer's head disappeared under the counter. He mumbled incoherent words as he rifled about before emerging with a small docket book. 'We use one of these each quarter.'

Taylor held out her hand and said, 'Please, may I see?'

Docket book in hand, she flicked through the square block like a bank teller tallying notes. 'Looks like only three paying guests yesterday. Not a good night from a possible twelve to rent out. Maybe...' she said with a dose of sarcasm, '...the receptionist forgot to enter everything, huh? Let's compare these payments with the register. Jack, who have you got down for Room 201?'

'One sec...' Jack turned to the required page. 'No one. Only rooms 207, 211 and 212 are signed for. Messrs Brown, Jones and...here's a good one...Citizen.' Jack slowly raised his narrowing eyes. 'So explain to me, sir, if you can, how come there's a dead man in Room 201, which had the key sticking out of the lock, when, according to your ledger, it was…FUCKING…EMPTY?!' Jack roared and thumped his fist on the countertop.

The owner took a step back, hands defensively in front of his face. 'Jesus, I dunno. Maybe he was moved there afterwards?'

'Bullshit. I've seen plenty of crime scenes, and I can tell you this man was killed right where we found him. Try again.'

Greer's lips quivered as he tried to think of a reason. 'I can't explain it, sorry.'

'Back in a minute.' Jack dashed up the staircase to Room 201. He quickly greeted Proctor and Carla, who were placing items in clear plastic evidence bags. The photographer was there too, preparing to leave. He gave Jack a nod of recognition before edging past him at the doorway. 'Hey, Margaret.'

The chief forensics officer spun around. 'How are you getting along?'

'Not great. The official records of this joint leave a lot to be desired. We can't even establish who was renting out the effin' rooms.'

She nodded. 'Good luck with that.'

Jack noted the stockings had been removed from the body. McAdam was still a gruesome sight to behold, but in some way a touch of dignity had been restored. 'Pick up organised?'

'The meat wagon's on its way.'

Jack flinched slightly at the gallows humour. 'In your professional opinion, was McAdam killed here or moved from somewhere else?'

'Oh, he definitely died on this bed. Now, he could have been knocked out in another location and then brought here, but that would have attracted attention a killer would want to avoid. My money is on the whole scenario unfolding within these walls.' She waved her hands about demonstratively as if Jack didn't know what walls were.

'Thanks. I thought the same.' As he turned to head back to the reception, he noticed the key still protruding from the lock on the outside of the door. 'You gonna bag this up, Margaret?'

'Of course.'

Jack asked for a spare rubber glove; Proctor extended a box of them. He snapped one on, extracted the flat silver key and put it back in the lock, gave it a turn. It didn't budge. He tried again. Stuck. 'Bloody hell.'

'What's the problem?'

'I'll be keeping this for now. It's the wrong key.'

---

'OK, MR GREER.' Jack brandished the mysterious key an inch from the man's nose. 'What's going on? This key doesn't fit the lock to Room 201.'

'I dunno, lemme see.'

Jack held it between the thumb and forefinger of his gloved hand. Greer pulled a pair of reading glasses from his shirt pocket, stretched his neck forward. 'Hmmm. Can you turn it around. There. The "R" engraved on the reverse side means it's for…this room. Reception.'

'So if we take the key hanging on the corkboard under the letter "R"…' Jack grabbed it, examined both sides. 'Well, lookee here. It's engraved with 201!'

'There you go.' The owner smiled, folded arms across his chest. 'A simple mix up. What of it?'

Jack paced back and forth, scratching his head. He stopped, placed both hands on the counter. 'What of it? I can think of two scenarios. One, someone gave the killer access to Room 201, mistakenly put the wrong key back in the lock and returned the other one to reception. Meaning an employee of yours could be an accomplice to murder, knowingly or not.'

'Fa-a-a-rk!' Greer croaked. 'No way. Not possible.'

'Very possible,' said Taylor. 'Was it you? You said business was poor. Maybe you got paid handsomely to turn a blind eye.'

'No way. You must be out of your mind!'

'Now, I think I can guess the second scenario Detective Lisbon had in mind. The murderer somehow managed to gain access to the reception unassisted by your staff and grabbed the keys,' Taylor pointed to the corkboard with various-shaped keys hanging from hooks, 'let themselves into Room 201, and mucked up when they've made their escape after killing McAdam.'

'But why would they even put the key back in the door? And then return what they thought was the reception key to its rightful spot?' said Greer, shaking his head. 'Makes no sense to me.'

'Me either, I'll admit,' said Taylor.

'Nor me.' Jack sucked air through his teeth. He then asked Greer to write down the contact details of all his staff, whistled for Wilson to leave his post at the front entrance and return the keys of interest to Proctor to bag up. The owner whined about the inconvenience of not having them. In response, Jack told him to get the locks changed if he was worried about security, even though his admissions so far indicated it was a low priority.

'That's all for now,' said Jack, shrugging on his lightweight cotton jacket. The frustration of dealing with this fool was making his temples throb. Plus the fact he was missing out on his lunch date with the Amazonian Marietta Szabo. There had been a couple of insistent buzzes going off in his pocket, texts from her he wasn't keen on reading. 'Please don't re-open the hotel until further notice. Constable Wilson is staying behind to keep order. Got me?'

The man made a face like a kid whose teddy had been snatched from its grasp. 'C'mon. I need to be trading to make a dollar. Not even a couple of regulars drinking at the bar? Every sale counts.'

'No one unauthorised comes in. No exceptions. Other officers may be deployed here later to assist the constable. I'd like you to hang around and not leave until the forensics unit has left.'

'We'll be in touch,' said Taylor with an amiable smile. She stood and brushed a stray fleck of ash from her black trousers. 'We'll require a formal statement from you down at the station at some stage, so don't leave town.'

Greer nodded. 'Where would a broke man like me go?' He unscrewed the cap of a 750ml bottle of Bundaberg rum and tipped a large measure into his mug. 'This is going to kill my business, I tell you.'

Jack turned on his heel, snarled at the man. 'Wrong word choice, sunshine. A man has been *killed* for real. You better be squeaky clean from now on or I'll be back to make your life a living hell.'

The detectives walked out of the reception area to the sound of a man whimpering and gasping, the sparking up of a match.

'Was that necessary, Jack?'

The DS shrugged. 'Probably not.' He chucked three pellets of gum in his mouth, bit down hard. 'And I strongly doubt he's involved in the murder.'

'Then why?'

'Grubs like him only understand a firm hand, Claudia. And you know what?'

'What?'

'He'll be installing CCTV next week, mark my words.'

'But he can't afford it.'

Jack burst out laughing. 'Don't you believe it. Word on the street – that tightwad is one of the richest men in Yorkville.'

## Chapter Six

THE HOTEL GASNIER'S housekeeper Ms Mercy Valdez sat opposite DC Taylor in the former's modest rented bungalow cottage in the working-class suburb of Provan. Chintz curtains, portraits of the Lord our Saviour in various styles and sizes, scented candles burning on every window sill. A shrine to Catholicism. A gently humming air-conditioner blew a cool breeze directly over the DC's head which bounced off the wall behind her and spread like floating gossamer about her neck and shoulders.

Taylor accepted a rattling cup of hot tea with a smile. 'Thank you.' She blew a cloud of steam across the top of the fine china cup, took a tiny sip of the scalding hot brew. She put the cup down on a small side table. 'Not having one yourself, Ms Valdez?'

Not changed out of her maid's uniform, the witness flopped into a green vinyl armchair. She stared into space, teeth softly clicking and fingers running over each other in her lap. 'No. I...I...can't...drink or eat.' She made the sign of the cross in front of her face. 'It's all too much...' A tear formed in the corner of one eye.

Taylor got off the sofa, approached the woman with careful, slow steps, took her by the hand. 'Is there any medication in the house you could take to calm down?'

'No. I don't take drugs of any kind. Only natural products.' She gazed up at the detective pleadingly. 'All I want is to go to bed and try and forget what I saw. Can you come back another time?'

'I'm sorry, but this is too important to wait. I need you to tell me everything you can remember about what happened this morning.' Taylor mustered her best caring expression. 'The sooner we can do this, the sooner I can leave. I'm worried about your state of mind, though. Does anyone else live with you?'

'No. All my family are in Manila. I'm trying to get my son over here on a work visa, but it's very difficult.'

'Friends?'

'I have a girlfriend, but she's out of town. I'll be OK on my own, don't worry.' Valdez offered a watery smile. 'I don't mind my own company.'

Time to get tougher. 'You might think you can simply sleep this off. But you've seen something today that's going to haunt you for years to come.'

Valdez's chest heaved faster as she struggled to keep it together.

'I strongly recommend that you see a doctor,' Taylor continued. 'Would you like me to call one for you?'

A vigorous shake of the head. 'Thank you, but it's not necessary.'

Taylor pursed her lips. The woman's refusal was irrelevant. After the interview Taylor would arrange for a doctor to drop by. Whether they were admitted inside the house, that was another matter. But at least Taylor would have tried.

'Please,' Valdez huffed. 'Ask your questions and leave.'

Taylor's mobile buzzed in her pocket as she flicked over the page of a small note pad. She chose to ignore the message.

'How long have you been working at the Hotel Gasnier?'

'Too long.' Valdez immediately waved her hand in apology. 'Sorry, two years this February.' She whispered, 'I hate it.'

'What is it you don't like about working there?'

'Everything! It's a dirty, disgusting dump. When I first started I worked nights on the reception. Sometimes I had to fetch booze and cigarettes and snacks from the bar and take them to the animals partying upstairs. The filth that goes on in those...' She paused, screwed up her nose like she'd recalled a vile smell. 'Anyway, I convinced Mr. Greer I wasn't cut out for that kind of work and he agreed to let me do the cleaning every morning and clock off at lunch time when the...you know...men started rolling in with their floozies.'

'And that line of work suited you better?'

'Hardly. Can you imagine the disgusting things I find when I'm cleaning those rooms? At first it used to turn my stomach, but I kind of got used to it. Until today...Oh my God!' Her hands shot to her head. 'I'll never go back there. Never! Even if I have to return to the slums of Manila.'

Taylor waited while Valdez blew her nose and took a couple of deep breaths.

'What did you do when you found the deceased?'

'I'd just finished cleaning room 202 across the hall when I noticed the key was in the door to 201. It was, let me think, just after 11:00am. I thought whoever hired the room simply left in a hurry and forgot to remove the key. Anyway, I walked in to find him...all tied up like that. At first I thought, you know, it was some kind of kinky bondage game and the man was supposed to figure a way to untie himself. But then I took a closer look at his face.' She made the sign of the cross. 'Those bulging eyes...like a zombie. Oh my God!' She uttered a single screech which morphed into prolonged, soft sobbing.

Taylor took the opportunity to read the text message she'd received moments earlier. Jack. Urging her to get to the station ASAP. She answered with a pre-programmed response – on way – then ordered a taxi. When Valdez stopped crying Taylor said, 'Then what happened?'

'I raced downstairs to tell Mr Greer. He started to panic like me. When he managed to calm down he organised a taxi to bring me home.'

Taylor tucked the spiral notepad back in her handbag and thanked Valdez for her co-operation. Gave her the usual spiel about possibly needing to provide a formal statement and a warning to stay in town. Valdez had no objections or complaints, she just wanted to be left alone.

As Taylor jumped into the cab, she was struck by the feeling Valdez was keeping something back. Was she protecting someone? Her boss? This was a question she – or better Jack – could put to her down at the station. But first she contacted the hospital and made an urgent request for a doctor with the nicest bedside manners to pay Ms Valdez a visit.

## Chapter Seven

**THE OFFICE WAS ALMOST EMPTY.** No raucous banter, no politically incorrect jokes, just the intermittent *bring bring* of phone calls and oaths of frustration as rookie Constable Damien Wells battled to answer them. But there was only so much one man could do. Unanswered calls got diverted to the Cairns Police Communications Centre, which worked around the clock and had enough staff to handle overflow from Yorkville. Constables Semmens, Smith and Trevarthen had taken the 4X4 to the Yorkville Grand hotel and were currently in the car park, awaiting Batista's go-ahead to question a number of guests in relation to McAdam's death – the parents, coach and other players.

Batista held his head in his hands, stared at the space between the edge of his desk and the floor. Jack took the opportunity of the pause in their conversation to sip a chest-hair-inducing espresso he'd purchased from the café next door. A half-eaten cinnamon donut sat surrounded by crumbs in a saucer. He took a bite of the sweet treat, wiped grains of sugar from his chin with a napkin. The pause was going on too long. 'You alright, sir?'

'What?' Batista raised his head, thrust out his chiselled jaw. 'Of course I'm alright. Why wouldn't I be? Now, what were you saying?'

'You sure you're OK? You don't look too flash, sir. Quite pasty, if you don't mind me saying so. Not sleeping properly?'

The chief rubbed his chin. Jack observed a series of tiny cuts where Batista had nicked himself shaving, a drooping of the eyelids, slumped posture. 'I appreciate your concern, DS Lisbon, but I'm absolutely fine. Just a bit overwhelmed by the scale of what's ahead of us. The station phone line's been running hot.'

'I know, I can hear it.'

'It was worse earlier. McAdam's worried parents want us to go out looking for him.'

'Jesus.'

'Exactly. He was supposed to meet his coach and his mum and dad for breakfast at 9:00am and then head off for a practice hit-out. I, ah,' ... his eyes averted Jack's gaze... 'decided to play dumb until he was brought back to the mortuary.'

'Sir!' Jack slapped the desk. 'Once the timeline gets out and they realise you weren't straight up with them, things might get a bit tricky, to put it bleedin' mildly.'

'I...ah...shit. I don't know. I wanted a pair of uniforms to tell them in person. It's always better that way. I'm just about to give Trevarthen and Smith the go-ahead to pass on the bad news.'

'Sure, sir.'

'And, of course, I wanted the parents to identify the body in the mortuary, not where he died.'

'Naturally,' Jack nodded.

'Proctor's made the victim look as presentable as possible for the ID. She's done a sterling job as usual.' The Inspector shook his head slowly. 'I saw the crime scene photos. Christ, how could anyone…'

Jack walked around the desk, put his arm around the chief's shoulder, gave his back a pat. 'C'mon, sir. You need to focus.'

'I know, I know,' came the absent rely. 'Where's Claudia, by the way? There's a mountain of work to do. I want her here for the media stuff.'

'She took a cab to interview the maid. A Filipina woman who's apparently on the superstitious side. She freaked out when she found McAdam. I thought Claudia talking to a female witness might produce better results. Especially after that moron Greer wound me up with his nonsense. Claudia's coming back here when she's done.'

Batista pushed back in his chair, nodded for Jack to resume his seat opposite. The boss had never been a fan of "man hugs". 'We need her back quickly, though. No one can deal with the press vultures like she can…' Batista's phone jangled on the cradle. He stared at the ID display and held up an index-finger. 'One second, I have to take this. It's the new Assistant Commissioner.' The previous AC for the region, Ray Hook, had passed away from a heart attack during the last big murder case in the Deep North. Hook was a corrupt prick and no one missed him. The new one, Jennifer Landacre, was seen as a breath of fresh air, and Batista rated her highly.

Jack fired off a second text to Taylor while Batista was chatting to the top brass. *Hope you're on your way. Batista's in panic mode!*

'Landacre's organised four detectives on loan,' said the

Inspector after hanging up on the call. 'Two are flying up from Brisbane, another two are making the short trip from Cairns. They'll all be driving here together later tonight for a briefing.'

'There's a ton of people to question, door knocking, desk work.' Jack sucked in his cheeks. 'Is four enough?'

'Landacre will approve more if I put in the request – up to a point.' An unsure laugh. 'Apparently there's plenty of research going on right now behind the scenes, officers looking into McAdam's life, acquaintances, possible enemies, motives. Any early suspects in your mind, Jack?'

'At first glance Depp seems the obvious one. He threatened McAdam publicly. But, geez, that was a spur of the moment outburst. No way he could plan and carry out a grisly murder like we've just seen, what, overnight? It's so unlikely as to be ludicrous.'

'But not impossible.'

'Yeah. When you think you've seen everything in the job, something new lobs up.'

'Was that a tennis pun?'

'What?'

'*Lobs.*'

'Oh, shit. Sorry.' Jack slammed down the rest of his coffee. 'You know what else?'

'What?' Batista frowned.

'This will turn into a nation-wide investigation. There are people currently outside this town who could have had it in for McAdam.'

'A jealous rival, you mean?'

'Yeah. Perhaps someone didn't like the thought of an arrogant upstart like McAdam taking the crown. Some tennis experts have been saying if he got to number one, he'd be holding down the position for years. Another possibility – he's pissed someone off on social media. He's said a lot of offensive stuff to other players. Borderline libel. You know how precious these high profile folks are. Someone might've decided to skip the proper legal process of suing him and taken a more direct route to shut him up.'

'That's a definite possibility.'

'Lots of them are prima donnas with an inflated sense of their own importance. They've got more money than you and I can ever dream about. Plenty to pay for a discreet hitman. Then there's the whole world of sports gambling to consider.' Jack paused to crack his gnarled knuckles with a sequence of loud pops. 'How's this for a scenario. A high roller has McAdam killed to doctor the odds for the Aussie Open, or to make sure McAdam didn't become world number one.'

Batista's face twisted like someone was ringing it out over a sink. DS Lisbon was clearly introducing too many elements into the equation. 'Fuck it!' exclaimed the Inspector. Jack's eyebrows shot up. The Inspector was no prude, but him busting out the f-word was rare. 'It's going be tough to cover every scenario. But we handled the murders of those MMA fighters a couple of years ago well, didn't we?'

'Yeah, we did.' Jack leaned back in his chair. 'But that was a local competition. Peanuts in terms of stakes. If sports gambling's a factor, this has global ramifications. I'm not sure our modest little station's going to be the one to crack it.'

Batista sighed heavily. 'Then it's a good thing were getting the extra bodies, isn't it?'

'Perhaps. But like I said, it mightn't be enough. I–'

'Was that fast enough for you?' Taylor appeared behind Jack's shoulder, cardboard tray of take-away coffees in hand.

'Bleedin' heck. I only just texted you.'

'I was already back. I got your last message when I was buying these.'

'We'll have to drink those in the car. It's time to meet the parents. Sir, will you call the uniforms and ask them to break the news, or would you like me to call them on the drive over?'

Batista sighed. 'No, I'll call them. Then the Grand Hotel, tell them to make sure all guests involved in the tournament stay put. I'll also be getting in touch with Clyde Pilmer, if I can track him down.'

'I heard he's staying in one of the penthouse apartments at the Grand,' said Taylor.

'Thanks, Claudia. It's imperative he cancel the tournament and advise all ticket holders. OK you two, make tracks.'

'Yes, sir.'

'One last thing, Lisbon.'

Jack eased an arm into a jacket sleeve, turned back to face the chief. 'Yes?'

'The parents are going to be in deep, deep shock. Go easy on them, OK?'

Jack forced a grin. 'Don't I always?'

---

TWO BLOCKS from the Yorkville Grand Hotel Jack radioed Constable Kylie Smith. Had they received their riding instructions from the boss? 'Yes we have, DS Lisbon,' said Smith. 'Aden and I are on our way up to the McAdams' room. Constable Semmens will be waiting for you in the lobby.' There was a nervousness in her shaky voice. She'd been more relaxed under shotgun fire from a violent biker gang. Smith wasn't ready for this job. Jack exchanged a look of understanding with Taylor. A change of plan was required.

'Leave the McAdams to me and DC Taylor.'

'But the Inspector said we—' Jack heard the ding of an elevator on the other end of the call.

'New orders. I've got another job for you. Less traumatic.' He heard Smith suck in a breath. 'I'll fill you in when we get there. We're just pulling into the hotel now. Wait for us in the atrium bar.'

'Yes, sir.'

Jack hung up, shifted down a gear to negotiate the tight corner into the hotel's spacious car park. Although it wasn't peak tourist season, thanks to the Pilmer Challenge the lot was almost filled to capacity.

The Kia Stinger cruised past a line of waiting taxis. The waving tops of coconut palms danced shadows on their roofs, a baking heat mirage rose from the asphalt. The beginnings of rain clouds were gathering on the horizon, the deep gunmetal grey variety that often presage a tropical storm. In this part of the world, skies could be cloudless one moment, the next you were being assaulted by a torrential downpour or ducking hailstones as big as oranges. The forecast said no heavy rain for the next few days but Jack was doubtful. But for those hoping to witness Roderick McAdam on centre court, the weather was as irrelevant as last month's spent pay check.

As Jack nosed the car into a spot near the entrance that civilians would earn a ticket for parking in, Taylor tossed out a thought bubble. 'If this investigation expands, it's going to require travel. There're tennis tournaments going on everywhere right now. Two important ones in Adelaide and Brisbane as we speak. Then the Australian

Open, of course. We might be adding to our frequent flyer points.'

'Don't get too excited,' said Jack. 'I'm not sure the QPS has that much money to chuck about. If leads point across borders, we'll be leaning on other state's forces and the Feds. Plus, you're assuming the killer's closely linked to this...' Jack thought for a moment '...milieu.'

'Say what?'

'Y'know. Milieu. It means...ah...environment or something.'

'Yeah, I know what it means. I'm surprised you do. Have you been reading the great philosophers?'

'Yeah, I have 'n all.'

'Which ones?'

'Ah...Rembrandt I think it was.' Jack switched off the engine. 'C'mon. Let's get inside and find Smith and the others.'

The officers sat on a semi-circular lounge in the sunken atrium beneath a glittering chandelier, light bouncing off thousands of facets. Smith stared into space, the two men consulted their mobile phones. Guests wandered about, laughing, chatting, dragging suitcases, scurrying self-importantly here and there. Jack ignored his colleagues for a moment as he and Taylor marched to the check-in, elbowing through a group of guests sporting white zinc cream on their noses, Hawaiian shirts on their backs, and orange towelling hats on their heads. Tennis "groupies".

A flash of police badges, a hasty phone call by the officious woman to Batista to make sure Jack's unusual orders were legit. The Inspector must have turned on his urbane charm, as the receptionist became all serious nods and deliberate scribbles on notepaper, clearly excited by the prospect of being involved in something momentous. She then made a series of calls to the guests Batista had named. At that moment, Taylor received a call from the Inspector. The DC spoke to him for two minutes while Jack concentrated on the receptionist's conversations. To the ones who answered her, she explained that a serious incident had occurred and they needed to make themselves available to police. She told them to either stay in their rooms or hustle back there pronto. On the last call, Jack overheard a vociferous woman demanding to know what the hell was going on. He beckoned for the receptionist to hand him the phone.

'Detective Sergeant Lisbon here. To whom am I speaking?' He already knew the answer.

'Veronica McAdam. Is this about my son? Where is he, what's happened? I'm losing my mind with worry.'

'I'm really sorry, but I can't reveal anything over the phone.' Unintelligible shrieking. *The woman knows the truth.* 'We'll be with you in a few minutes, please don't leave your suite. Thank you.' He hung up while she was in the middle of yelling something. Rude, Lisbon, but there was no other way.

'This is going to be a tough job,' said Taylor with a slow head shake.

A printer hummed briefly before the receptionist retrieved a list of names, room and mobile phone numbers matching up with McAdam's parents, his coach and the other two players still staying at the Grand Hotel enjoying Clyde Pilmer's largesse. And Pilmer himself in the presidential penthouse suite. 'Want me to keep trying to contact the people who didn't answer?'

'No, we'll follow them up.'

Jack took a photo of the list on his phone, sent a group MMS message to his colleagues, tucked the piece of paper into his pocket. Taylor's phone chirped in her handbag almost immediately. Jack spotted the officers waiting in the atrium, each looking intently at the screens of their mobiles.

'Oi,' Jack barked as he and Taylor approached. The three uniforms jumped in their seats. He established all had received the list and allocated them to the following persons of interest: Semmens – Sean Depp and eliminated player Cory Troutman; Trevarthen – McAdam's manager Peter Gosling and would-be finalist Hugh Marshall; Smith – Clyde Pilmer.

'What's wrong, Smith?' Jack was struck by her milky pallor. 'Don't think you can handle one of the country's richest and most powerful men?'

She shook her head as she stared at her feet. Jack clicked his teeth. 'C'mon, Kylie. You didn't want to deliver the death notice. Now you're scared of Pilmer. You want to go back to the office? I can get the rookie, Constable Wells, to take your place, and you can play office administrator for the rest of the day. Is that what you want?'

'N-no, sir.'

'From what I hear, he's a down-to-earth kind of billionaire. It's a straightforward assignment. If you've seen him on the TV, you'll know he loves to talk. Just ask him who he thinks did it and he'll have plenty to say.'

'Yes, sir. That's all?'

'Basically. Keep him company until we're done with Mr and Mrs McAdam, then we'll drop by to keep the pressure on. While he's prattling away, stand there looking tough with your arms folded across your chest and your Glock turned towards him.'

'Sir?'

'OK, maybe that's pushing it. But don't let his status

intimidate *you*. End of the day, he puts his pants on one leg at a time, same as everyone.'

'Yes, sir.'

'If he makes or receives any phone calls, pay attention to everything he says, OK?'

'Got it, sir. Is he...aware of what's happened?'

'Should be.' Jack turned to Taylor. 'When did the chief say he was informing Pilmer?'

'Immediately after we left his office,' replied Taylor flatly. 'And he just confirmed it to me five minutes ago. Apparently, Pilmer was stunned, which is not unexpected, but he's promised to stay put and keep the news under his hat. He'll make a public statement about the cancelation of the tournament only when we give him the green light.'

'Right then.' Jack looked at Smith again. 'Play it by ear, alright? Remember your training. We aren't far away if you need us.' He addressed the two male constables. 'You blokes got any issues with your assignments?'

'Not an issue as such, DS Lisbon,' said Constable Aden Trevarthen, a heavy-set man turning to fat. Too many soft drinks and sugary donuts. Jack had let himself go to the pack many years ago before getting back into shape. He liked Trevarthen as a man and as a policeman and had visions of the constable repeating Jack's past errors. He had offered to be the constable's gym partner to help steer him back on the right path, first session pencilled in for tomorrow night. Some serious sparring sessions would soon see the kilos melt off the man.

'What then?'

'Are there specific questions you want us to ask?'

'Didn't they teach you how to use your initiative at the academy?'

'Well, yes. But—'

'No buts. This isn't the first murder case you've all been involved in. Yes, it's high-profile and the heat's gonna be turned up once the press get wind of it later today. But for now – apart from Smith who'll be babysitting Pilmer – I want you two to get the spadework done. Find out alibis, where were they last night. What are their potential motives for offing McAdam, if they've got no motive, who do they suspect had it in for the lad.' Jack stopped, pointed a finger at each male constable. 'Use your common sense. Get every detail you can out of them, see if the news sends them into shock. And if they don't seem shocked, make note of that too. Once you feel there's nothing more to be got out of them, send me a text, then head back to the station. I'll call you when we're done and we'll work out what to do next based on all information gathered. What you learn could be very important. Understood?'

Curious faces in the foyer turned to follow the five police officers as they strode purposefully to the bank of elevators. Within the hour, many guests would be checking out of the hotel and heading to the airport. Jack's job, and that of his team, was to ensure that others went precisely nowhere.

## Chapter Eight

WHEN HE WORE a London Metropolitan Police uniform all these years ago, Jack would have removed his hat and tucked it under his arm before informing a parent their child had passed away. No hat today, but he had decided to don a tie. A dusty, sombre dark blue number from the back of the wardrobe. He hadn't worn one for so long it was impossible to get the knot to sit squarely in the space between the ends of his shirt collar. For some reason it kept wanting to stray off centre. As the lift stopped on the eleventh floor for a man to exit, Taylor redid the knot so it fit snugly in place. Her deft skill sparked an illogical and jealous curiosity in Jack; was there a new tie-wearing boyfriend on the scene she hadn't told him about? Whatever, as a sign of thanks he volunteered to make the death announcement. It must have been Jack's lucky day, because, in addition to correcting his wardrobe malfunction, Taylor offered to relieve him of that burden, too.

At the top floor – the 20th – the detectives and Constable Smith alighted, Trevarthen and Semmens having stepped out of the elevator on lower floors to interview the three remaining tennis players and McAdam's coach, Peter Gosling. There were four luxury suites at the top, one each rented out to Clyde Pilmer, Mr and Mrs McAdam, the victim, and a Chinese businessman totally unconnected to the tennis tournament.

Now, to face the unpleasant music. A rap on the door, a deep breath and a step back. The door flew open, as if poor Mrs McAdam had been lurking there from the moment Jack ended their phone call. It was all Jack could do to keep from thrusting his hands in his pockets, his fingers clenched and unclenched, he blinked like a teenager on a first date.

No introduction was necessary, as the ground for their arrival had already been prepared. Taylor spoke, gently and with reassurance. 'Are you Mrs Veronica McAdam?'

Mrs McAdam gave a rapid nod, her dangling emerald earrings bouncing about underneath a severe, short blonde haircut. She reminded Jack of one of his youthful heart-throbs, Annie Lennox. No "Sweet Dreams" for this woman. Streaks of black eye makeup lined her damp cheeks, her plump lips quivered.

'May we come in, please?' Taylor prompted as the woman stood rooted to the spot.

'Just a moment. ADRIAN!' She turned, repeated the name, louder if it were possible. 'Come here, darling.'

An impish man in mottled jeans and a black polo shirt, three or so inches shorter than his wife, appeared from behind a dividing wall, glass of something clear in his hand. Ice clinked as he came closer. Jack would have bet anything it wasn't water in the tumbler. 'I'm here, darling. Is it the police? What have they said?' It was then he clocked the detectives, still standing outside in the hallway, like they were at attention on a parade ground awaiting instructions on what to do next. He took his wife by the elbow, guided her backwards through the dimly-lit reception alcove lined with potted monstera deliciosa, Jack and Taylor ambling a metre behind. The hall opened up to a bright floor space twice as big as the interior of Jack's entire apartment. The mother half-collapsed on a chrome and leather dining chair. 'Don't tell me, a horrible accident? He's so reckless.' Veronica scrabbled about trying to fill a glass from a decanter on the table. Her chunky silver rings clanked on the polished marble surface of the table. Her husband grasped the back of her chair, the detectives also standing. It was bad form to sit when you were bearing sad tidings.

'It's worse than that, I'm afraid.' Taylor's tone was professionally sympathetic. 'Your son has been found dead in a hotel on the outskirts of town. We suspect foul play and have launched an investigation. We're sorry for your loss.'

'No! It's not him!' cried Adrian McAdam. 'There must be some kind of mistake.'

Jack said, 'There's a minuscule chance it isn't Roderick. And that's why–'

'Of course it's a bloody mistake,' said Veronica. 'It's someone who looks like him, that's all.'

'I hate to say it, but that is highly doubtful,' said Taylor. 'Your son is famous and very recognisable to many people, two witnesses and us included. But, as my colleague DS Lisbon was about to say, we would like one or both of you to accompany us to the mortuary to officially identify the body.'

Adrian McAdam drained his drink, wiped his hands on the front of his trousers. 'Let's go, then.' His voice was now devoid of all emotion. It reminded Jack of a cheap robot program used to voice-over video clips.

'Are you sure?' said Taylor. 'We'd like to ask some questions first, if that's alright.'

Veronica was back on her feet, handbag over her shoulder. 'My husband is right. If you want to ask questions, you can do it after we've seen...our boy.' She burst into tears, struck by the realisation the police were telling the truth, before throwing her arms around her husband's neck. He inclined his head, temple veins raised and throbbing, into the crook of her neck. They hugged firmly and seemed in no hurry to break their embrace.

Jack whispered to Taylor, 'You think you can take the two of them to the mortuary on your own?'

'Don't you want to put questions to them now?'

'Like they said, they ain't talking till they've seen their lad. And it's only courteous to respect their wishes. Besides,' he brandished a plastic swipe card. 'I'd like to have a snoop around the victim's hotel room, which is just around the corner.'

'Where'd you get that from?'

'The receptionist. I asked her for it while you were chatting to Batista.'

'Did you ask her for anything else?' The rising inflection, the faintest hint of jealousy. Or was Jack imagining it? One day he'd make his move on Taylor, but he could never find the right moment. Now was definitely not the right moment. Jack just shook his head with a pressed-lip smile. The couple slowly disentangled themselves, Mrs McAdam asked if they could please get on with the process before bursting into tears again.

'DC Taylor will drive you to the mortuary,' said Jack, summoning his deeply-buried soft side. 'I'll join you there in an hour or so. May I just take the opportunity to personally extend my sincere condolences.' He offered his hand to Mrs and Mr McAdam in turn, which they accepted with tiny nods and blank stares.

A minute later, they and Taylor were gone. Jack strode around the circular corridor of the tower until he reached room 2003. He placed the hotel card in the slot until the green light glowed and shoved open the door.

Inside, he stuck the key in the corridor wall slot to activate the lights, which flickered for a moment before revealing a room that was a replica of the one Roderick McAdam's parents were staying in. At first glance, neat and tidy. *Nothing to see here.* He pulled out his Samsung mobile and started to record a video as he began to explore the room. Either Yorkville or Cairns forensics would give the place the once over, but as usual, Jack wanted his own record for reference.

It was clear housekeeping had not serviced the room in the interval between the occupant's last visit and his death. The king size bed was unmade, pillows scattered and sheets crumpled, empty soft drink bottles and the crust of a toasted sandwich on a plate sat on a side table. A red-and-black suitcase the size of a medium refrigerator stood by the floor-to-ceiling windows with a view overlooking Yorkville's busy Esplanade. Jack put down the phone and flicked on a pair of disposable gloves before flipping the suitcase on its side and unzipping it; inside were six plastic-wrapped tennis rackets, three pairs of brand new tennis shoes and some random sweatbands and hand towels in side pockets. There were no clothes strewn across the floor, as one might expect from a nineteen-year-old male. Perhaps an indication of the discipline of a professional athlete? Such a trait wasn't in accordance with his tempestuous on-court persona. Maybe that was all an act, though? Could a tennis player be an actor in the same way as, for example, a wrestler? An idea worth fleshing out. The coach would be the logical person to ask about that.

A translucent green Xbox was connected to the giant wall-mounted TV, a matching controller sat on the deep-pile carpet. There may be some clues on the gaming devices, perhaps incriminating DNA. Additionally, there was a plugged-in closed laptop on a chestnut writing desk with a panoramic view over the harbour. Jack teased open the computer. A password prompt appeared. The device would be bagged up as evidence, its contents analysed. As would the complimentary hotel pen lying beside a note in neat handwriting. It simply said *Hotel Gasnier 11 PM Room 201*.

Jack continued the inspection. He opened three bedside drawers to find carefully folded t-shirts and shorts, rolled-up socks and boxer shorts. In the walk-in robe he found a range of expensive-looking dress shoes, long and short-sleeved shirts and trousers, pressed to military exactitude, waiting patiently for an owner who would never return.

The note was a good start, but Jack wanted more evidence.

And then, there it was, in the ensuite. Big, bold letters across the mirror, written with bright red lipstick, its holder still in the sink. BYE ROD. GONNA STRING U UP LIKE A TENNIS RACKET U PRICK. Rounded off with a crudely drawn penis and testicles.

Jack removed his gloves, made a call to Proctor. No answer. Then Batista. 'Is Proctor available for another job? I can't get hold of her.'

'You kidding, DS Lisbon? She and Clara are still at the Gaz. They haven't had a break. Clara texted me earlier, though. She says the room's got more DNA in it than a railway station public toilet.'

Jack winced at the apt comparison then quickly explained what he'd found, emphasising the violent language and the cock-and-balls signature on the mirror. 'So, in essence it's not a crime scene, but it needs a forensics go-over. A bleedin' thorough one, too.'

'I'll pass the message on. Have you heard anything from the other officers?'

'No. I'm heading to Pilmer's suite. It's on the other side of the tower.'

'Is Taylor still with you?'

'No sir. She should be at the mortuary, if not she ain't far away.'

Batista said he'd call the hotel and request they turn over all their CCTV footage from last night. Jack would pick it up on his way back to the station, also obtain any records of in-house phone calls, room service deliveries made to McAdam's suite. Now he was about to join Kylie Smith at Pilmer's suite. Before hanging up, Jack took photos of the hand-written note and bathroom mirror and forwarded them to the Inspector.

'You get them, sir?'

'Oh my God. Coupled with the MO, this is looking like a Charles Manson-style killing. The press is going to have a field day.'

## Chapter Nine

CONSTABLE NOAH SEMMENS fiddled with the switch of his Axon body-worn camera, or BWC, before knocking on the door. Would he use it or not? Practically all uniformed constables wore them these days. In addition to a ton of other equipment that made beat cops feel like pack mules. He didn't particularly like the intrusiveness of the cameras, but sometimes they were good insurance against false claims of police brutality. One such BWC had came to his own rescue late last year when a thug attacked him without warning and then accused Semmens of provoking the altercation. A review of the footage resulted in the man being prosecuted for the assault *and* making a false accusation. In the end, for this interview with weedy tennis player Sean Depp, Semmens decided to leave it off.

The door was opened by a beaming Depp. Large, uneven teeth dominated an elongated baby face that appeared not to require regular shaving. 'Oh,' he said with half a smile. 'I was expecting a round of toasted ham and cheese sandwiches.'

'No, I'm afraid this is official police business.' Semmens introduced himself before being ushered into a stock-standard hotel room that shouted "beige".

'Yeah, I know,' Depp crouched and clicked his fingers with a loose-wristed flick, like a wannabe rapper. 'I was joking. Tell me what it's all about, officer. Must be serious. I was told not to leave my room. Thought a pandemic had broken out.' He gave a throaty chuckle.

Semmens was bemused by the fellow's carefree attitude. He'd seen the TV sports report of "the incident" at the Yorkville Tennis Centre. Depp should still be seething after being cheated of his big prize. Something was up. *Let's see if the news rattles him.*

'I'm sorry to have to inform you, but a terrible tragedy occurred overnight.'

'What kind of a tragedy? Don't tell me – Roderick McAdam got eaten by a crocodile? I hear they're real hungry bastards up this way.'

Semmens took a deep breath. 'As it happens, it does concern the man you mentioned. He was murdered at the Hotel Gasnier some time last night.'

'What the...?'

'A full-scale homicide investigation has been launched, and speaking with you is part of the process.'

'Holy shit. I was kidding about the crocodile. This is some kind of practical joke, right?' He stared over the constable's shoulder. 'Is there someone out there in the corridor ready to burst in with a TV crew?'

'I'm afraid it's not a prank, Mr Depp. I'm obliged to ask you a couple of standard questions in relation to the crime.'

'Why me?' He shrugged with his palms up. 'I've got nothing to do with it. I barely know the guy.'

'Don't be alarmed.' Semmens mentally noted the use of the present tense. *I barely "know" the guy*. Murderers tend to use the past tense when referring to their victims. Which indicated Depp had no prior knowledge. 'Nobody's accusing you of anything. We're talking to everyone involved in the tournament who's still in town. Other persons of interest interstate and overseas will also be questioned.'

The colour drained from Depp's face, his frivolous attitude finally over. He struggled to breathe before stumbling to a seated position on a two-seater couch. 'Holy crap. This is huge!'

'Indeed.' Semmens had a change of mind. 'You OK if I switch this thing on? He pointed to the camera mounted in the middle of his chest.

A look of doubt furrowed Depp's brow. 'What the hell's that for?'

'It could save you a trip to the police station to make a statement if what you say is already recorded.'

'Wait...what? I thought you said I wasn't under suspicion.'

'No, I didn't. I said no one was accusing you of anything.'

Depp gulped. 'Do I need a lawyer?'

Semmens shook his head. 'Of course not. This is why I'd like to turn on the camera. To avoid...misunderstandings.'

Depp nodded rapidly. 'Sure. Ask your questions.'

'Can you account for you movements yesterday?'

'That's easy. I played a game of tennis against a bloke you're telling me has been killed. Witnesses number in the millions, if I'm to believe the ratings figures. After that I came back here, had a swim in the pool, then I took a shower and went to the restaurant. I never left the hotel once I got back here after the match. Woke up fairly early, had breakfast delivered around 7:00am. Then I took a stroll around town, checked out some cafes on the waterfront. People even asked me for my autograph, can you believe it? Totally surreal for an ordinary person like me.'

'Can anyone confirm your movements?'

'Sure. The guy who hands the towels out at the pool, the staff in the restaurant and the cafés I visited. Oh, and I ordered a bottle of the most expensive cognac the hotel has in stock. It was delivered to my room at about 10:30pm. I can show you the docket if you like.'

'Why did you order the cognac? Hardly a day for celebration after you...you know, didn't win the money for breaking McAdam's serve. In fact, the whole world saw you screaming at McAdam, threatening him.'

Depp waved the matter away like he was shooing a fly. 'The misunderstanding was resolved quite nicely, thanks to Mr Pilmer. I'm more than satisfied with the outcome.'

'How do you mean?'

'Pilmer could see the injustice. About 8:00pm last night he rang me, said he'd watched some replays and could see the ball was out and I should have won that game. Most apologetic he was. About the bad call and the way the security guards handled me.'

'From what I could see, they defused the situation perfectly.'

'Perhaps,' admitted Depp. 'But I have to give Pilmer a big thumb's up. Can you believe the money is already in my account? And d'you know what else? I didn't even have to pay for the booze.' Depp pointed at a half-drunk bottle on a writing desk. 'Pilmer's taking care of that, too. He offered to pay for an upgrade to a better room, an offer I fully intend to take advantage of later this evening. All in all, not a bad day's work.'

'So, you're saying you had no animosity towards McAdam, is that right? From what I could see, he taunted you pretty good when that second serve was called in. That would give you a solid motive to seek revenge. Humiliation in such a public manner. I know I'd be fuming.'

'Would you like to try this Hennessey Paradis, officer?'

Semmens shook his head and smiled politely. 'And you put on a massive turn for the whole world to see. I've already seen some memes on the Internet. Pretty hurtful stuff.'

'So what? It's the price I'm willing to pay for my allotted fifteen minutes of fame. Oh, and the cash.' Depp helped himself to peanuts from a glass bowl. 'At the time, of course I was pissed off, who wouldn't be? If those security goons hadn't grabbed me, I would've rammed my fist down that spoiled brat's throat.'

Semmens smiled to himself. McAdam would have easily handled the smaller man.

'I know it's bad to speak ill of the dead,' Depp continued. 'But McAdam was a massive arsehole.'

'You said you hardly knew him.'

'How well do you have to know a man who doesn't bat an eyelid when he cheats you out of a fortune to know he's an arsehole? It's pretty fucking obvious, isn't it?'

Semmens pointed at his camera, raised an eyebrow and inclined his head to one side.

'Look, I don't care if I swear while you're filming me. I really don't. I'm sad McAdam's dead, despite him being a prick. Do you have any idea who did it?'

'Too early to give details, I'm afraid.'

'How did he die, can you at least tell me that?'

'Ditto my previous statement. Is there anything further you'd like to add which may help us with our enquiries?'

'I've got nothing. Perhaps look into the pro tour. His behaviour is atrocious. It's well known he's immensely disliked by his competitors.'

*There it is again. Present tense.*

Depp grabbed more nuts before adding, 'It *is* a tragedy, like you said, officer. His parents are going to be…I can't imagine…just…devastated. Do you mind?' He unscrewed the cap of the outrageously expensive alcohol, poured himself a generous three-finger slug. 'But let's not dwell on the negative. It's worked out just fine for me. I feel for Hugh Marshall, though.'

'And he is…?' Semmens knew exactly who Marshall was.

'The fella who was going to play in the final tonight. I rated him a chance of taking a set off McAdam. A slim chance, but he was easily the best of the rest of us, know what I mean?' A mobile buzzed on the writing desk. Depp picked it up. 'Pilmer's just let me know the tournament's officially cancelled. Public announcement to follow later, I imagine. I'd love to be a fly on the wall in his room right now.'

'Why's that?'

'For the drama and the spectacle, Constable Semmens. Isn't that why we're all here on this planet?' He raised his glass and grinned. 'To Roderick!'

---

CORY TROUTMAN WAS a different kettle of fish altogether. Semmens congratulated himself for the unspoken joke as the man approached, a dark shadow emerging into light. The man didn't look much like a tennis player. Overall, he had a physique more suited to darts. At about five-five tall and sporting the beginnings of a pot belly, he came trotting along the corridor, wet flip-flops almost tripping him up. Lank black hair flapped about his face like curtains in the breeze.

'Sorry I wasn't in my room as requested,' he huffed. 'I had my phone switched off while I was at the beach. Man, that sand gets hot! I just checked my messages a minute ago. What's the problem?'

Inside hotel room 313, Semmens repeated what he'd told Depp. The man burst into tears at the news, waving his fingers like a fan in front of his sweaty face. A series of borderline effeminate *Oh my Gods* accompanied much hand wringing and pacing. If he was in any way connected to the murder of Roderick McAdam, Troutman was the world's best actor. Could he account for his whereabouts last night? Yes, he was in the hotel disco on the ground floor from around 9:00pm until 2:00am. He bought drinks at regular intervals which he signed to his room, which would prove he was there. Prior to that he had dinner at the hotel restaurant and before that he attended what was to become Roderick McAdam's swansong appearance in the world of tennis. To his utter disappointment, Troutman failed to pick up at the disco, saddened that none of the handsome local men even recognised him as a round-one loser in the Pilmer Challenge. He was rather inebriated and keen to get out of stinking hot Yorkville and back to his day job as a hardware salesman in his hometown of Newcastle. Did he have any thoughts on who might have wanted the world number 10 dead? He could only think of one person off the top of his head – Sean Depp.

CONSTABLE ADEN TREVARTHEN had been looking forward to tonight's gym session with DS Lisbon. The way things were panning out with this investigation, their little get-together would most likely have to be shelved. There would be overtime money to help with the mortgage and young Cornelius's school fees, but sparring with Jack would have been a thousand times more rewarding than any extra pay. In Trevarthen's eyes Lisbon, the ex-pat Englishman, was an inspiration, almost a hero. Not just because of his remarkable record of collaring and convicting criminals, but also because of his personal transformation. Trevarthen had seen photos of Jack as a young man: a fit, muscular boxer. He'd also seen pictures of when the DS had gone to seed. Today, in his mid 40's, Jack was ripped and shredded like a professional athlete. If Trevarthen was going to be totally honest with himself, he'd stopped caring about his own health just like Jack had at a similar age. The standards of fitness in the Queensland Police Academy had been high, but once you graduated, it wasn't hard to turn to flab. Especially after a few years on the beat, where cynicism and demoralisation can eat into your soul and stifle any desire for self-improvement. The default coping mechanism of many cops was booze and drugs and overeating. Trevarthen would never let that happen to him.

As McAdam's coach Peter Gosling opened the door, thoughts of tonight's scheduled sparring session with the DS fell through a trapdoor in Constable Trevarthen's mind. His job right now sucked. He suddenly envied Semmens, informing men not closely connected to the deceased of the recent tragedy. Imparting the news to a person in

McAdam's stable was shaping up as a tougher assignment altogether.

The coach radiated a sober maturity, his slicked-back silver hair and neatly trimmed moustache giving him an almost military bearing. He was dressed casually in fawn chinos and a salmon Ralph Lauren polo shirt. Trevarthen guessed the man to be in his late 50's to early 60's. Gosling wore an expression of worry tempered with curiosity, the deep furrows in his tanned face contracted. Tennis people are always tanned, Trevarthen thought to himself. Out in the sun all day, playing or training or coaching. Despite the signs of superior physical health, the man exhibited emotional pain, like he'd been contemplating all manner of horrible scenarios. He must be guessing the worst – his charge has been missing for many hours, and now the cops land on everyone's doorstep after instructing them not to go anywhere. It didn't take a genius to figure out something was terribly wrong.

After a pause of perhaps five seconds during which the men stared blankly at each other Gosling finally said, 'Yes?' There was a tremor in his voice.

'Ah...I...um...' Trevarthen stammered. For the life of him he couldn't think of the right words to say.

'He's dead, isn't he?'

Hat tucked under his wing, all Constable Trevarthen could do was nod slowly. He took a deep breath to compose himself. 'May I come in?'

Inside room 711 they sat in silence for a moment at a small round dining table while Gosling mumbled a prayer. Not a religious person, Trevarthen nevertheless closed his eyes and clasped his hands together, and repeated "amen" after Gosling when the short prayer concluded. He opened his eyes to see Gosling leaning forward, elbows resting on the tabletop, fingers steepled. 'Can you tell me what happened?'

'At approximately 11:00am today Roderick was found dead in the Hotel Gasnier, located on the edge of town.'

'Was it a drug overdose? I know the younger generation like to experiment with drugs. He's been going to parties on tour that I disapprove of, mixing with the wrong element. I know he's young, but still, he's a professional sportsman. I told him over and over not to—'

Trevarthen reached out and grasped Gosling's shaking clasped hands. The initial calmness was devolving into rambling. 'Please. I'm not meant to tell you too much. All I can say is we strongly suspect foul play. An official announcement will be made later today, after Roderick's parents have ID'd his body.'

Gosling unsteepled his fingers, held his face in shaking palms.

'Mr. Gosling? You all right?'

'Just give me a moment.' The man bolted to the ensuite and slammed the door behind him. Sickening sounds of dry retching echoed inside the hotel room.

A few minutes later Gosling was back at the table with a box of tissues, a foil of painkiller tablets and a glass of water. Crying, fainting and wailing were reactions the Constable expected, not a hurling fit in the bathroom. He jotted the fact down in his notebook. He thought for a moment about switching on the BWC, then discounted it. Let the man speak freely.

Gosling blinked a few times and said, 'Please forgive me for that reaction. Roderick was like a son to me.' He poked three pills out of the packaging and swilled them down. 'I'm going to need something stronger than aspirin before today is out. This is just...oh my God, it's...' His voice trailed off into silence.

Trevarthen waited for the man to stop staring at the wall and to look back at him before asking, 'Do you have any other clients apart from McAdam?'

'Clients?'

'Surely you haven't put all your eggs in one basket.'

Gosling shook his head slowly. 'When Roderick turned pro a few years ago, he and his parents asked me to stay with them on a full-time basis. I was honoured. The kid's so talented, you know. It was Roderick who made me look good, not the other way around. There were plenty of other coaches on the market with more experience and track records, but we were like family, I guess. I've been with him since his parents brought the kid along to his first lesson when he was only five years old. I never considered him to be "a client".' He let out a gush of breath. 'More like the son I never had.'

'You've got no family of your own?'

A weary shake of his silver head. 'No time to settle down. I've been teaching kids to play tennis since I was a young man myself. None of them took off in a big way. And then, Roderick comes along and changes everything.'

'I assume you've been paid well for your services.'

'Oh, yes. I can't complain about my salary.'

'Would it be impertinent to ask how much you get paid?'

Gosling scratched a spot under his right temple. 'Is that relevant?'

Trevarthen shrugged. 'It could be. I mean, murders often have a financial motive behind them.'

'Now, come on a minute.' A look of real worry added creases to Gosling's already creased face. Trevarthen's experience told him the sudden change in expression perhaps wasn't brought on by pangs of guilt, but by an irrational fear that he could even be considered a suspect. Like when a tourist who's done nothing wrong suddenly gets all nervous when faced with a customs official. Gosling continued, 'You gotta be kidding, right? Like I said, I loved that kid.' A tear escaped the corner of his right eye, which he dabbed at awkwardly with a knuckle.

'Of course, I understand. We have to ask these questions, nothing personal. Every scrap of information is potentially important. Another question I'm obliged to ask relates to your whereabouts last night. Can you account for them?'

'Yes. I had dinner with Veronica and Adrian McAdam and Mr Pilmer, then we had nightcaps in the bar until about, hmmm, 11:30pm. Then I came back here and...' he snapped his fingers '...out like a light.'

'Thanks for that.' Trevarthen hummed absently as he drew an elliptical doodle on his notepad. A silence might prompt Gosling to volunteer some thoughts of his own. The gambit paid off.

'You know,' said Gosling almost conspiratorially. 'If I were hunting the person who murdered poor Roderick, I can tell you a good place to start looking.'

The officer had a suspicion he knew where Gosling's finger was going to point. 'I bet you're going to suggest other players on the pro tour, right?'

But Constable Trevarthen had guessed wrong. Way wrong.

---

THE LEAD from Gosling would be passed on to Lisbon and Taylor. In the meantime, there was the Tasmanian Hugh Marshall to deal with. Constable Trevarthen was keen to get this interview over with ASAP. He was hating the process; especially for this case where the onus of responsibility on him seemed enormous. After more detectives arrived tonight, he'd be free of this awful work and back to the bread-and-butter stuff of policing – assaults, traffic infringements, drug deals and robberies. At least, that's what he hoped.

Trevarthen carefully placed his hat on the glass-topped coffee table, licked his finger and flipped over a page of his jotter. 'I guess you're miffed about not getting the chance to win a fortune, now your opponent's dead.' It was a challenging remark, and one probably not worthy of Trevarthen, but one never knew where a hand grenade might land and what shrapnel of information it could produce.

'No, not at all.' Marshall either subdued a hostile reaction to the provocation, or he was still numb from the news. Or he was lying. He sat with a straight posture on a sofa by the window of the characterless sixth-floor hotel room. Dressed in blue jeans and a black t-shirt, a thick novel lay open face-down on the coffee table. "Poor Fellow My Country" by Xavier Herbert. Trevarthen had never heard of the book or its author, but the sheer size of it told the policeman Marshall was no fool.

Trevarthen noted the room had a view facing the ocean and waterfront life, rather than the tin-roofs of warehouses faced by the rooms on Troutman's side of the building. 'I'm rather keen to get home. Back to my job studying marine creatures.'

'Of course. But we may request you to stay in town a little longer than you'd planned.'

'Why?'

'For further questioning. This is a high-profile case. Everyone's going to be under the microscope.'

'Whatever. I'm prepared. I'm no stranger to murder.'

'How so?' Trevarthen leaned forward in his seat. DC Taylor had sent him some notes in an email, but he was keen to hear it from the man himself.

'My parents were killed when I was a teenager. The cops in Tasmania even suspected me at the beginning of the investigation.'

'Should we suspect you now?'

Marshall's face twisted in incredulity. 'Only if you're as dumb as the dickheads in the Hobart CIB.'

'Why do you say that?'

'I've got no motive. Like you said. Now I'm no chance of winning the prize money. If there's anyone I'd be inclined to do in, it's whoever killed McAdam.'

'Logical.'

'Of course it's fucking logical!' Marshall's hands shot to his forehead, he stood and began pacing. 'I've been training my guts out for months. Ever since I got the invitation to this bloody circus. It was a long shot, sure, but you gotta be in it to win it, right? When I saw how close that idiot Sean Depp got to breaking McAdam's serve last night…'

'He *did* break serve,' interrupted Trevarthen.

'Yes, technically. It was a travesty the way he got ripped off. With McAdam gloating! Anyway, after I saw Depp could do it, my confidence was through the roof. A life-changing opportunity was in my grasp, now…gone. So, yeah, I'm mighty pissed off the man was killed.'

*Trevarthen made a note. At first said not upset by missed chance to win money, then mighty pissed off.*

'Is it just yourself you feel sorry for? What about McAdam and his family?'

Marshall dropped his head. 'Yeah. I'm sorry for his family. They'll never get over it, just like I'll never get over losing my mum and dad. The bastard who killed them is still out there somewhere, having a laugh 'cos he got away with it. This time, I hope you catch whoever did it.'

'So do I,' said Trevarthen. 'Let's get this out of the way. Do you have an alibi for last night?'

A shake of the head. 'I was alone all evening. Lemme see, I ordered dinner through room service some time after 8:00pm, watched a movie on cable TV – a murder mystery, as it happens, then went to bed with my book. Fell asleep around midnight, I guess.'

It was no surprise lone tennis players "on tour" had no one to back up their versions of events. On the plus side, staying in a hotel made claims easier to verify with swipe cards and cameras dotted about the place. Trevarthen continued. 'From what you've already said, I guess you can't think of anyone who'd want to murder McAdam?'

'No.'

'Others have suggested some of his rivals on the pro tour would want him gone.'

'No way,' Marshall scoffed. 'I mean, he's a grade-A dickhead, but he's not that insufferable you'd want to kill him for it.'

'I meant for selfish reasons. For example, to prevent him from taking top spot.'

Marshall nodded as the penny dropped. 'Ah ha. Yes, I see what you mean. From what I understood Roderick was set to claim number one ranking if he won the Australian Open and other results went his way.'

'But players climb the rankings then tumble down again all the time. No one's ever been killed for it, as far as I'm aware.'

'True.' Marshall walked to the bar fridge, pulled out a can of ice-cold local beer. He offered one to Trevarthen, who declined despite being sorely tempted to say yes. 'But you know what they say, constable.'

'What?'

He raised the can in mock salute. 'There's always a first time for everything.'

## Chapter Ten

THE MAN WAS EVERYWHERE. His face was recognisable to every Australian who owned a television set. Or a computer or a mobile phone with an Internet connection. Even if you only read a newspaper once a month you were aware of him. With his brash manner, constant postulations on political and economic issues via his extensive media network, and even appearances on rival networks simply because he was a ratings magnet, he was an extrovert-on-steroids who grated on many people. One of those people was Constable Kylie Smith.

Clyde Pilmer was a big, jowly man bordering on obese who loved publicity almost as much as he reputedly loved Turkish delight chocolates, Pepsi and fish & chips. His was a face Constable Smith disliked immensely. Of course, she hadn't mentioned this to DS Lisbon; he would have ripped her a new one for letting her prejudices get in the way of doing police work. So she had begrudgingly accepted the assignment of "babysitting" the billionaire. However, she resolved to use her initiative and ask some probing questions before Lisbon arrived. Maybe she'd strike it lucky and weasel key intelligence out of Pilmer. Either way, she was sure the meeting with Big Clyde would leave a bad taste in her mouth for days to come.

At least, that was her belief prior to meeting the man in person.

Now, she was already under his charismatic spell and he'd barely said a word besides *Come in*. Must be some kind of evil magic. Everything she'd seen, read and heard about the man told her he was a bad guy whose only goal in life was to feather his own nest, kicking in the head of anyone stupid enough to get in his way. Contrary to expectations, he radiated a cheerfulness that made you forget about all the bad stuff he'd been accused of for three-plus decades.

'A drink, officer? I can get you anything you like. I've already had two rum and colas. This news is just horrifying! Anyway, did you say yes to a drink?' His tones were rich and velvety.

He was hinting at alcohol, but she never touched it on the job. 'I'll have a glass of water, please.'

Pilmer smiled and snapped his fingers. A figure appeared from behind a wall that separated the reception area from the kitchen. The muscular man, plugged into a visible white earpiece and dressed like an agent from Men in Black, took the order with a curt nod and an obedient *Right away, sir*.

Unsure where to start, Smith decided to begin with expressing condolences and regret that Pilmer's tournament would have to be cancelled.

'The tournament be damned!' was Pilmer's unexpected response. 'Yes, it's going to be a huge inconvenience and a disappointment for so many people. But a man's been murdered, for goodness sake! The only important thing now is to find whoever did it, and quickly.'

The conversation paused as the security man brought Smith her drink on a platter.

'Have you spoken to anyone about this yet?' she asked.

Pilmer's bushy black eyebrows furrowed as he shook his head. 'No way. Inspector Batista told me...' a mobile chirped in his baggy shorts. He looked at the screen before holding his finger up. 'That's him again. One second.'

Smith placed her glass on a polished timber coffee table and took a couple of steps back. She remembered DS Lisbon's advice, stood by the door, arms folded across her chest. Instead of angling her Glock to face Pilmer, who was lumbering about the suite while he spoke to Batista, she made sure the goon could see it. He'd taken up position by the floor-to-ceiling window overlooking the ocean and was staring at Smith with the blankest expression she'd seen outside of department store mannequins. She bugged her eyes at him but he remained impassive. Not able to get a reaction from the robot, she turned her attention back to Pilmer, who had his chunky mobile pressed close to his ear.

'When did you say the press conference is going to be held?' said Pilmer. 'Great, that gives me time to tidy up and join you.' *A pause.* 'Why? Because I want to make a statement at the event.' *Pause.* 'Why is it not possible? How about a donation to the–' *Pause.* 'C'mon, Inspector. People know me, they're likely to respond better if...' *Pause.* 'Right, fair enough. Will do. Bye.'

'What was all that about?' Smith dropped the door-bitch pose, retrieved her glass. The suit turned on his heel and was gone again.

'I need to light a fire under my press secretary so she can

set a few wheels in motion. Can you give me a moment again, please?'

Smith had to admit to herself, the magnate was certainly polite. 'Sure.'

Pilmer called out to "Wendy!", who, like the body guard, materialised as if from nowhere. In her late 60's to early 70's, Smith guessed, the primly dressed secretary listened hard as Pilmer issued half a dozen instructions she was to carry out immediately. Among them, alert everyone involved in the tournament that the event had to be cancelled due to unforeseen circumstances – Wendy didn't enquire as to what those circumstances were – and also instruct the ticketing company to send out a mass SMS and email campaign. Ticketholders needed to know they'd be wasting their time coming to the arena. Full and immediate refunds were to be issued to all customers, no questions. She was also to contact McAdam's parents and request a meeting at a time of their choosing. Wendy scurried out of sight, heels clacking on the tiled floor, and vanished into what Smith presumed was an office at the far end of the expansive suite.

'Why do you think McAdam was murdered?' Smith decided to go the direct route once the efficient Wendy had closed the door behind her. 'You're a smart man. You must have a theory.'

'Seriously,' he extended his arms like a gliding albatross. 'I have no idea. I can only speculate it was some sicko looking for a thrill.'

Smith put a forefinger to her chin. 'Interesting idea. But why would such a killer pick him?'

'Why not? Think back to John Lennon, Gianni Versace. Famous people murdered by their own crazed fans. And

Rod's got plenty of fans as well as detractors. Especially among females.'

Smith nodded. She had to admit, the deceased was a handsome young fellow, although if the constable were to get excited about a tennis player, it would most likely be a female one. Pilmer's theory certainly had merit. 'A deranged stalker.'

'Exactly.' Pilmer sipped his drink with fat, fumbling fingers. 'Perhaps Roderick thought he was safe from such things in his sleepy hometown. But are we safe anywhere in this world anymore?'

'Probably not,' admitted Smith. 'Even Yorkville can be quite dangerous at times.'

'But that's, and I don't want to sound snobbish, restricted to the lower socio-economic classes, isn't it?'

He did sound like a right royal snob, but his assessment wasn't inaccurate. 'To an extent,' was all she'd concede on that point. 'Did McAdam have security around him?'

'Here in Yorkville? Not at all.'

'How about when he was staying in other places?'

Pilmer ambled to a cream three-seater leather lounge, flopped his considerable bulk into it, droplets of rum and cola leaping from his glass. 'Probably. Once you get to the top level of any endeavour, you need people looking out for your safety. I do.' He waved a hand at his own goon. 'Rod, well, you know his reputation for being a hot-head on court, got under people's skin with his antics. Some fans of rival players take exception to that kind of behaviour.'

'Has he received any threats since making the big time?'

'I'm unaware of any. But these are questions best put to his coach and parents. I'm not even that big a tennis fan myself, to be honest.'

'Then why did you organise the Pilmer Challenge?'

'I won't lie to you. Publicity for my business. Seeing my enterprise grow, that's what drives me, it's what gets me up in the morning. I do the things I do in the commercial world because for me it's like breathing; I'd die without it.'

'It's good to be passionate about your career.' She wished she still had the bouncy spring in her step she had after graduating the academy. That was long gone. The job was generally a chore.

'Indeed it is. People think I'm greedy, not satisfied with what I've got.'

Smith couldn't resist saying, 'I've heard that.'

'Nothing could be further from the truth.' A defensiveness crept into his tone. 'Have you heard about the money I donate to charity?'

'Um…'

'Of course not. And you know why?' Pilmer didn't wait for an answer. 'Because I don't make a big song and dance about it like many others do. I'm not interested in winning brownie points. I make my donations on the quiet, and I don't even claim them as tax deductions. I could write off millions of dollars, however I choose not to.'

Smith was about to question him further about all this altruism when there was an urgent triple-rap knock on the door. Pilmer clicked his fingers and the goon flashed by and opened it.

Jack Lisbon with a grim look on his face.

## Chapter Eleven

TAYLOR CAST her eyes around the cold, white-tiled room. A shiver ran up her spine; the gruesome procedures that went on here were more the cause of her goosebumps than the cool temperature. Jack was forever teasing her about her queasiness, about how "unprofessional" it was for a cop to want to puke at the sight of blood. It was an issue she'd grappled with all her life. She'd had sessions with hypnotists, acupuncture, aversion therapy, the lot. Nothing worked. It was one of those ingrained personality traits no branch of science could modify.

Stainless steel surgical implements gleamed on orderly shelves, glints of light from high-wattage globes bounced off bottles of all shapes and sizes. Black and flesh-coloured rubber tubes and other gear the DC could only speculate about hung neatly from hooks. Taylor never felt comfortable in the mortuary when Doctor Margaret Proctor wasn't there. The woman engendered a calming influence among the blood and guts of death and the smells of industrial-strength cleaners and formaldehyde. On the plus side, the

Inspector was with her this afternoon to help make the task of officially identifying McAdam a less traumatic one. At least for Taylor.

The body lay stretched out on the metal slab, raised on a hoist roughly to average waist height. Taylor and Batista stood on one side, the McAdams on the other. A pristine white sheet covered the body completely. Taylor had not seen the corpse since she and Jack had looked at it back at the Hotel Gasnier.

Adrian McAdam blinked repeatedly and shuffled his feet. The corners of his mouth curled downward as he appeared to be combatting the urge to let loose with tears. Veronica McAdam dabbed the inside corners of her spider-veined eyes with a white handkerchief. She'd done a lot of crying on the drive over from the hotel. Neither she nor her husband spoke loud enough for Taylor to hear anything as she drove, only clutching at each other desperately and occasionally whispering throughout the brief journey back to the station.

'Are you ready to look at him now?' said Batista to both parents at once. His face and quiet voice worked in tandem to produce empathy. 'I have to warn you, he won't be looking his best.'

Taylor observed Veronica exchanging a look of apprehension with her husband before they each gave their consent with a mumbled "yes". Taylor reached out to grasp the sheet, her hand shaking slightly. Batista edged his left shoulder against her body and deftly nudged her aside. He whipped the sheet down as far as the deceased's jugular knot – just far enough to see the lad's face, which was all that was required for an identification.

Proctor's best efforts at making Roderick "presentable", which were, as usual, of the highest standard, could not prevent Veronica from unleashing a primal shriek that made Taylor wince and grit her teeth. A side glance to gauge the father's reaction. He stared uncomprehendingly for a fraction of a second then quickly turned his back, fingers interlinked behind his head, as if he was being taken hostage. 'NOOOO!'

After about a minute, the parents had calmed to the point of being ready for the next phase in the process. 'Would you like some time, just to be with him?' said Batista. The couple nodded in silence. 'I hate to say this, but please try and resist the temptation to touch him.' He could barely look at their eyes, wide with disbelief.

'Why not?' said Adrian.

'Surely you've completed a post mortem by now?' said Veronica.

'I'm sorry. There are legal reasons you mustn't. His body may have to be examined again. The investigation has barely begun and we can't take any chances with contamination of evidence.'

'He's not evidence, he's my son!' said Mrs McAdam.

'I know, I know, I...I mean...we...' Batista struggled to find the words.

Taylor came to the rescue. 'It shouldn't be too long before we can release him to you and you'll be allowed to touch him. I promise.'

'We'd like to start making arrangements for a funeral,' said Mr McAdam.

'I understand. The coroner will grant a handover of the body once it's deemed there are no further examinations required,' said Batista. 'I can't guarantee it, but I'd say no more than a week.'

That assurance seemed to placate the parents.

Taylor and the chief stood several metres away, maintaining a solemn silence. Mother and father, raw with grief, held hands and looked down upon their slain son.

'We've seen enough now,' said Mrs McAdam.

'We'd like to ask you some questions before you go back to the hotel,' said Taylor. 'Do you mind?'

'Of course not,' said Mr McAdam. 'We'll answer any questions you have. And then we'll be heading home to Cairns. We're not staying in this hick town any longer than necessary.'

'Of course,' said Batista. 'It's only a short drive from here, so I can see no reason to require your presence in Yorkville.'

Batista opted for his own office rather than the formality of one of the interview rooms. While the McAdams had been paying their respects to their son, he told Taylor he was confident the parents would turn out to be a hundred percent innocent of involvement. She agreed – for the moment – although she knew from bitter experience that even the least likely suspect could turn out to be the culprit. She was acutely aware of one horrific statistic: in Australia parents kill their children at an average rate of one a week. Known as filicide, the numbers are dominated by parents of young children. The crimes often take the form of murder-suicides. A case of "If I can't have the kids, no one can!" when custody-denied dad was the murderer, neonatal depression when it was the mother. The McAdams fell well outside of those categories, however other – rarer – motives existed for parents to do in their offspring. Those morbid thoughts were interrupted by Constable Damien Wells as he carried a fold-up chair into the boss's office for Taylor. The McAdams occupied the two armchairs across from the Inspector's desk.

'Normally we'd be joined by our lead detective for this

interview, but he's been unavoidably detained with Mr Pilmer,' said Batista. 'This tragic case has meant we're having to spread our limited resources. But be assured, we will not rest until we've found out who killed your son.' The Inspector offered an avuncular smile. Jack had texted Taylor and the chief to report he'd be busy with Pilmer for the next hour or so and suggested they conduct the initial interview of the parents without him. Jack had a feeling the magnate might be good for a lead or two. He'd also given Constable Smith a commendation for not being intimidated and gaining Pilmer's confidence, words which made Taylor smile. The gruff ex-boxer was getting softer as he aged.

'Are you referring to Detective Lisbon?' said Adrian McAdam. When the Inspector confirmed that was the man he meant, McAdam added, 'Excellent. I've heard of his clean-up record. Second to none.'

'That's correct,' said Taylor. 'But we work as a team here. Jack has capable backup.' She meant herself and her tone probably gave that away.

'Of course,' said Mr McAdam.

'Also,' continued Batista, 'we're getting extra investigative resources from Cairns and Brisbane and...'

'I think you may have to look further afield than that.' Taylor detected a hint of something more aggressive and insistent creeping into Mrs McAdam's voice.

'Why?' said Taylor. 'Do you think someone *ordered* this murder?'

Adrian McAdam glared at the DC, then the Inspector. 'You know, I've just realised. You've told us precisely nothing about what happened to our son.'

'That's right,' said Veronica McAdam. 'How did he... die?' She dabbed a runaway tear from her cheek.

The Inspector rubbed a hand across his face, as if

suddenly very weary. 'It's not a pleasant topic, but one we must confront. I apologise for not telling you earlier.' As Batista laid out the gruesome details of the murder, the faces of Mr and Mrs McAdam crumbled. Each new fact was like a knife to the heart. Their anguish was palpable, and Taylor now scrubbed any notion mum and dad were monsters after their kid's money. And there certainly was plenty of that to be divvied up at some point. When he'd finished speaking the hard words, Batista buzzed Constable Wells to bring in a pot of tea, chocolate biscuits and a jug of water. A good idea, Taylor thought. The poor parents looked like diabetics with dangerously low sugar levels and mentally ready to snap.

'From what you said before, it seems you have your own ideas about who might have wanted to harm Roderick,' Taylor prompted.

'If you'd been following the pro circuit,' said Adrian, accepting a mug of tea from the tray Wells brought in, 'you'd be aware of a running rivalry between Roderick and Stefan.'

'Who's Stefan?' said Taylor. 'I have to plead ignorance of the players names. Now if Jack were here, another matter altogether. He's a sports nut, big time.' She offered a watery smile, trying to appear supportive while not being "jokey". It was a dangerously fine line to tread when dealing with the recently bereaved, especially when trying to coax information out of them.

'Then it'll be terrific when Detective Lisbon is able to free himself from other duties and get on the case…'

'He *is* on the case,' defended Batista. 'In fact, he sent me these photographs from your son's hotel room.' The Inspector laid his mobile on the desk. The parents shook their heads as they stared at the paper note and the horrific message on the mirror.

'Damn that hotel manager!' said Veronica McAdam. 'He wouldn't let us into his room. There was a "do not disturb" sign hanging on the door handle this morning. He said privacy concerns prevented him from letting us in. It's not Roddy's habit to hang up DND signs. When he's not playing tennis or training, he's on that damned Xbox. Someone else put the sign there. We knocked and called out, over and over. When Roddy didn't answer and all our phone calls went unanswered, that's when we called the police.'

Batista nodded slowly. 'Unfortunate, but the manager was probably in his rights to do what he did.'

Adrian McAdam exhaled through puffed cheeks. 'Bloody rules! Anyway, does your Detective Lisbon have any ideas about this disgusting message?'

'We're yet to discuss the matter, but I'm sure he does. What do you make of it?'

'Well, they're taunting, aren't they?' said Mrs McAdam. 'I can't imagine the sick sort of mind that would do something like this. Can you, Ade?'

'Definitely not. And why isn't Detective Lisbon here?' said Adrian McAdam impatiently. 'Pilmer's not going to be of any damn use!'

'I appreciate your anger and frustration. Unfortunately, though, we can't all be everywhere at once. Yorkville's a small town. We've only got two full-time detectives in our CIB unit and a handful of uniforms. Every one of us has only one focus at the moment. Your son.'

'I apologise, Inspector,' said Adrian McAdam, setting his tea on the chief's desk. 'It's just, I don't know, I figured my wife and I to be more…central…to our son's murder than Clyde Pilmer.'

'Pilmer may have vital information. And if he does, DS Lisbon will get it out of him. But be assured, DC Taylor is an effective deputy. In fact, the last murder enquiry was solved thanks to her keen observation skills. Jack got most of the credit in the press, but it was all down to Claudia here.'

Taylor felt herself blush to the roots of her hair.

'Very well. Let me fill you in on Stefan Krepper.' Adrian McAdam explained, in rapid sentences, that Krepper, a Swede, had enjoyed a long run at the top of the rankings, and only had to win the upcoming Australian Open to beat Roger Federer's streak of 237 weeks as world number one. 'Roddy was tipped by many to snap that winning streak.'

'Forgive me,' said Taylor, partly to ask a question but also to get a break from frantically writing notes. 'But that's speculation.'

'Perhaps,' said Mrs McAdam. 'But our son hadn't lost a match in six months. He was in better form than any of the other players. He was all set to become the youngest ever world number one as well.' Pride made her eyes glow through the tears.

'All due respect,' said Taylor again. 'But I saw how he lost his serve to a man who's a rank amateur.'

Adrian McAdam waved the suggestion away. 'Pfft. Theatre, Detective Taylor. He was playing up to the crowd. All part of Pilmer's plan, you can ask him yourself. We were at meetings with him where he explained that Roddy was supposed to give them a chance of winning, if not a set then at least break his serve, but then snatch that chance away at the last second.'

'We all saw Depp's reaction last night. Surely that could

not have been staged. Depp was genuinely angry. Perhaps that could have motivated him to…kill Roderick.'

Adrian McAdam shrugged. 'I strongly doubt it. Pilmer rang me to let me know he'd arranged to pay out the other lad. And told him about it. Depp was jubilant, apparently.'

'When did Pilmer make that call?'

'Early in the evening. Why? Does that make a difference?'

'Depending on the time-of-death analysis, it could. If Depp had been informed of his reversal of fortunes before the murder took place, the motivation to seek revenge for the way he was wronged would have disappeared.'

'He can't be a serious suspect,' said Veronica McAdam. 'It's someone higher up. Someone with a longer-term benefit to be gained. And that someone, I'd bet anything on it, is that fucking Swedish bastard! Look into him.'

'He's in Melbourne ahead of the Australian Open, isn't he?' said Batista.

'Physically, yes. But he's rich and powerful. He could've organised a hit.'

'Does that sound like a serious scenario?' Taylor tapped a pencil against her open notebook. 'I mean, you heard the horrible details of the murder. That doesn't equate to a — she made a pair of air quotes — "hitman's" MO. A contract killer wouldn't go to that level of…sophistication.'

'That's your department, MO's and the like,' said Mr McAdam. 'If you don't mind, we'd like to go home now.'

'Of course,' said Batista. 'How are you making the journey? I'd recommend against driving for a while.'

'I can drive,' insisted Mr McAdam. 'Our own car is at the hotel.'

'But after what's happened, are you—'

'Yes, I'm sure!'

'Very well. Your decision. One last thing, I'll be appointing Constable Kylie Smith your police family liaison officer. She'll keep you up-to-date with the progress of our enquiries. Feel free to contact her at any time.' He handed the McAdams a card with the station's main number on it. 'Call the general line and we'll redirect to her.'

Taylor escorted the broken couple to the exit and then sedately drove them back to the hotel. Not a word was spoken in the vehicle until the police radio crackled to life as they entered the Grand's car park. Two minor traffic accidents on the outskirts of town, a spot of road rage reported. Trevarthen and Semmens accepted the call and took one job each.

'So much for our son being the only focus!' said Mrs McAdam.

A totally unfair observation, thought Taylor. But she understood the woman completely.

## Chapter Twelve

CONSTABLE KYLIE SMITH looked more comfortable than Jack had expected. Slender shoulders back and standing in an at-ease position, her face broke into a smile as the detective entered Pilmer's luxury suite. Not so much relief as gratitude to Jack for turning up and taking over. DS Lisbon greeted his colleague with a friendly wink, simultaneously extending his hand to Pilmer, who came striding across the room.

'You must be the legendary Detective Jack Lisbon,' boomed Pilmer. 'Your fame precedes you.' Then in a more subdued tone, 'A pity we weren't meeting under more auspicious circumstances.'

'I'd say you were a lot more famous than me, sir. And yes, the circumstances are tragic. I'm hoping you can shed some light on a couple of matters for me.'

'I've already spoken at length to your delightful colleague, here.' Pilmer gestured to the crimson-faced constable. 'She's been most efficient, a credit to the Yorkville Police.'

The man certainly knew how to lay it on thick. 'She is indeed. I won't take up too much of your time. I have to get back to the station to help coordinate the investigation. First, I'd like to show you something. Kylie, come with us please.'

Travelling in a semi-circle around the tower, they soon reached Room 2003. Jack led them straight into the ensuite and flicked on the light.

'Jesus, what the...?' said Pilmer. 'I don't believe it.'

'Me either,' added Smith. 'Apart from the fact it's disgusting, how could someone get in here to do that unless they had the key, like you? Does this mean a hotel staff member is involved in the murder?'

'Possibly,' Jack agreed. 'But there's another scenario.'

'What?' said Pilmer, his monumental frame almost teetering from the shock of the message on the glass. 'Roderick wrote that himself?'

'No, of course not. However my gut tells me McAdam knew his killer and he was lured to his death.'

'Really?' said Smith. 'So, what, you reckon the victim has let someone in here, that person had scribbled this... filth...on the mirror and then McAdam's followed them out. That doesn't make sense.'

'How about this?' said Jack. 'McAdam and the person he let in, let's assume it's the killer, were about to head off together. Then at the door the killers says, oops, I forgot something inside. You wait for me at the elevator. Or downstairs, doesn't matter. Then that person goes into the room alone, quickly writes the message on the mirror, comes out again, hangs the do-not-disturb sign on the door and leads McAdam off to the Gaz, and to his death.'

'Impressive deduction, sir,' said Smith. 'And the handwritten note?'

'Perhaps it was slid under the door at some point, or the killer gave it to him personally. An invitation to something at the Gaz that Roderick couldn't resist.'

'But why the message in lipstick?' Pilmer rubbed his jowly cheek. 'To what purpose?'

'It's a mocking gesture,' said Jack. 'There's a level of hatred here I haven't seen in a long time. The killer wants everyone to know McAdam was a horrible person and deserved to die.'

Pilmer's hand went to his mouth. 'But...you can't show the world this image. It's...an outrage to the man's dignity.'

'Let me tell you, it's almost a love letter compared to the way he was killed.'

'What? And how did he...'

Jack put a finger to his lips and shushed Pilmer, then led the way out of the bathroom into the open space of the suite. He sat at the long smoked-glass dining table, beckoned for Pilmer to do the same. Smith remained standing behind the DS. 'I can't tell you about the killer's MO right now. The Inspector may choose to reveal that information publicly. Even a picture of that godawful message, I dunno. And he'll decide on the timing of such a revelation.'

'That's his prerogative, I guess,' said Pilmer, fiddling with his chunky Rolex Oyster-Perpetual that probably cost more than Jack's car.

'You bet it is,' said Jack. He craned his neck around. 'Kylie, can you briefly fill me in on what you asked Mr Pilmer and his responses?' He pointed to a spot to the right of Pilmer. 'Sit next to our friend.'

Smith swiftly took a seat, plucked a notebook from her pocket and summarised the exchanges.

'Terrific,' said Jack when Smith had finished. 'Now, sir.

Can I just ask a couple more questions before we leave you in peace? It's been a helluva day and I'm sure you have a lot to organise with cancelling the tournament and whatnot.'

'Sure.'

Over the next five minutes, Pilmer told the officers that last night after the tennis he'd enjoyed a dinner with the McAdams, minus their son, who, they assumed was in his room playing the Xbox he was addicted to. Peter Gosling was also at the dinner. They had a relaxing evening at the hotel's five-star restaurant *The Crocodillio* enjoying lobster mornay and champagne – at Pilmer's expense – then a few cocktails in the piano lounge listening to a horse-toothed crooner performing covers of Billy Joel numbers.

'Sounds like a ball,' said Jack with open sarcasm. 'Now, what have you got to say about the disgraceful way the tennis officials cheated Sean Depp out of his money?'

'Sorry?'

'Was that part of the plan? Lure the unsuspecting chumps from around the country with no intention of rewarding their efforts? Just to put on your circus?'

'Now, wait a minute. That was all an honest mistake.'

'Bullshit. Every man and his dog could see the ball landed out, but, somehow, every one of the officials saw differently. Can you explain that?'

The big man's eyes darted about. 'No, I can't. Like I already told Constable Smith, I'm not into tennis. All that official stuff is out of my hands. I swear there was no instruction from me to fix the results one way or the other.'

Jack drummed his fingers on the table. 'So, poor Depp goes home empty handed?'

Pilmer shook his pumpkin-sized head vigorously. 'Nope. When people started contacting me about this very matter I had a good hard look at the replay. Even I could see an error had been made. A costly one. So I rang Mr Depp and made amends.'

'How?'

'I asked him for his bank details and made a transfer immediately. Even bought him a bottle of cognac. It's the least I could do.'

'Very noble of you. Speaking of which, you had to reschedule the final because McAdam didn't like playing in the hottest part of the day. Were you upset by the demand from the McAdam camp?'

Surprise twisted Pilmer's lips. 'What are you insinuating? I got so mad at having to make a change to the program that I'd...what...kill someone?'

'Of course not. I just meant that—'

'If anything,' Pilmer interrupted, 'it would've worked out better for the advertising companies in terms of higher TV ratings. It would've made sense to run all the matches early morning or later at night for the American viewers. It was my mistake from the outset. But there's not going to be a final now is there? So it's a moot argument. My only desire now is the same as yours. To find and prosecute whoever killed Roderick.'

Jack assessed Pilmer's words as genuine. It *was* utterly ludicrous to propose that a switch in the program irked the organiser so much as to push him to murder. The DS thanked Pilmer and said all the persons he mentioned had already been interviewed – including Depp – and Jack would make sure their stories matched. He also requested Pilmer not to leave Yorkville for the next 72 hours. It was a randomly invented period, but Jack made it sound like a legal requirement.

'I'd planned on being in Adelaide on Sunday morning

for a meeting with my Brazilian partners,' pushed back Pilmer. 'My private plane is waiting at Cairns airport.'

'You'll have to reschedule that one, I'm afraid. Or have an online meeting. I hear they're all the rage these days.'

'Really? No, I need to be there. Online meetings with interpreters need a lot of preparation. They can be a bloody nightmare, things are misunderstood.' He pulled out his cell phone. 'Listen, I'm just going to call my lawyer to see if I'm legally obliged to stay in Yorkville. All right with you, Detective?'

The billionaire had called his bluff. It was clear why the man was a success. Polite and canny with it. But DS Lisbon had his own negotiating talents. 'Look,' said Jack with a sigh. 'Your lawyer will tell you you're under no obligation since you haven't been charged with anything and you aren't *officially* a suspect, but think of the optics.'

'What do you mean?'

'Well. I'd hate to have to tell my friend Holly Maguire at Channel 11 that Clyde Pilmer's business interests take precedence over a murder enquiry. It would look like you're running away from something.'

'Oh dear.'

'Please, do the right thing and wait the 72 hours like I've asked you, and then after that I don't care what you do.'

'Gotcha.' Pilmer offered a flat-mouthed smile.

As the officers walked back to the bank of elevators in the middle of the tower, Smith whispered to Jack, 'That was about the coolest thing I've ever seen. You certainly put him in his place, sir.'

Jack pressed the button to call the lift. As the ping went off he turned to Smith and said, 'I'd rather put the killer in their place. Copperhead Jail.'

## Chapter Thirteen

WAITING to receive at least some preliminary information from an overworked Margaret Proctor and her assistant Clara Littlejohn, Jack, back at his desk, tapped his fingers on the desk. For some reason The Stranglers' frantic tune "No More Heroes" thrashed in his head. With the boss on a call to Assistant Commissioner Landacre and Taylor dropping the McAdams back at the Grand Hotel, Jack decided to hit the phone. First up, Constable Ben Wilson.

'Sir?' came the clipped response.

'Update me,' came the equally clipped reply.

'On?'

'Waddaya mean "on"? What's happening at the Gasnier?'

'Right, of course. Forgive my scatterbrain, sir. The heat's sapped all my energy.'

'Yeah, tell me another story. We all feel the heat. Now—'

'No, I mean Greer closed the hotel and left me standing outside. There's some shade under the roof that runs around the veranda, but there's absolutely no breeze. I'm not sure how much longer I can hold up.'

'Why didn't you ask the bloke for a spare key?'

Silence.

'Wilson?'

'Didn't think of it, sir.'

Jack had a lot of time for Wilson. He was a wiz at maths and science and remembering arcane minutiae of the criminal code, but sometimes the basic common-sense stuff let him down badly. 'I'm sending Trevarthen to pick you up.'

'Thanks, sir. Appreciated.'

'When did he leave?'

'Who?'

'Rudy Greer, for fuck's sake! Geez, the heat really has fried your brain.'

The sound of Wilson swallowing hard. 'About half an hour ago. He's been turning dodgy-looking men and half-naked women away all afternoon. None of them were happy about it. Some of them scurried off in a real hurry when they saw me in my uniform and the crime scene tape, even tried to hide their faces. Must have thought it was a raid by the vice squad. Rather amusing to watch.'

'So glad you've had some fun among all your suffering. I guess Greer wasn't in the best of moods either.'

'Correct. He was real angry when he left. Jumped in his Rav4, swearing at the top of his head, and sped out of the carpark, dust flying everywhere.'

'He'll get over it. What about the forensics team? They say anything to you?'

'Proctor looked pretty tired after they packed up their gear and headed off. Same with her offsider.' A pause. 'D'ya know if she's single, sir?'

'No, I don't bleedin' know, Wilson! Keep your mind on

the job. Need I remind you of the enormity of this case? I repeat, did they say anything?'

'Proctor told me they'd collected so much evidence it would take a long time to examine it all. Maybe a month. She said because of the high turnover of guests and...you know...the kinds of activities that go on in the Gaz, there's going to be a lot of DNA, hundreds of sets of fingerprints, you name it.'

'Just perfect.' Jack had anticipated this scenario. Perhaps it was going to be another of those cases where science doesn't play the decisive role in solving the crime. 'Anyway, hang in there, son, relief's on its way.'

After dispatching Trevarthen, with an order to drop Wilson at his home for a cold shower and change of uniform before they both came back to the station, Jack fished out a tatty business card from his wallet. He punched in the number.

'Hello?'

'Mr Greer. DS Jack Lisbon here. I need you to answer a couple of questions for me.'

'Are you serious?'

'Yeah. First, why didn't you offer my Constable a spare key to the front door? He's been cooking on the veranda of your shit-hole pub all afternoon.'

'What's he been cooking? Sausages?' The man took a pull on a cigarette and chuckled, bringing on a racking cough.

'Don't be a smart arse,' Jack snapped. 'You know what I mean. Why no key?'

'He, ah, never asked for one. What else you wanna know? I'm a busy man.'

'I'm going to need an official statement from you.'

'I already told youse everything before.'

'That was just a chat. Frankly, I don't like you and I don't trust you. I wanna make everything nice and official. Same goes for all your employees.' Jack clicked on his mouse and the criminal record of Garth Greer appeared. Nothing too serious, a couple of assaults, latest one a year ago. Then the brother Derrick. A string of traffic offences and two counts of possession of excessive amounts of cannabis. 'Especially those sons of yours.'

'Come on. They're good lads.' The man sounded pissed off. *Good.*

'Don't make me laugh. Now, once I'm off the phone to you, ring them all and ask them to contact the station ASAP. We'll make appointments to question everyone who works for you. I suggest you also gather all your financial records and bring them in. We've got specialists who can analyse all that stuff in a jiffy. If things don't stack up, I'm referring you to the Financial and Cyber Crime Group to have a long, hard look into your affairs.'

'Financial crime? Look, I may not keep the best records, but—'

'OK, the Tax Department, then. You're a drain on society not paying his fair share. I'll get you one way or another. If it's not for involvement in the murder of Roderick McAdam, then it'll be for fraud.'

'Why have you got it in for me, Detective? What have I ever done to you?'

'Nothing. But there's been a horrific murder committed on your premises, and as far as I can see, your main concern is the effect it's having on your business, not solving the crime. I feel you need a readjustment of perspective about what's important.' Jack ordered Greer to write down the station's direct number, made him read it back aloud. 'And if it takes a prosecution for that to happen, so be it!'

Jack disconnected the call, confident he'd got further under the man's skin. Greer's financials would surely be of interest to the tax authorities, his preference for cash-only payments a magnet for a zealous investigator. The man's sons sparked something in the reptilian part of Jack's brain. Ugly brutes, they had appeared in court more times than they'd been convicted. Which could mean they had good legal representation rather than them being innocent of the offences they were alleged to have carried out. Accessory to the armed robbery of a Cairns liquor store was one such charge they had successfully evaded. A quick search of the data base made Jack grin. The Greer brothers' lawyer in the robbery case was none other than Denise Hutchinson, a woman Jack had dated, rather unsuccessfully, a couple of years ago. He was just about to give Denise a call when a little white envelope icon flashed in the bottom right-hand corner of his screen. Then another.

The first was from Marietta Szabo. Subject line. *Call me ASAP*. Preview mode revealed a short message expressing Marietta's disgust Jack didn't ring her to cancel their lunch date or respond to her attempts to contact him. His phone log showed a couple of missed calls from her and some unread and unanswered texts. He shot a hand to his forehead. *Dammit*. Not to worry, she'd figure it all out once the press conference went to air and, hopefully, forgive him. If not, no great loss. *Taylor. It was Taylor he wanted.*

The second email demanded more attention.

Proctor's "very" preliminary findings.

## Chapter Fourteen

JACK CLICKED OPEN THE EMAIL, which had been cc'd to Batista and Taylor. The chief forensics scientist's initial conclusion was that the cause of death was ligature strangulation. The victim was most likely subdued using stupefying substances, however this remained to be confirmed. Time of death using the new method developed in the Netherlands – in the neighbourhood of 04:15–04:45, Friday 7 January. Proctor's own quick blood analysis found traces of alcohol, cannabis and another substance she believed could be Flunitrazepam, aka Rohypnol; a full laboratory analysis would verify what that mystery substance was. She sent the following specimens taken from the corpse to the lab for analysis: blood, urine, vitreous humour from the eye (to confirm the time-of-death estimate), gastric contents, bile, liver and hair from the head and pubic region.

Dry scientific reports were one thing. Hearing it direct from the horse's mouth another. He placed the call to Proctor.

She answered after half a dozen rings. 'Did you get my

summary report?' She was breathy, as if she'd sprinted up a flight of stairs to answer the phone.

'Yes, and thanks for doing it so fast.' He paused to take a sip of cold coffee. 'So it's definite that he choked to death?'

'At this early stage and pending proper toxicology tests and all the other analyses we have to run, I would say so. Substances were probably used to daze or even knock McAdam out, but if that occurred, he's eventually woken up and suffocated himself. It's clear in this particular ligature strangulation that the pull of the legs drew the stockings tight around McAdam's neck.' The snap of Proctor's fingers echoed down the line. 'Lights out.'

'Any other proof?'

'Yes. I observed haemorrhaging in the corneas, what's also called conjunctival petechiae. The same thing had affected the skin around the eyes, turned it a reddish hue. All of which tallies with a good old-fashioned garrotting.'

'So the drugs didn't kill him first?'

'It appears not. You'll just have to be patient if you want watertight stuff for a prosecution. I'll prepare a more detailed report once we get *all* the results back.'

'Yeah, Wilson told me it could take a month. That's damned annoying.'

'I'm sorry. The toxicology might be quicker, about a week. But the DNA salad we unearthed is going to take some sorting out. And that's not even getting into the fingerprints. Imagine a game of naked twister with hundreds of participants.'

Jack felt his face flush. 'I'd rather not. What about the roach ends and the glass with the lipstick on it?'

'That's all part of it, Detective Lisbon. All bagged up and waiting their turn under the microscope.'

'Any way of speeding the process up?'

'No.'

'You can't have a word in the ear of the Head of Forensic Services? She's a mate of yours, isn't she?'

'No chance. Besides it being unethical to jump the queue, that other incident in Cairns is going to take precedence now.'

This was news to Jack. 'What incident?'

The whistle of a kettle in the background. No doubt Proctor was fixing herself a herbal tea concoction based on a druid recipe from the Middle Ages. 'The boat fire in Cairns.'

Then he remembered. 'Actually, I did hear that story on the car radio. I thought it was a minor problem that got taken care of.'

'Check the update.'

Jack clicked on the internal webpage with the latest police news from around Queensland. What he saw made him gasp. A small fuel fire on a charter boat quickly spread after the skipper said he had it under control. A Canadian tourist drowned along with the skipper, another person was in a critical condition in Cairns Private Hospital with third-degree burns, survival chances slim.

'Holy shit, Margaret. McAdam's case just slipped down the ladder of priorities.'

'It may turn out to have been an unavoidable accident, but…'

Jack understood the "but". A massive investigation would be required to determine if there had been foul play or, at the least, negligence in relation to the boat fire. And negligence meant the involvement of the coroner and the laying of criminal charges. Mr and Mrs McAdam would be most displeased their son's murder wouldn't be the sole focus of the police now.

'I've got another job for you,' said Jack. 'Are you keen on some Saturday work?' He explained what he'd discovered in Room 2003 at the Grand.

'Hmm. Tempting. I'd rather enjoy my day off, though. Today was exhausting.'

'I appreciate that, Margaret. But with the incident in Cairns, where else can I draw on the manpower to do a sweep of McAdam's room?'

'Oh, all right then.' She was being totally disingenuous. Nobody loved their job more than Proctor.

'I'll be taking Clara with me.' Not a question, a statement.

'Of course. Double-time pay for both of you. I've already cleared it with Batista.' He hadn't.

'We'll be there at 7:00am sharp.' Jack could hear the sound of her dog Watson barking in the background. Made him wonder if he needed one for company. He'd always liked Australian Kelpies.

'OK, thanks, Margaret. You're a champion.'

'There's one thing I'm curious about, but it doesn't seem to have a bearing on the victim's demise,' said Proctor. 'I wonder what you make of it.'

'What's that?'

'McAdam's left arm. It's much larger than his right, but totally normal looking, if you know what I mean. I'm not sure I've seen anything like it before.'

'Well, that's where being a sports fan trumps being a clever-clogs scientist.' Jack explained that the bigger arm was a common phenomenon among full-time tennis professionals. More so in the old days of heavier wooden racquets, but it still happened. As a boy, Jack had been fascinated by Argentinian Guillermo Villa's massive left arm, which was so pronounced he thought it was a deformity.

'Fascinating,' said Proctor.

'Yeah, it is 'n all.' Jack looked up, grateful at the opportunity to terminate a call which had now outlived its usefulness. DC Taylor was back, again with a cardboard tray of coffees from the Good Bean in one hand, that was good. A worried-looking Joe Batista by her side, not so much.

## Chapter Fifteen

'ARE THE OTHERS BACK YET?' Jack asked Batista, eagerly accepting a cup from Taylor. He'd not managed to ingest his usual quota of caffeine today, which partially explained the bollocking he'd handed out to Rudy Greer. Also the fact the man was a complete prat.

Batista shook his head slowly. 'That charter boat fire has thrown a spanner in the works in more ways than one.'

'No doubt. But you didn't answer my question, sir.'

'I was getting to it. I've sent Noah Semmens up to Cairns to help out with that matter.'

'What?'

'The fire started 50 metres off the dock. There were people dining at pier-side restaurants at the time, meaning potential witnesses. I couldn't say no to the request with two people dead and a third hanging on by a thread. But we're only one constable down.'

'What about the two detectives from Cairns we were promised?'

'We'll have to scratch them. But we are getting the two from Brisbane.'

Taylor took a seat at her desk, which sat at right angles to Jack's corner workstation. 'At least that's something to be grateful for.' She logged onto her computer, keen to read the mini-report from Proctor.

'You know who the detectives are?' said Jack.

Batista consulted a text on his mobile. 'Tania Wycombe and Mike Steger. I'm assured they're both top-class investigators. Their flight arrives shortly. I've told them to get here for 9:00pm for a debrief.'

The Inspector's words drew an enthusiastic nod from Jack. 'I know Wycombe and Steger from my days down south. They'll do a good job.'

Batista's body began to rock almost imperceptibly from side to side. The motion often foreshadowed an urgent request. 'Speaking of sterling jobs. Claudia, I need you to bash out a statement for the press and our social media profiles. Ask the main media outlets to assemble here at 7:00pm for a press conference. It's already'... a glance at his watch ... '5:30pm.'

'That doesn't give me a lot of time, sir.' Taylor's eyebrows knitted together.

'I've already jotted down the main points I'd like to address. It'll just be me and Jack fronting the jackals. Pilmer wanted a seat at the table, can you believe it? Even in tragedy that oaf looks for an opportunity to get his mug on the television.' Batista handed Taylor a slip of paper with bullet-pointed items. 'If you think of anything I've missed, add it. Just make sure to email me the draft for approval before you hit the send button.'

'Got it, sir.'

# Drop Shot

WHILE TAYLOR TAPPED at her keyboard, searching for the right words to describe the horrific crime recently carried out in sleepy Yorkville and what the police were doing about it, Jack and Batista retreated to the boss's office to take a preliminary look at the CCTV footage from the Grand Hotel. Jack pulled out a USB flash drive with more storage than a dock full of shipping containers. Batista plugged it in, navigated his way through the folders until he found the files covering the last 24 hours.

'Is this a long enough timeline, do you think?' said Batista, adjusting his reading glasses which, as always, kept sliding down his elongated nose whenever he bent his head forward. Every now and then he'd shove them back to the bridge.

'Should be. We can look at more footage later if we come up empty. There's files going back all week, see?' Jack took control of the mouse, clicked a back button and added, 'My bad, it's for the month. But seeing it's only the seventh of January today, a month's as good as a week to a blind bat, eh?'

'Your humour defies all logic, Lisbon.'

'Monty Python reference, sir.'

'Don't remember that one. Anyway, where do we start?'

They decided to split the viewing by area: foyer, elevator banks and corridors of the floors on which McAdam, his parents and Pilmer had rented rooms. They decided against the areas on the lower floors where coach Gosling and the journeymen tennis players were staying – for now, at least. The main focus – the 20$^{th}$ floor. Jack and Batista agreed it would take about 10 minutes to drive from the arena to the hotel, but for now the victim's movements from the end of the match had not been verified.

'Sir, did you and Taylor ask the parents where Roderick went after the match?'

'Dammit, DS Lisbon, no. I believe we omitted that rather obvious one. We were too focussed on asking them who they thought might have done it.'

'I don't feel like disturbing them right now. I can get the same information out of the coach.' Jack looked up Gosling's mobile number from the CIB's intranet database and put through the call.

'Yes?'

Jack quickly introduced himself.

'Have there been any developments?' The coach's voice was tired. Perhaps he'd been drinking.

'There's going to be a live press conference at 7:00pm. Should be on all TV channels. We'll be informing the McAdams about it. I advise you to watch it, too. It might spark some thoughts that could assist the enquiry.'

'Will do.'

'For now, though, can you tell me if Roderick went straight back to the hotel after the match with Depp or if he went somewhere else?'

'Back to the hotel. He couldn't wait to get out of the stadium. He refused the usual requests for interviews and autographs, which he normally does without complaint. It was that line-call incident that did his head in. Roddy was pretty annoyed with himself about the way he'd handled it, actually. I think on reflection he regretted not conceding the point to Depp. But he's got this massive ego, you understand?'

'I understand,' said Jack a touch too impatiently. 'The

whole world knew about it. How long before he arrived back at the hotel then?'

'He had a quick shower at the arena and then we headed back to the hotel in one of our hire cars right after that. I went to my room and Adrian and Veronica went to theirs. Later we met Pilmer for dinner.'

'And Roderick?'

'Back to his room and onto the Xbox. At least that's what we assumed. We never...saw him after that.' The man sounded like he was on the verge of tears.

'Thank you. That's a great help.'

Jack estimated Roderick McAdam's arrival at the hotel at about 6:15pm. To play it safe, he and Batista agreed to start their initial viewing of the video from 6:00pm. After 47 minutes at x8 speed, in order to get through as much as possible as quickly as possible, and with eyes growing weary, Jack's heart missed a beat. The time and date stamp at the top of the video showed 00:15:36 Friday 7th January when McAdam placed the swipe card in the slot to enter his room. He wasn't alone. Jack clicked harder on the mouse than perhaps was necessary, stopping the video. He jabbed an index finger at the screen. 'That's him, there, sir. Look.'

'Who?'

Jack rewound the footage and played it again at normal speed. 'See?'

'Yes.'

'Let's run it a bit longer.'

Jack adjusted the speed to x4. At 00:42:11 McAdam exited his room and headed for the lift, a spring in his step. At 00.44.09 the featureless figure in dark clothing and huge sunglasses who entered with McAdam reappeared outside Room 2003. No spring in that person's step. On the contrary, his – and it was clearly a male – body language was furtive. But the thing that made Jack sit up and take notice most of all was the stranger placing the "do not disturb" sign on the door handle. *The scenario he'd developed for Smith and Pilmer was on the money.* Then the man stopped halfway towards the elevators and ducked down the fire escape stairwell.

Jack paused the video again. 'One moment, sir.' He raced to Taylor's desk, tapped her on the shoulder. She jumped slightly in her seat, cursing under her breath.

'You could at least warn a person before you sneak up like that, mate. You scared the crap out of me.'

Jack ignored the mild rebuke. 'You haven't finished that press release have you, sunshine?'

'Almost. Why?'

'You're going to have to add a paragraph or two.'

'OK. What needs to go in?'

'I think we've got the killer on tape.'

## Chapter Sixteen

INSPECTOR BATISTA APPEARED resplendent in his uniform, shirt neatly ironed, tie just so. The press room was packed with reporters, camera operators and photo journalists from the local channels and the *Yorkville Times* newspaper. Accredited independent journalists were also in attendance. Crews from Cairns TV and the *Clarion* had also made the ninety-minute journey down the highway to cover the press conference. The sister city's media must have been torn, Jack thought to himself. Which event to give the most cover? The murder of a world-famous athlete or a tragedy in their own backyard? In the end, the outlets had sent second-string journos to Yorkville – Jack didn't recognise any of them – and kept their top talent at home to report on the boating accident. The cliché was true – news is 99% local.

Batista cleared his throat before pulling the fluffy black microphone closer to his face. He looked left to Jack, who nodded in support. He gave the mic a couple of test taps, took a deep breath and began speaking. 'As you were made aware an hour or so ago, our beautiful town has played host to a terrible tragedy. One that will have reverberations around the country and around the world. Late this morning, the body of tennis player Roderick McAdam – a product of Yorkville who made his name internationally – was found in the Hotel Gasnier. We suspect foul play and a murder investigation has been launched. I'd now like to hand over to the lead detective on the case, DS Jack Lisbon.'

Jack turned to the Inspector, thanked him for the introduction. Unlike Batista, Jack was casual – almost a slob by comparison. Ever-present cotton jacket, some stubborn coffee stains near the wrists, checked shirt with frayed collar, the same navy tie he'd worn when they gave the McAdams the bad news. Again, Taylor had helped him get the knot right. He'd leaned in extra close as she helped him this time, deeply inhaled the subtle smell of her perfume, of *her*, and almost melted. *One day, Jack.*

Arms waved in the air, microphones bobbed over the sea of heads. Voices called out with questions; it was all fuzzy static in Jack's ears. He never understood why reporters persisted in this childish behaviour. They would have to wait to be called upon in an orderly fashion.

'OK, I'm going to run through what we know, show a couple of photographs and a short video, and then take questions from the floor. There's a lot to get through, so please be patient.'

Jack began with what the police – more properly maid Mercy Valdez – had found at the Hotel Gasnier. Taylor's press-release had not contained the gory details of McAdam's death that Jack now revealed. The strangulation by nylon stockings, the lipstick on the glass, the remains of drug paraphernalia. A projector showed images from the crime scene – but not the body. That would be an affront to both the victim and his parents. Then photos of the threatening message with the crude penis drawing on the mirror in Room 2003. Silence fell over the assembled media as one horrific detail followed another. 'As you can imagine, we are dealing with a very sick mind. A twisted individual who must be apprehended as quickly as possible.'

'Do you have any leads yet?' screamed out a familiar voice. Holly Maguire, Jack's media nemesis from Channel 11. She was famous, among other things, for wearing high heels that required extraordinary balance, a quality missing from her salacious reporting. Jack pretended not to hear the question, which he considered rude and inappropriate coming only minutes into his spiel.

The unbidden question, however, acted as a catalyst for other reporters to yell out unintelligible ones of their own. Jack stared blankly ahead, ignored them all, waited for the crowd to settle, which took a minute or two. He then took the opportunity to drain a glass of water, wiped his lips with a napkin.

'The investigation is pursuing several lines of inquiry,' Jack continued. 'We would ask anyone who saw Roderick McAdam in the company of another person between the hours of 6:00pm yesterday and the estimated time of death, being around 5:00am today, to please come forward.' He gave the direct number for the Yorkville station and the generic crime-stoppers number for the state of Queensland. He looked at his briefing notes, prepared by DC Taylor, before proceeding further. 'The victim was last seen alive – not counting CCTV, which I'll be showing shortly – at the first time I mentioned, 6:00pm yesterday, in the lobby of the Grand Hotel. He had just arrived from the tennis centre with his parents and coach, and then they went their separate ways. Please, pay close attention to the clip we're about to show you. The video is also on the QPS website and our CIB Facebook page.' Jack called upon Ben Wilson to start the short video from the section of CCTV footage Jack and Batista had isolated depicting McAdam and the other man.

'That could be anyone. Totally unrecognisable from that clip,' called out Johno Peroni, a seasoned sports journalist from Channel 3 who doubled up as a crime reporter when required.

'We're confident the person is a male,' said Jack.

'Wow. That narrows it down to half the population,' said Holly Maguire, the observation greeted with muffled laughter. Jack would have gladly ejected her from the room had he the authority to do so.

'We can, however, state categorically that this is a man of average build, weight approximately 85 kilograms. The height we can estimate fairly accurately since we know McAdam's precisely. The second person is almost as tall as the victim, which would make him around 185 cm, or 6'1" in the old language.' Jack then asked for questions from the floor. He ignored Maguire and Peroni and all the other eager hands waving in the air, choosing instead old stalwart scribe from the *Yorkville Times*, Fiona Wagstaff. She had been working the courts and police beat for over three decades and was renowned for her insightful reporting, especially when it came to white-collar crime and political corruption. Wagstaff had ruffled a few feathers in the QPS, but Jack admired her for her grit, gumption and honesty. The rest of the pack of hyenas were only interested in TV or radio ratings or the circulation of their newspapers, and boosting their own inflated egos.

'Do you have any other footage of this suspect?' said Wagstaff in her clear, school ma'am voice. 'I'm getting on in years, but I reckon even the younger ones would be hard pressed identifying that chap. It's almost as if he's cased the joint earlier and made certain his face wouldn't be picked up.'

'I'd have to agree with you on that point, Fiona.' Jack smiled. 'Like I said, we are dealing with a sicko. Often people like that are meticulous planners and it can take a while to catch them.' Jack chided himself for that last remark, which would not be words the McAdam parents would want to be hearing. *Better soften it a wee bit.* 'The good news is we have footage from the Grand going back to the day Roderick McAdam checked in. As we speak, a dedicated team of officers in Brisbane is painstakingly watching every frame captured by security cameras. The task is labour intensive and takes time. If they identify better images of this person – or other persons we think might be associated with the victim, taxi or Uber drivers, for example – the footage will be released immediately. Facial recognition software will help us narrow down the search.'

'Is there no CCTV from the Hotel Gasnier?' yelled out Maguire. 'I mean, that's where the poor fellow died, isn't it?' This question could not be ignored.

'Good question, Holly,' said Jack begrudgingly. 'Sadly, the owner of that particular establishment, which is well known around the community for all the wrong reasons, has taken the view that modern technology has no place in his business...' The DS curled his top lip under his front teeth before adding, '...in a similar manner to the way he manages his books.' Jack felt Batista's bony knee under the table bang into his own. Jack knew that he'd gone too far and the comment was out of line, but just let Greer try and sue him. The man wouldn't have the guts.

'What about forensic evidence? Any leads in that direction?' Again Wagstaff.

Jack blinked a couple of times. How much to reveal? He exchanged a quick whispered word with Batista. He turned back to the throng. 'OK. We are currently analysing the fish-net stockings used to murder Roderick McAdam, hopefully retailers can assist if they were purchased recently. DNA evidence retrieved from the crime scene, as well as items discovered at his hotel room, including a laptop computer, are also being examined. The CCTV footage indicates the person of interest may have known McAdam, and there could be a trail of email exchanges or chats between the two on the laptop. We—'

'What about mobile phone communication?' interjected Peroni.

'Yeah...' Jack scratched his cheek. 'Unfortunately, we've been unable to locate McAdam's phone using tracking software, however we have served production notices on his service provider so we can examine calls and messages. We'll also be speaking to relevant financial institutions.'

'Why?' said Wagstaff.

'A matter of procedure. Financial motives, blackmail, for example, have to be considered too. If there were regular large payments going out of an account that suddenly stopped...you get the idea.'

Wagstaff put her head down and scribbled something; it seemed she was out of questions. Jack quickly took a sip of water, the mob again turned into braying donkeys. He looked up and saw a familiar face, one that wasn't marred by hostility.

'Yes, Corbyn, you were next I see.' He wasn't "next" at all — Jack chose to speak to whomever he wanted as he saw fit. The man was Corbyn Howard, a former professional basketballer turned independent journalist. He'd assisted the Yorkville CIB in cracking the case when a famous sports coach was mowed down and killed in a hit-and-run murder. Howard ran a sports blog that had begun as a hobby but then morphed into a massive business. He'd grown his base from a handful of supportive locals to millions of subscribers around the globe. For the Yorkville CIB, Howard was fast becoming a greater asset than any of the legacy media. Maguire and Peroni reputedly hated him for his popularity, but that was too bad.

'Thanks, DS Lisbon. I appreciate you inviting me to this gig.'

'Not a problem. You're a sports journalist, the victim was an athlete, so it made perfect sense. Fingers crossed your legion of followers might have some information useful to our inquiry.'

'I'm already getting hundreds of comments on my live feed, it's insane.' Howard, sitting in the front row on account of his height – and also because Jack wanted him close – furiously finger scrolled a laptop. 'Some people are suggesting the police should be looking at other players jealous of McAdam. He was poised to win the Australian Open, maybe become world number one, and then, boom – he's dead.'

'Thanks, Corbyn. We'll be looking into all possibilities, including interviewing other top tennis players currently in Melbourne ahead of the Australian Open. At this stage, and let me emphasise we have only just initiated our enquiries – we haven't pinned down anyone with motive and opportunity.'

'Maybe it was a "hit" job.'

'Maybe. The MO, though, is nothing like those used in what the press like to call "execution-style murders". This was way more elaborate and with that message on the mirror...well, suffice it to say, we will be looking closely into all his professional and personal relationships, recent and past.'

'What about his Twitter account?'

'What about it?'

'He was suspended a couple of times for his provocative Tweets towards other users, mainly his opponents, but even fans sometimes. He didn't hold back on his language. A lot of people hated McAdam.'

Stirrings in the crowd. In some ways, Howard knew more about the victim than the cops. But Jack wasn't fazed. 'We've got our IT specialists onto it as we speak. I'd like to emphasise that we've only just begun our investigation. Early days.' He laughed awkwardly.

'With no leads and no suspects, it doesn't look like you'll be wrapping this one up in a hurry, does it?' Maguire injected unbridled sarcasm into her words, which were an accusation more than a question.

'Don't be too sure, Holly.' *Time to end this circus.* 'We're chucking the kitchen sink at this case, with top detectives from Brisbane assisting us every step of the way.'

'What about Pilmer? What's he got to say about his much-vaunted "challenge" crashing to a halt?' said Johnno Peroni from Channel 3. He was cut from the same cloth as Maguire, vain as a peacock and loved the camera pointed at his face.

'You're free to talk to him yourself,' said Jack. He added cuttingly, 'However I'm sure, like the rest of us he's more gutted that a young man in his prime has been murdered.'

'And Depp?' Peroni wouldn't be stopped. 'The man made a public threat against the deceased. Surely he's your number one suspect.'

Jack turned to Batista, gave him a raised-eyebrows look that said, *you mind stepping in?* The chief shuffled some papers. As a parting word he said, 'We appreciate your help in getting the message out about this horrific crime. We'll keep you updated as and when more information comes to hand. Keep an eye on our social media presence. As I always say, it's a two-way street, so contact us immediately if you get any tips from the general public. Thank you.'

As Constable Wilson unplugged the TV monitor and rolled it away, Jack and Batista turned off their microphones and hustled out of the press room. On the back landing they breathed in the warm evening air. It smelled of rich moist earth, tropical fruit, frangipanis and ylang-ylang trees. Reminded Jack why he loved living in this Northern paradise. 'What did you make of that?'

'More questions were raised than we could answer.'

'Tell me about it.' Jack unwrapped a pack of nicotine gum and gnashed down on two pellets.

'We're like the man with the wheelbarrow, DS Lisbon.'

'Meaning?'

'We've got a job in front of us.'

## Chapter Seventeen

HE POPPED a can of ice-cold beer, ripped open a bag of his favourite salt and vinegar chips and settled in for the show. He'd chosen to watch Corbyn Howard's live feed online instead of one of the TV channels. With the web broadcast you could follow the comments from viewers as the press conference unfolded, make comments yourself if you wanted to. Which he absolutely would *not* be doing. Confidence is one thing, recklessness another.

He took a slug of beer before he checked the stats in the top right-hand corner of his laptop. Unbelievable, there were already over 25,000 people registered as watching and the spectacle hadn't even started for real. Just technicians setting up, chairs scraping as journalists jockeyed for position, camera operators looking for prime spots to set up their gear. Indistinct background chatter poured out of the speakers. Another mouthful of beer as the number of viewers ticked over 30,000. The sheer numbers of eyeballs Howard attracted to his live podcast was incredible. The former basketballer was fast turning into Australia's version of Joe Rogan.

He munched a mouthful of crisps as he watched the bland introductions and opening statements from the police. He couldn't help but smile. Then, without much ado, came the gory details of the murder. The news made some of the reporters screw up their faces in disgust. Some seemed to have trouble keeping their eyes on the photographs. And they weren't even that graphic! The police were showing just enough to convey the way McAdam died, but not enough to drive home how horrible that death had been. Never mind. At least *he* knew – he was there to witness it, after all. And then came a cropped version of the message he'd written on the mirror. The cops had castrated the message – no cock and balls! What the fuck?

Now, what's this? A video. No doubt some "incriminating" footage from the Grand Hotel. Oh dear, what a joke. The bumbling constable's gone and banged the trolley with the TV into the wall. What an absolute dickhead! Then he drops the cord before he plugs it in, hits his head on the metal rack on the way up. Must have stung the way he's furiously rubbing his forehead. Where do they recruit these idiots from?

The senior officers were just as pathetic. Utterly clueless. Inspector Batista, a long streak of misery. A giant praying mantis, fidgeting with his cuffs. The entire town knew he was henpecked by his wife Marjorie. How on Earth could a man like that run a police station properly? And then there's his sidekick, Detective Sergeant Jack Lisbon. Even tough guy Lisbon, with his crooked, battered nose and scarred eyebrows, was completely out of his depth in this case. Reading notes from scraps of paper, proving what he, "the Person of Interest – the POI – accompanying McAdam", already knew. That the law had no idea who the POI was, and no matter how hard they tried, they'd never catch him. No wonder the Yorkville Police were getting help with extra detectives flying up from Brisbane. But even so, the POI had covered his tracks well enough to avoid arrest. *They'll still be scratching their heads over this one long after I'm dead.*

Look at that flustered detective, not able to handle the media's barrage of questions. He ignores them like he's so superior. Now he's copping flack from Holly Maguire, then that wanker Johnno Peroni's having a go. If the quality of police officers in this town was poor, what could you honestly say about the press? The worst in the entire country. Small-minded scandal mongers. But they do have their moments. What did loudmouth Maguire just say? *"Doesn't look like you'll be wrapping this one up in a hurry, does it?"* Gold! How Lisbon managed to capture dangerous criminals – especially murderers – was a mystery in itself. The POI was sure the lovely Detective Constable Claudia Taylor had more than a hand in solving most of the crimes. Just listening to Lisbon's lower-class London accent was enough to make you want to puke.

Just like Roderick McAdam had puked up his late-night snack of Rohypnol washed down with a shot of vodka, and then a fat reefer for dessert. He'd coughed like an amateur smoking the joint, but, as ever, he had to prove he was super cool. What the POI had offered up was a volatile mix a smart kid like McAdam ought to have declined. Mind you, the POI had told McAdam the tablet was something else. Speed. And so the trusting moron was soon putty – more like jelly – in the POI's hands.

And now, look at the fools showing that clip of the POI with Roddy in the hotel corridor. *Not even my own mother would recognise me from those blurry images.* Now he knew what they meant by the term "grainy" footage. That stuff was grainier than a sack of rice. You'd think a swanky five-star hotel like the Grand would have invested in a better system. Wouldn't have mattered if they had, though. Even the best high-definition security cameras would have failed to capture his image distinctly. He didn't know if the machines recorded sound, so he made sure to say nothing in their vicinity or to speak in a whisper. As an extra precaution, every time he approached a camera he either ducked his head or – for a bit of sport – turned around and moonwalked backwards. He'd love to see the cops' faces when they stumbled upon those sweet moves. They'd still have no clue who he was.

Roderick himself suspected nothing out of the ordinary was going on when the POI turned up at the hotel to take him to the party – these days lots of people went to parties wearing dark glasses. The pair the POI had purchased at an out-of-town service station – with cash – were huge, covering half his face. They could almost be termed "novelty" sunnies. They wouldn't lead to him, though. People were buying these bad boys in their thousands as part of a promotion for the local rugby league team.

He set his beer down on a coaster and leaned in to listen harder. What is that Lisbon twit saying now? Blackmail could be a motive? Jesus, these coppers are desperate to hang their hopes on anything. A song his dad used to listen to ad nauseum played in his mind. "Desperado" by The Eagles. Described the cops perfectly.

But Lisbon was right about one thing.

The man they sought was good at planning. Oh yes, the planning was spot on.

He'd made sure to study each and every camera he could find in the Grand, did a number of "dry runs" weeks before the big finale. Of course, he could have missed a few, but the chances were infinitesimal. A bit of research – how he loved the research – was enough to find out the chain that owned the Grand in Yorkville used one of the simplest CCTV systems around. Such research was not required for the Hotel Gasnier, however. That stinking dump was the perfect place to carry out all manner of illicit activities and the logical place to bring McAdam for his final "checkout". Things might change now, though. That twit Greer might be thinking of getting out of his business altogether after this catastrophe. A new owner would surely turn things around, add some respectability to the place. The best outcome for the health of the town, though, would be to knock the fetid building down with a wrecking ball.

The night he'd gate-crashed the pre-Challenge launch party, casually "bumping into" Roddy McAdam was a cinch to pull off, too. A boozy function in a huge red-and-white marquee erected in the tennis centre carpark. Not a security camera in sight, everything totally relaxed, tropical North Queensland style. If the event had taken place in a bigger city with more formal conditions of entry, body guards at every turn, he would have failed to complete his mission. In laid-back Yorkville these challenges didn't exist. Getting in was a breeze. He had no ticket, but a confident "I'm with catering" and a brisk stride were enough to get past the indifferent man at the entrance.

Once inside the tent, full of people swilling sparkling wine and nibbling canapes and cheese on toothpicks, the POI figured it would be easy to find his target. Simply look for the biggest group of people and McAdam was sure to be at the centre of everyone's attention. This assumption proved wrong. It turned out the biggest bunch of people surrounded Clyde Pilmer; a certain breed of bootlicker always looking to ingratiate themselves with the rich and powerful. In fact, it was Roderick who had somehow recognised the POI through the crowd and made the initial approach. Bonus. The fly had flown straight into the web.

At this point in the game, to contemplate a tennis analogy, the POI wasn't 100 percent sure he'd be able to pull it off. Everything had to go exactly right. Luckily, everything *did* go right. A few short days later, the trap he'd laid on that opening night slammed shut on Roderick McAdam.

Bang!

Mission accomplished.

POI nibbled on the last of his chips as the press conference concluded, wiped his hands on a paper towel and drained his can of beer. How he relished the awkwardness of the sweating cops, winding the event up when the questions started to get hard. He resolved to watch a replay of the event later on the police's website. Now, though, there was another video he was dying to see again. He fetched a coldie from the fridge, cracked it open... *psshhhhhhh*... and for about the tenth time this evening clicked on the YouTube link – the tail end of Roderick McAdam's last match. The clip started with McAdam serving what everyone thought would be another easy game. But not to be! The challenger gave him a run for his money. The POI fast-forwarded to the best bit. The bit that made it all worth watching. The bad line call.

*Here it comes. Yes!* The POI stood and applauded as weedy runt Sean Depp leapt over the net – barely clearing it – and waved his puny little arms in McAdam's sneering face. What a shame the security guards intervened and dragged Depp away. The man was completely in the right.

But it didn't matter.

Justice came a'visiting in any case.

## Chapter Eighteen

DS LISBON BREATHED a sigh of relief when the cavalry arrived. An injection of manpower that instantly doubled the investigative capabilities of Yorkville CIB. All it took to raise Jack's spirits was the sight of the two smartly dressed detectives, Tania Wycombe and Mike Steger, striding into the office. Their shoulders-back, jaw-set body language instilled confidence. It was like they owned the place despite, to Jack's knowledge, neither of them ever having visited Yorkville before.

The arrival of the two familiar faces took Jack's thoughts back to his year as a junior detective in the state capital. A career stepping stone to his move north, to the far-flung tropical region that eventually won his heart.

Prior to donning the plain clothes again, Jack had endured a short stint as a uniformed constable patrolling the rough streets of Brisbane's western suburbs. It was his first job in the Queensland Police Service after migrating from the United Kingdom. Not many knew the truth, that he hadn't departed the UK by choice. Rather, he'd left the

London Met under a dark cloud of suspicion. For years, Jack had stunk of corruption and stale booze. One day, his bad ways caught up with him. Not DC Taylor, not Batista, not even his ex-wife were aware of the real circumstances under which he fled his home country. Jack was determined to do everything to prevent them or anyone – apart from a handful of trustworthy allies back in the Old Dart – from finding out about the heinous crime he committed in London, a cold-blooded murder he'd miraculously gotten away with. Not a day went by that he didn't imagine a phone call, a tap on the shoulder, the words *you're nicked!*

So far, so good.

Jack extended his hand first to the bespectacled Wycombe, a ginger-haired and heavily freckled woman who exuded an air of studiousness. About five years younger than Jack, she'd been responsible for helping to clear up a number of cold cases stretching back to the mid 1960s, evil child abductors and serial killers among them. She had the uncanny ability to find sense in clues others had stared at again and again and failed to notice their significance. Awarded multiple commendations, the Yorkville CIB could not have wished for a better assistant.

Unless that assistant was Mike Steger. Resembling Rambo with a cleft chin and possessing the brains of a champion Mastermind contestant, Steger was almost a caricature. Again, a stellar record as an investigator. He grabbed Jack's extended hand, almost crushing it. Taylor looked on, smiling wistfully. Jack did the introductions before Batista interrupted the banter-filled conversation and called everyone into the Operations Room.

With only rookie Wells manning the front desk and Semmens and Smith on stand-by for any callouts, the crowded bullpen was humming. The atmosphere reminded Jack of his days back at the London Metropolitan Police.

Batista had been busy while Jack and Taylor went over their case notes, preparing for the meeting. The whiteboard was covered in names written with magic marker, arrows, sticky notes, all arranged in the Inspector's own chaotic manner. The blow-ins from Brisbane brought along thick briefcases, Jack hoped full of data on persons relevant to the investigation.

The Inspector clapped his hands. 'Right, it's getting late, so let's get cracking.'

'I'm prepared to stay as long as required, sir,' said Jack, swinging his legs back and forth as he sat on a modular trapezoid table. His statement was a challenge to the others to offer similar sentiments. He wasn't disappointed as his colleagues all agreed that they too would stay the journey. To midnight or later if need be.

'Terrific. Before we start, I'd like to call upon Detectives Steger and Wycombe to present the results of their back-room work.'

'Thanks, Inspector.' Steger the alpha male took up position to the right of the whiteboard. Jack wasn't surprised the man didn't open his briefcase; he was renowned for having a photographic memory. 'We started from the premise that you'd have local territory covered, so we honed in on the pro tennis players in Melbourne, plus a few other key figures in the victim's life living in Australia and abroad.' The man spoke in an animated fashion, heavy on the hand movements like many natural communicators.

'That's a lot of ground to cover,' said Taylor. 'Where do you begin to even narrow it down?'

'The usual way,' replied Steger. 'We got underpaid

constables to spend hours on computers to look into every nook and cranny of the people we identified.'

The bullpen laughed as one. Even the uniforms.

'Any areas in particular?' said Constable Ben Wilson.

Steger narrowed his eyes. 'As DC Taylor rightly pointed out, the territory is vast. Luckily, many of the people we looked at have very public profiles. They're cleanskins as far as criminal records go – so far – but their biographies and online personas are easy to access. The problem arises in terms of the amount of data you need to trawl through. Algorithms that target keywords in social media posts, for example, come in handy for this kind of work.'

'And what did you come up with?' asked Batista.

'If I may?' Steger gestured at the whiteboard.

The Inspector nodded. 'Of course, we'll come back to my musings later.'

Steger deftly flipped the revolving whiteboard over on its central pivot, revealing a clean slate. With a fat black marker pen he wrote the names of the top five ranked tennis players in the world. He drew a double circle around the top name. Stefan Krepper. Then single circles around numbers 4 and 5. Dragan Stojanovic and Lucas Khumalo.

'OK,' Jack chewed the end of a Bic pen. 'Krepper was brought up as a prime suspect by Adrian McAdam. You agree with that assessment?'

'This is what we know.' An indirect answer. 'Swedish. Thirty-one years old. Lots of fans, has a reputation for philanthropy. No real "haters", as the younger generation says. Krepper only needs to make the semi-finals of the Australian Open to achieve the longest reign at the top spot. But there was an obstacle. McAdam. Bookmakers had McAdam as clear favourite to win the Australian Open as he hadn't lost a match for six months and had beaten every other player in the top five in their latest encounters. McAdam could also have snatched top ranking, but it was a long shot.'

'Didn't the cards have to fall in a prefect sequence for McAdam to do that?' said Taylor.

'Correct. And a rather unlikely scenario. Still, although there is no historical animosity between the victim and Krepper, the man should be interviewed.'

'Too bleedin' right he should,' said Jack. 'Doing everything to ensure he broke Federer's record could have been a big motivation for Krepper. Even if his public image is squeaky clean, we gotta grill him.' He took a sip of Gatorade. 'Now, what about the other two players?'

'Lucas Khumalo is a South African, pride of the nation.'

'Why?' said Taylor.

'He's black, so he's a trailblazer for that country in the tennis world. Khumalo also had a chance of taking number one ranking, but it's so remote as to be laughable. For that to happen, all the other players in the top ten would have to lose in the first round. Virtually impossible.'

'Yeah, that was never gonna happen,' agreed Jack. 'And Stojanovic?' said Jack.

'An interesting character. A firebrand, like McAdam, loves to stir the pot. The two men had an online spat last year when the Serbian accused McAdam of taking performance enhancing drugs. Said the kid was too young to be defeating more experienced players without assistance. It's rubbish of course. They have stringent drug testing requirements on the pro tour. McAdam rose to the challenge, said Stojanovic was simply jealous of a more talented rival. The tweet battle went on for about a month, then petered out.'

'Sounds like normal trash-talking among athletes,' said Trevarthen, making his first contribution to the discussion.

'I agree.' Steger tapped the end of the marker pen against the name. 'But here's the rub. If Stojanovic were to reach the final and defeat Krepper, he would sneak over the line and steal the top ranking.'

'Not possible,' said Jack. 'I checked this myself. Krepper and Stojanovic are on the same side of the draw, so they couldn't possibly have met in the final.'

Steger shook his head. 'Guess what?'

'What?'

'With McAdam out of the picture, Stojanovic has been moved across to the opposite side. Now he can theoretically face Krepper in the final.'

A hush fell over the cops as the realisation dawned. 'Holy shit,' said Jack. 'Could someone – hypothetically Stojanovic – know that would happen if McAdam was *eliminated*?'

Steger shrugged. 'Unless he had a crystal ball, I don't see how.'

'Perhaps he has a contact in the administration. Knows someone involved in organising who plays who at the Open,' said Trevarthen.

Steger had to admit that was a scenario worth exploring.

'Me too,' said the Inspector with half a smile. 'We now have a solid suspect among the elite players. Brilliant.'

Another short silence.

'Agreed,' said Jack. 'But where's the proof?'

'That's what you get paid the big bucks for, DS Lisbon,' said Batista. 'Find the evidence!'

Jack ignored the chief, addressing Steger. 'Are there any

digital trails linking any of these three men with McAdam in a private scenario? Phone calls, texts, anything like that?'

'Perhaps Tania could speak to that question.' Steger sat in a plastic chair next to a bubbling watercooler.

Wycombe clicked open her briefcase and retrieved a clear plastic sleeve containing a number of printouts. She assumed the spot vacated by Steger. 'Thanks, Mike. As you all know, we've had virtually no time to work on this properly, but there are some preliminary results we can base further enquiries on.' She stepped forward and handed sheets of paper to all the officers. Jack scanned the pages. Lines of names and numbers in no particular pattern. 'Unfortunately,' Wycombe continued, 'they don't reveal much. Family contacts of the deceased and their details, estimated net worth of the McAdam family and their associates, names, addresses and phone numbers of former schoolmates. The same parameters for the tennis players that Mike spoke about, also Clyde Pilmer and his coterie. For a more thorough examination of people's financial records and communications a judge has to give us the OK to serve production notices on the relevant banks and service providers.'

'In other words,' said Jack. 'You've got nothing even slightly incriminating.'

Wycombe shrugged. 'Not yet. But we might be able to get a magistrate to co-operate if Inspector Batista thinks my next recommendation warrants implementation.'

*For fuck's sake*, thought Jack. *Can't these people speak simple English?* The words he spoke aloud were more polite. 'And what recommendation is that?'

'Mike and I reckon that you, Jack, should fly to Melbourne ASAP and put some pressure on these prima donna tennis players.' *So, she can keep it simple when she wants to.* 'Inspector?'

'I agree. It's a good idea and one I'd already contemplated,' said Batista. 'Taylor can go with him.'

'Sir?' said Taylor. 'Why wouldn't Melbourne police assist us?'

'I'll be making a request to Vicpol for help, sure. But you and Jack are leading the investigation, and as such I want you in the faces of realistic suspects rather than chasing leads. Others can do that. Plus you've both seen the body up close, dealt with the parents and, most importantly, it's Yorkville's bloody jurisdiction!'

Wycombe resumed her seat as Batista took a deep breath after his little outburst. Composed again, he flipped over the whiteboard. It was his turn to give a rundown on the case. He admitted the Yorkville team only had sketchy and incomplete knowledge to go on. 'In terms of forensics, I trust our pathologist's hunches. She's almost always right and final test results generally agree with her early findings. So, we'll assume the victim was knocked out with Rohypnol before being tied up. It's a Schedule 8 drug and can only be prescribed by a doctor.'

'So there's a doctor involved in this?' asked Constable Wilson. 'Disgusting!'

Jack shook his head. 'Possibly, sunshine. Most likely it's been obtained illegally for a high price on the street.' He turned to Taylor. 'Have we had many cases of roofies floating about Yorkville?'

'Did you say many or any? Because I can't recall a single prosecution for it.'

'Me either.' Jack made a mental note to ask his mate Dave, the barman at the Pelican Pub on the waterfront, if he'd heard of roofies circulating around the bars and clubs.

'What else?' said Steger. 'Anything on the stockings that choked McAdam?'

'We're going to have to wait a week minimum for the full DNA results, but unfortunately there's no label on the stockings. Proctor tells me a fibre analysis could pinpoint a brand, which could lead to a retailer and a salespoint, but she's not hopeful. With online buying these days, it's simply a rabbit hole. A serious crim would have paid cash in any event.'

'Still worth a try though, right?' said Taylor.

'Oh, don't worry.' Batista's posture stiffened. 'We'll be exhausting every avenue. In fact, we're sending Proctor and Clara Littlejohn to the Grand tomorrow to have a good hard look at Room 2003. Pity about the boating accident, otherwise that location may have already been swept using Cairns station's resources. On the plus side, Jack retrieved some items, including this handwritten note and laptop.' He pointed at photos of the items, affixed to the whiteboard with sticky tape.

'What about the humans?' said Jack.

'What?' said Batista.

'Sorry, chief. I meant the witnesses 'n that.'

'Of course.' Batista gave an overview of what each of the officers had learned after speaking to key persons of interest – whose names were written in block letters on the whiteboard – which ones could be dismissed and which were worth keeping a close eye on.

'For the most part, these people were able to give plausible alibis and could back them up with evidence, such as receipts for room service and corroboration by others. Let's start with Depp. Despite his outburst, he got his money, so motive evaporates. Cory Troutman, according to Constable Semmens, is the most unlikely suspect he's ever encountered. Also scrubbed. Hugh Marshall, the guy who would've played McAdam in the final, was desperate to try and win the money, had trained hard for the event. No motive.'

Wycombe stopped writing notes as the Inspector paused. 'I'd like to add that the other eliminated players who returned home early — there are twelve of them — are still being looked at by our people down in Brisbane. If they turn up anything, they'll contact us.'

'They'll find nothing on them,' said Jack dismissively. 'Those club players are a bunch of ordinary blokes who enjoyed a fleeting moment of fame, not criminal masterminds.' said Jack. 'I wouldn't be wasting time on them at all.'

Taylor backed up Jack's assessment. 'I've done some online research into them — superficial at this point, yes — but I'd be super surprised if any of them were linked to the murder.'

'Right,' Wycombe sighed. 'I'll deprioritise that one. We can still run some background checks using AI, though. I'd hate for one of the also-rans to slip through the cracks because we dismissed them too early.'

'OK,' said Batista a little loudly, perhaps detecting some heat creeping into the conversation. 'I'd like to round things off by giving a green light to the parents and coach Gosling. DC Taylor and I are in agreement their grief was genuine and, on the surface at least, they could only lose by the death of Roderick McAdam.'

'So that's it then?' said Kylie Smith hopefully, her eyelids drooping slightly.

'Just about. Constable Trevarthen, can you tell us what Peter Gosling told you?'

'Sure.' He consulted his notebook. 'Apparently, a woman called Anne Cumberland had been stalking the victim for the last two years. She's a year younger than McAdam, at just 18, but Gosling seemed to think the woman was unhinged enough to—'

'One second, one second,' said Steger, rubbing the cleft in his chin. 'That name's on the list Tania handed out.'

*There's that photographic memory again,* thought Jack. Still, he cross-checked the list, and there it was. 'So she was a school chum of his?'

'Yes,' said Wycombe, consulting the relevant piece of paper. 'She attended Yorkville Central Primary with him, but they went to different high schools. Let me see…'

Batista coughed into his fist. 'Excuse me, but I'm sure Constable Trevarthen can elucidate. He got all the details from Gosling. Aden, proceed…'

'Thanks, sir.' He flipped over a page of his notebook. 'Anne Cumberland was the deceased's girlfriend right up until he joined the pro tour just after he turned seventeen. They lived in the same street as small children and were inseparable. But when Roderick got a sports scholarship at St Finian's in Cairns, the whole family sold up and moved house. Apparently distance was no barrier to the young lady. She'd save up from her part-time job at KFC to catch the bus every weekend to Cairns to watch through a cyclone fence when he was training. Roderick realised he was destined for bigger things and he basically got sick of her, told her to stay away. She wouldn't, until Adrian McAdam intervened and told Anne's parents he'd take out a restraining order if he had to. She stopped coming, all right, but she began to send letters to his home address, mysterious little gifts would arrive on the McAdams' doorstep. She's been quiet for the last year but Gosling thought—'

'I know exactly what he thought,' said Jack. 'Same as I would. Roderick being the centre of attention, back on home turf, could have brought back the old feelings and made her snap.'

Batista finished tapping something on his mobile screen and glanced at Wycombe and Steger. 'I'd like you two to have a chat with this Ms Cumberland tomorrow. Up for it?'

'Most definitely,' Wycombe replied with alacrity. Her Brisbane colleague gave a nod. 'I was afraid it'd be all deskwork with your team out in the field.'

'Nope. We need you and Detective Steger out there rattling cages. I'll need the rest of you to step up, too, with a briefing tomorrow morning. I've just booked Jack and Claudia on flights to Melbourne tomorrow morning.'

'Not the redeye special, I hope,' said Jack.

'How does a 06:15 check-in sound?'

'Bloody terrible!'

'I agree completely,' Batista grinned. 'Your flight's scheduled for 10:45. So you can both drop in here at sparrow's fart before you head for the airport.'

'You got him a good one, sir!' said Constable Wilson, chuckling under his breath.

Jack didn't feel like joining in with the lame joke. Instead, he shrugged on his jacket and headed for the door. 'I'm gonna need my beauty sleep.' He turned to face Trevarthen. 'But before that, you and I are going to slug it out in the ring.'

A look of alarm crossed the constable's face. He glanced at his watch. 'At this time? Seriously?'

'You decline, I won't ask you again. Coming or not, sunshine?' He didn't wait for an answer. With keys in hand and five metres from his car, Jack heard the man's jogging footsteps and laboured breath. *That's a good lad.*

## Chapter Nineteen

THE 24-HOUR HEALTH CENTRE, despite the late time of 10:30pm, proved a drawcard for a handful of hardcore gym junkies. Not everyone was interested in hitting the town, getting drunk at a bar or staying home watching TV. Jack's gym hours were erratic at the best of times, so a late visit was nothing new. A 5-km daily run along the Esplanade or the botanical gardens in the cool of the early morning was non-negotiable, barring illness, but the weights, the skipping rope, the heavy bag and punching the bodies and heads of strangers at The Iron Horse, that could happen any time. Even 2:00am, when the insomnia was at its worst or bloody memories of South London wouldn't leave him in peace, was an acceptable time for a visit.

'I appreciate you making this offer.' Trevarthen slung his Puma sports bag onto a wooden bench. 'I hope you're going to go easy on me, sir.' An apprehensive laugh.

'Call me Jack.'

'Are you sure?'

'Let's do it this way. When you're out of uniform, drop all the formalities. OK?'

'Suits me, Jack.' Trevarthen paused for a moment. 'Geez, it feels weird saying it, though.'

'You'll get used to it, sunshine.'

'Call me Aden.'

'Sorry.' A half shake of the head. 'It's sunshine until you can last three rounds with me in the ring – without chucking in the towel or collapsing with a coronary.'

'You're on!' The total lack of confidence in Trevarthen's words reminded Jack of crims he'd charged who reckoned their lawyer would get them off, no worries, but were now languishing in prison.

On the way to the boxing ring they passed a man with liver-spotted hands and thinning hair, maybe in his late 60's, straining to bench press what Jack considered a modest weight. Fair play to him, though, the fellow was improving – last time he was lifting less. Even slight improvements are positives. Jack stopped and turned to Trevarthen. 'How much can you bench press?'

Trevarthen shrugged. 'No idea. Probably more than that bloke, I'd say.'

Jack chuckled. 'I wouldn't bet on it.'

Inside the ring, Trevarthen, dressed in a navy blue singlet and cotton cargo shorts performed a couple of symbolic stretching exercises. He shuffled his feet awkwardly, trying to look the part but failing miserably.

'One sec,' Jack barked and Trevarthen froze. Jack wriggled the man's headgear, a full-face guard on loan from Jack, from side to side. It had added padding to protect the forehead, cheeks, ears and even the back of the head. The guard was sitting a tad loose and Jack tightened the Velcro straps until the thing wouldn't budge. 'That's better. Are you looking to get knocked out on day one?'

'What? No!' came the muffled reply through a brand-new mouthguard that would need several hours of use to wear in properly. 'I've never tried one of these helmets before.'

Jack grabbed the man's wrist. 'Don't worry, I won't aim for the head. I need you healthy for this investigation.'

The look of relief that washed over Trevarthen's pasty, sweating mug nearly made Jack burst out laughing. 'Don't mean my aim is always true, though.'

The alarm crept back into Trevarthen's eyes.

'Easy up, sunshine. You're in zero danger. Promise.'

Jack then checked his colleague's gloves, also borrowed and also loose, and tugged on the straps. 'Right, just concentrate on defending yourself this time around. If a fighter can't defend, he's a bad fighter. Now, feel free to throw a punch at me if you like, but you'll just be wasting your energy 'cos I'll block whatever comes my way. OK? Three rounds of three minutes each with a minute's rest in between.'

'That sounds doable.' Those three words would soon come back to haunt the Constable.

Jack activated a timer app on his phone and set it under the ropes next to a turnbuckle, put his gloves on then tapped Trevarthen's. 'Dukes up. Let's go!'

---

A TOWEL FLAPPED over Trevarthen's heaving chest. 'Oi! Wake up.' Jack was thinking about calling an ambulance when the man opened his eyes wide as if waking from a nightmare.

'What's happening? Where am I?'

'You fainted, sunshine. Don't panic.' Jack reached out and yanked Trevarthen to his feet.

'So it wasn't a KO then?' Trevarthen patted his head. 'Did you knock the headgear off?'

'No, you pillock. I removed it when you passed out. And the mouthguard. I said I was gonna go easy on you and I did.'

'Easy? I could barely stop you from punching me in the guts. You must have hit me a hundred times. Oooh…' He clutched his stomach then bent double, gasped for breath. 'I think I'm gonna be sick.'

'C'mon. Stop being a drama queen.' Jack put his hands on the man's shoulders, guided him back to the wooden bench. Trevarthen, sweat dripping from every pore, wobbled on unsteady feet before his substantial buttocks made smacking contact with the seat. Jack rummaged in Trevarthen's bag, found a banana, a packet of sweet chocolate biscuits and a bottle with something orange in it. He fished out the bottle, mottled with condensation 'Here, drink this.'

The contents of the bottle quickly disappeared into the vanquished boxer's neck. 'I think my blood sugars are dropping. Did you find those chocolate bikkies?'

'Yeah. I chucked 'em in the bin. And what's that drink?'

'Orange cordial, why?'

'It's nothing but liquid calories. No wonder you weigh what, 120 kilos?'

'Come on, sir! I mean Jack. I'm only 105 kilos.'

'Still twenty over what you should be for your height. You passed out after a short period of vigorous exercise 'cos you're a paunchy soft git with no discipline. Even that dolt Wilson's got more drive than you.'

Trevarthen's eyes stared at the floor. His breathing was laboured, either he'd been mortally offended or the truth was striking home. He looked up, eyes watery. 'You're right…Jack.'

For the next ten minutes, Trevarthen opened up about his personal struggles, his strained homelife, bringing up a lazy, rebellious son. Jack, to his surprise, listened intently, sharing his own experience of longing for a daughter who lived on the other side of the world. It struck him that he had no real friends in Australia apart from Claudia Taylor. And, if things went the way he hoped, one day she'd be more than that. Truth was, he needed a male buddy, someone to hang out with and shoot the breeze every now and then. Could that person be Aden Trevarthen? Maybe.

When Trevarthen and Jack stopped pouring out their hearts to one another, Jack said he'd be willing to help his colleague shed the extra weight and get into shape. Improved fitness, hopefully, would see improvements in other areas of his life. Two times a week to begin with, promoted to regular training partner if he reached certain goals and maintained them. They agreed to the deal with a handshake.

With their gear back in their bags and as they headed for the exit, a large TV monitor mounted above a vending machine showed a floodlit Holly Maguire against a backdrop of the locked and sealed-off Hotel Gasnier. Jack stayed Trevarthen with a raised hand. 'Let's just see what madam has to say.'

The men stood and listened as the journalist gave her report.

*I'm standing outside the infamous Hotel Gasnier, where hometown hero*

*Roderick McAdam was brutally murdered in the early hours of Friday morning. The hotel has been locked down and attempts to contact the owner to find out when he plans to open up again have gone unanswered. Police assure us they are doing everything they can to track down the killer. We can only hope they do find the perpetrator, and quickly. Our station has been bombarded by calls from viewers too terrified to leave their homes in the wake of the violent murder. Inspector Joe Batista promised to keep us informed of developments, and Yorkville has its collective fingers crossed for a quick breakthrough. The one question on everybody's lips is: Why was Roderick McAdam even at the downmarket Gaz when he was due to play in the Pilmer Challenge final the very next day?*

*Now, as far as the Australian Open is concerned, we have an update on that too. Despite calls from some quarters to cancel the event, organisers of the Australian Open have confirmed it will go ahead as scheduled. The image cut to a pre-recorded on-camera statement by the head of Tennis Australia, Sue Steele. While we sympathise with the parents of Roderick McAdam and grieve his untimely death, the show must go on. There is too much invested in an event this size to cancel it at the last minute. Many millions of dollars have been spent and thousands have travelled to this country specifically for our Grand Slam tournament. Again, we offer our deepest apologies to the McAdam family, but that's just the reality of the situation. In light of the recent tragedy, our security measures have been boosted for the Open. I'd like to finish by saying we all want answers, justice for Roddy. If anyone knows anything, please, please, please, call the police.*

'Ridiculous,' said Jack.

'What? Sounded reasonable to me.'

'No. I meant Maguire traveling to the Gaz to do the stand-up to camera there instead of in the studio or whatever. No wonder people have no time for the media these days.'

'She had a great question, though.'

'Yeah,' Jack sighed. 'Why the effin' heck *was* he at the Gaz?'

## Chapter Twenty

HE NOSED the vehicle into one of the prized spots shaded by a grand old Jacaranda tree at the far end of the car park. In autumn, or what passed for it in Far North Queensland, he wouldn't dare risk the Hilux's duco becoming damaged by the cascading purple blossoms. This time of year the tree was a good, leafy friend – the shade it provided meant early arrivals could park under its natural umbrella.

Today Jack was first by miles. The workout with Trevarthen late last night was a mild one by his own tough standards, although the exercise-deprived constable would no doubt be suffering the aftershocks this morning. Maybe he was still asleep. There was a good chance, since it was only 6:34am.

For Jack it had been a sleepless night. Maybe he dozed for an hour, he couldn't be sure. Most of the night was wakeful and he was pissed off about it. The chat with Trevarthen had somehow fertilised memories of his crime. The letter opener. The blood spurting out of the neck. The stolen money. The cover up. Instead of the flashbacks fading, they were as intense as ever. A course of self-hypnosis was the next remedy he'd resolved to try. Fingers crossed it would bring some benefit. Something had to!

Despite the lack of sleep, he'd still squeezed in the sacrosanct morning run – in the dark with a headlamp strapped to his head, croaking cane toads and chirruping insects for company. Then a shower and a shave, pack a small bag for his flight to Melbourne, and into the car, the roads all to himself.

Before opening up the station, he guzzled a coffee the consistency of freshly laid road tar from the nearby Good Bean café, where he scanned the morning edition of the *Yorkville Times* and the much thicker state-wide *Courier Mail*. Being Saturday editions, they were thick as bricks, chock full of useless lifestyle inserts and advertising. Reading about the murder of McAdam was taking a while, so he ordered an al fresco breakfast of a buttered croissant and a second brew, this time a gentler flat-white.

Tributes flowed from sporting greats and all manner of celebrities. A three-page spread featuring the kid's comet-like career – luminous but brief. Half-page colour photos with the lad in action and accepting trophies. Not a word about his brattish on-court behaviour, and quite right, too, thought Jack. He was a firm believer in not speaking ill of the dead. Thankfully, the newspaper articles contained no criticism of police, which was to be expected in a brand-new case. If the cops didn't crack it fast, though, the tabloids wouldn't hold back.

There was plenty off about this case, but Jack had to admit his least favourite journalist was on the money. The question posed by Holly Maguire was at once simple and complex. What could possibly have lured Roderick to the stinking Hotel Gasnier? Perhaps the Brisbane digital forensics guys would find something in the laptop, express couriered, that would shed light on the mystery. Or uncover a hidden ghost in the CCTV images. One could only hope.

Back inside the station, the rest of the team arrived within minutes of each other. Jack exchanged nods of greeting with everyone, a special smile reserved for Taylor. It only just dawned on him they'd be taking a trip together, sitting next to each other on a plane, arms touching in the close confines. They were scheduled to fly home in the evening, but who knew what turn the case might take? They may have to stay in Melbourne overnight. He swallowed hard.

Trevarthen, the last to arrive, flashed Jack a sheepish grin as he hobbled into the Ops Room, mockingly grasped at his ribs, which made Jack smile. Aden was a good bloke at heart. He would make a great friend.

Batista didn't waste much time giving the troops their instructions. Wycombe and Steger would turn up at Anne Cumberland's family home unannounced, hopefully catch the young woman by surprise and vulnerable to probing questions. Then, more visits, this time Rudy Greer and his sons, followed by the receptionist Joanne who had thus far avoided questioning.

'Aden, I'd like you to have another word with Peter Gosling. See if he can think of an answer to the burning question Holly Maguire rightly asked last night. *Why* did McAdam go where he did? Something tells me once we know that, it'll be easier to figure out the "who" part.'

'Yes, sir.'

He then ordered Smith to visit Mercy Valdez, ostensibly to check up on her welfare, but also to squeeze her a little. Taylor mentioned she thought the woman was holding something back. 'Give Valdez a nudge. Perhaps hint at…I don't know…visa issues if she withholds information. Be subtle about it though. And be prepared to chat with the McAdams if and when required as their family liaison officer.'

'Got it,' said Smith.

'What about me sir?' Wilson sounded a little miffed, thought Jack. He was, technically, the senior of the uniformed officers, and the boss was leaving it a little late getting to him.

'I'd like to make use of those brains of yours. I'm expecting an email in the next couple of hours from digital forensics with a report on McAdam's laptop, and on the security cam footage. They've also obtained phone records of the deceased. See if you can pick anything useful out of the data.'

'Yes, sir.'

Wilson conveyed more enthusiasm in the response than Jack was expecting. The extended period baking on the veranda of the Hotel Gasnier must still be preying on the lad's mind. Today's maximum would reach a scorching 36°C with high humidity, so the constable had probably drawn the long straw.

'Semmens.'

'Yes, sir?'

'Desk work for you, too, I'm afraid. Look into similar MO's in old murder cases around the country. It's so unusual there's a remote chance we're dealing with a repeat offender. A thrill killer.'

A nod from Semmens, also visibly relieved to have an indoor assignment.

The Inspector glanced at Wells, about to say something about his role, when the rookie's mobile went off. The ring tone indicated it was a redirected call from the Communications Centre. An emergency. Wells answered with a sharp hello, listened for a minute before his lips twisted into a frown of concern. 'OK, thanks.' He ended the call.

'That didn't sound good,' said Batista. 'What's up?'

'Road train flipped over on the Bruce Highway, blocking half the road.'

'Any casualties?'

'Truck driver trapped in his cabin, a number of injured people in another vehicle, freight scattered all over the place causing traffic chaos. Beer cans are exploding, I'm told.'

'Change of plans,' said Batista through clenched teeth. 'All uniforms to the scene. Now!'

Jack sucked in his teeth. 'You want us to reschedule our flights?'

'No chance. Get your arses to the airport.'

## Chapter Twenty-One

THE KEENLY AWAITED email from digital forensics arrived minutes after the four anxious uniforms squealed out of the carpark in the Ford Territory 4x4, haring to the crash scene 15 clicks from the station. Wilson took the wheel, declaring eagerness to be back in the action despite yesterday's flirtation with heat stroke. Jack and Taylor hopped a cab to Cairns Airport – thankfully in the opposite direction to the highway accident. Batista remained in his office with the Brisbane detectives, the new turn of events forcing an immediate rethink of his previous plan.

There was nothing for it but to make the best of the situation.

Batista's inbox was littered with emails, more than he'd ever seen. Dozens from news outlets around the globe, specialist tennis publications and sports websites, even social media "influencers", all begging for exclusive interviews with the chief. He ignored them and clicked open the email from the digital forensics unit.

A shared-screen version popped up on the large wall-mounted monitor in the Ops Room. The message itself didn't inspire a lot of confidence. In a nutshell, the analysts couldn't identify the suspect using even the most sophisticated facial recognition software. The disguise and physical actions used to elude the cameras worked, the technology had not. Wide-ranging searches of the victim's computer, financial and phone records also failed to uncover incriminating emails, texts or phone calls to or from suspicious numbers. Bank transactions all appeared legit, too. The unit's head wrote that their specialists were eager to start looking at the digital footprints of other persons of interest when production orders could be secured. He ended with: *Please find four major files attached. It's not a lead, but there is some entertainment value in the smaller file CCTV_Michael_Jackson.mp4*

The officers stared open-mouthed as the suspect danced the Moonwalk – rather skilfully – after he emerged, backwards, from the stairwell onto the second floor. He kept up the move before entering the stairwell again, when it became clear he was wearing a blue surgical mask now in addition to the oversize sunglasses. 'He's an arrogant son of a bitch.' Steger sucked air through his teeth before taking a sip of tea.

'You got that right,' said Wycombe. 'But it gives me hope. The cocky ones often think they've planned everything perfectly but trip up on something simple.'

'Should we look at the other files?' said the Inspector, his tone already intimating he wasn't keen. 'Is there any chance we're going to find something they haven't?'

'Maybe later,' replied Wycombe, thoughtfully resting her chin in the crook of her thumb and forefinger. 'Those guys are the experts. But, without blowing my own trumpet, I *have* been known to find treasure among the trash.'

'She sure has,' nodded Steger, a touch of comradely

pride in his voice. 'But let's get the interviews out of the way first. All of us could spend a little time raking over this stuff.' He pointed at the screen. 'But only if there's no breakthroughs working the old-fashioned way.'

Wycombe smoothed the top of her slacks. 'Mike's right. I'd put more faith in hard slog than on these preliminary findings.'

'Non-findings, you mean,' Batista scoffed, then checked his attitude. 'But I guess they can't manufacture evidence out of thin air, can they?'

'True, sir,' said Steger encouragingly. 'But like Tania says, another look if we hit a dead end is always on the table.'

'Right. You two best be off then.'

As Steger and Wycombe drove off, the Inspector couldn't help himself. He opened an enquiry from *Sports Illustrated*. Should he…? He scanned the request for an exclusive interview, marked the email as spam. His finger hovered over the key for half a minute before he deleted it. He drummed his fingers on the table for a moment, then picked up the phone and called Wilson.

'What's happening?'

'Geez, it's shocking, sir.' The constable's breathing was laboured. 'The place stinks like a brewery, hundreds of cans all over the road, popping like firecrackers.'

'How bad are the injuries?'

'The truck driver has multiple compound fractures of the leg. They had to use the jaws of life to get a woman out of another car, but her kids seem all right. Looks like all are going to survive.' Wilson explained the other uniforms were helping direct traffic, keeping accident victims calm until they could be attended to, and clearing the lost load from the carriageway.

'Don't be tempted to souvenir any of that beer, Constable.'

'No chance, sir. It's warm. Besides, the media are here filming everything. Getting in the way as usual.'

Batista ended the call with Wilson, said he'd be along soon to lend a hand, then rang his wife. It could be another late night.

## Chapter Twenty-Two

THE THUMPING TURBULENCE the aircraft flew into twenty minutes after take off was like nothing Jack had experienced. He felt his face muscles grow tense as his elbows ground into the armrests. Flight attendants struggled to get trolleys out of the aisles before they turned into bulldozers, overhead lockers rumbled as belongings banged together, frightened children wailed like banshees. The captain announced something over the PA but it came out as garbled nonsense. The tumultuous helicopter ride Jack took to the north of Scotland last year to rescue his daughter from kidnappers was nothing compared to this act of airborne violence.

He glanced to his left to check on Taylor's welfare when the Airbus A330-300 dropped like a stone. Jack felt the sharp tug of the seatbelt across his lap and his head jerk upwards, his coffee launched towards the ceiling. A second later, the spiralling paper cup landed on his meal tray and drops sprayed on his shirt. Thankfully the damage was minimal; he could buy a new shirt in Melbourne

But how was Taylor holding up? It was then, above the yelling and screaming of other passengers, he heard her laughing hysterically. She must be in shock.

'You orright, sunshine?'

'Never better!' she roared. 'Best fun I've had in ages.'

Jack shook his head as the plane suddenly regained its smooth trajectory towards their destination. She might be squeamish around blood, but the prospect of plummeting out of the sky clearly held no fears for Taylor. He reflected on the ability of humans to have diametrically opposed reactions to one and the same phenomenon. The shaking of the plane sent his heartrate into overdrive and made him think of impending death, she just laughed it off. He could stare at blood and guts and gore all day, it made her sick. And so it went.

After a light meal of salad sandwiches somewhere above the dry and dusty town of Cunnamulla in outback Queensland, Jack was wrestling with a cryptic crossword puzzle while Taylor retrieved her phone from her handbag, wedged tight under the seat in front.

Phone in hand she said, 'Are you curious about the road accident and how the guys are doing?'

'Yeah, I am 'n all. Tell me all about it. More insurance for cricketer.'

'What the…?'

'It's a cryptic clue.'

'No idea, I'm afraid. I can't get my head around those things.'

'Extra cover,' Jack mumbled as he filled in the blank squares.

'What?'

'It's the answer. It's like a riddle. Extra is "more", cover is "insurance". Geddit?'

A bewildered head shake from Taylor.

'Extra cover's a fielding position in cricket, innit?'

'It is?'

'Yeah. Everyone knows that.'

Taylor connected her phone to the inflight Wi-Fi. 'Except for people like me who don't know anything about...whoa!'

'What?' Jack placed the folded-up newspaper and pen on his tray. 'Sounds important.'

'We've been forwarded files from digital forensics.' She stood and retrieved her laptop from the overhead locker. 'I'll need a bigger screen to look at this properly.'

'What about the highway accident?'

'Oh, that. Batista says they're doing fine. No one died, all good.'

'That's all you have to say about it?'

'Yep. These files are much more interesting.'

'That's debatable. Here's an easy clue. Very apt for our current investigation. Terrain ruined coach.'

Taylor ignored his rambling, clicked through to the attachments, opened the phone call and message log.

'Trainer. Anagram of terrain,' said Jack.

Taylor again ignored his waffling and asked, 'Did you say Tania Wycombe was some kind of evidence-finding genius?'

'On her day, she's like Sherlock bleedin' Holmes.'

'Must be my day, then. Who am I?'

Jack shrugged. 'Miss Marple?'

Taylor laughed. 'I'll take that. Here, check this out.' She passed the laptop across the armrest.

Jack fumbled with the device before looking at the screen, his eyes blurring from the rows and rows of pixelated figures and names. 'Nope. Can't see it.'

She leaned across, her shoulder pressing into him, her cheek, lips, inches away. *How am I supposed to concentrate?*

'Late December last year, see? A bunch of missed calls from a number registered to—'

'Yep. I see it. G. Cumberland. That'll be that young lady Peter Gosling said had been stalking McAdam. But I thought her name was Anne?'

'Wait a minute.' Taylor clicked around the police databases. 'Here's a record of the restraining order application from Adrian McAdam that he subsequently withdrew. So, Geraldine's her first given name, Anne the second. She's choosing to go by her middle name. Like a couple of Australian prime ministers did.'

'Yeah? Never knew that.'

'Yep. Gough Whitlam was really Edward, Malcom Fraser was John.'

'Good work, sunshine. You know you might not be as smart as me in the crossword department, but—'

Taylor had her phone to her ear before Jack had finished speaking. 'Hello, Inspector Batista? I think you might want to pass this on to our Brisbane colleagues.'

---

WITH AN IMPRESSIVE COIFFURE of Brylcreemed silver hair, towering at about six foot four and sporting a half-melon paunch that strained at his belt, Detective Senior Sergeant Toby Horner of the Victoria Police struck an imposing figure. Jack figured him for a man approaching retirement age and not happy about it. A copper for whom the job meant everything. The type of man Jack never wanted to become. When it was time to exit the force – voluntarily next time and not shoved out as he was from the

London Met – DS Lisbon would need no encouragement. Horner's entire bearing, by contrast, said he was wedded to the job. He almost bowed as he extended his hand to Taylor, then Jack. Up close, old-school Horner gave off strong hints of Old Spice.

Horner made a call while his guests admired portraits of the Queen, the current supremely unpopular Prime Minister and a cast of top-brass coppers from yesteryear. Efforts had been made to soften the austere feel of the modern office; a wide chestnut bookcase lined with legal tomes graced the wall behind the their host, polished rosewood chairs and an antique coffee table occupied a far corner of the room. Horner hung up the phone with a clunk. 'Let's go. The car to take us to Melbourne Park is ready. The players you want to speak to are waiting for us at the Show Court Arena.'

'Why there?' said Taylor. 'Don't you have interview rooms here at the station?'

'Of course, but it's much easier this way. We've got them all together in the same location, practising before the Australian Open.'

'There's also no compelling reason for us to...ah, compel them to come to the station...at this stage,' added Jack.

'Correct,' said Horner, pressing the elevator button. 'Not a good look for Vicpol to be harassing international guests of their high status without good reason.'

The officers rode the elevator to the bowels of the blocky glass and steel edifice known as the Melbourne West Police Station, exited into a cool, brightly lit basement before stepping into the waiting vehicle, a black, unmarked BMW 3 Competition with windows so dark one might think they were painted on.

'Couldn't we have walked there?' said Taylor, buckling up in the back. 'It's only up the road a bit. This warm Melbourne weather without the humidity is perfect for a stroll.'

Horner, in the front next to the serious-faced driver, shook his lustrous mane. 'Lovely day for it, I'm sure, but it's a touch too far. You have this vehicle and its driver at your disposal for as long as you need it. And me as your guide slash chaperone.' He uttered the words with pride, as if any policing job would be an honour for him to carry out, even washing dishes in the officers' canteen.

Fifteen minutes later, they had negotiated the bustling tram-filled streets of Australia's second-largest city and pulled into the country's premier sporting centre. Melbourne Park was like nothing in the world — a massive complex playing host to all manner of sports: tennis, basketball and ice-skating to name a few. As a sports nut, Jack had always wanted to visit the iconic precinct, and now he'd got the chance the sheer scale of the place took his breath away. Thankfully, they had Toby Horner to guide them through the maze of alleys, arenas, gardens and outdoor courts.

The three officers walked briskly in bright, warm sunshine until they reached the refurbished Show Court Arena. Inside, Jack marvelled that this was only a secondary venue, yet it seated five times more spectators than Yorkville Tennis Centre's main court. The three tennis stars, sweating heavily, were waiting in the stands about twelve seats back from the court itself. Also present were three other men, also dressed in sporty attire but not showing the same signs of recent exercise. Jack assumed they were the players' coaches.

'I'd like to separate them for questioning,' Jack whispered to Horner.

'Understood.'

Horner breathed hard as he lumbered up the stairs two at a time, the heels of his shoes banging as he went, Jack and Taylor tucked in behind. He flashed his ID and thanked everyone for taking time out of their busy schedules and attending at short notice. He quickly established that the extras were indeed coaches. While Horner spoke, Jack studied the huddled group. Their faces portrayed a combination of curiosity and worry, a touch of impatience. 'To expedite our enquiries,' Horner continued, 'I'd like to ask one player and his coach to remain seated while the others wait their turn in the foyer.' He jerked his thumb towards the nearest tunnel out of the seated area. 'Don't care who goes first, but time is not our friend, gentlemen, so please decide quickly.'

'I'd rather we all stuck together,' said a man sitting beside Lucas Khumalo. His fruity accent was pure Cape Town, his tone defiant. A fellow used to getting his own way.

'Thanks Detective Horner, but we'll take over from here.' Jack somehow hooked his leg around the monolithic Horner and edged his way to the front. Taylor took refuge between two rows of seats as the switcheroo took place. Horner sat two rows from the assembled tennis folk, thigh flesh spilling over the sides of the plastic foldaway chair, and wiped his brow with a handkerchief. Jack introduced himself and DC Taylor as he eyeballed the men with a no-nonsense glare. 'I really appreciate your co-operation. But I'm gonna have to ask you all to forget about your hit-outs for now. You can resume in the evening if it's that vital.'

'Wait a minute. The Victorian Police liaison told us this would just be an informal briefing.' Again, Khumalo's coach.

'Never mind what they told you. This is my investigation, and the local constabulary are merely offering me and my colleague assistance. We make the rules, not Vicpol.' Jack scanned his audience, wide-eyed with a new emotion – indignation. 'So, since you, Mr...?' Jack stabbed a forefinger at the protesting coach.

'Habinski. Ron Habinski.' The man was almost scowling.

'Right. As I was saying, since you seem so keen to help us out, we'll start with you and your player, Mr Khumalo. The rest of you, please accompany DSS Horner into the foyer. I'll call upon *you* next,' he pointed at the lithe, blue-eyed Stefan Krepper, 'and we'll finish with Mr Stojanovic.' He nodded at the more muscular Serbian, whose jet-black hair was millimetres away from being a mullet. Both Krepper and Stojanovic wore granite expressions, elbows resting on their knees like a pair of delinquents. 'If I have reason to believe any of you are lying to me, I'll be arranging for formal interrogations within the cosy confines of a police interview room downtown.'

'I'm pretty sure none of us has legal representation in this country,' said Krepper, waving a hand to encompass his adversaries. 'So that is an unlikely scenario, isn't it, Detective Lisbon?'

The Swede's got some balls, thought Jack. Or it's that sense of entitlement all elites have. 'That's the great thing about Australia, son. It's an orderly, democratic country that can provide a lawyer for anyone.' Jack winked at Krepper. 'Even tourists with tennis racquets.'

'Look,' said the South African with the attitude. 'These men are serious athletes, not "tourists" as you put it. They haven't got time to waste running all over town answering your questions. They've got nothing to do with what happened to Roddy McAdam, I can guarantee it.'

'Maybe not,' said Taylor. About time she made her "good cop" contribution, thought Jack. The players and coaches needed to like one of them, and it sure as eggs wasn't ever going to be Jack. 'However,' she continued. 'They may know something that can lead us to the perpetrator.'

Stojanovic held up his hands in appeal. 'We've already spoken to each other about this. Many times. McAdam was a jerk, but so what! No reason to kill him. Honestly, we haven't got a clue about this murder.'

Taylor nodded. 'I understand. But there could be a thread of information locked away deep in the recesses of your subconscious. DS Lisbon here is an expert in unlocking those pathways, aren't you Detective?'

'Too bleedin' right I am. Now, please do as I asked or we'll all be taking a drive down to Spenser Street. Got me?'

Another attempted protest, this time from the Swede, was too much for Jack and he cut it off before the words could leave Krepper's mouth. 'Stop! Just stop!' Jack's hands shot to his head. The dissociation of these people from reality was unbelievable. 'One of your own has been murdered. Do you people even understand that? Do you even care?'

The players and coaches watched Jack open-mouthed. Perhaps his point had been made. Whatever the case, four men stood and meekly followed the waddling Horner through the tunnel and out of sight.

First up, the South African. Khumalo's eyes widened like a flower opening to the sun. His hands shook and his eyes darted all over the spectator stands as if he was looking for someone to come and rescue him from the nasty policeman. Jack locked his gaze on coach Habinski. 'I'm letting you stay as a courtesy to your lad who, truth be told, looks as nervous as all fuck.'

'What DS Lisbon means...' intervened Taylor, picking up on Jack's cue for her to be the nice one again, '... is that nobody has to cope on their own. Now tell me, Lucas, how has the death of Roderick McAdam affected you?'

Tears welled in the corners of Khumalo's soft brown eyes, his bottom lip trembled. 'To be honest, I'm thinking of pulling out of the tournament. It's not right somehow...I... oh geez.' The waterworks came hard and fast, the man's chest heaved as he let the emotions out.

Habinski placed a comforting arm around his charge's shoulder. 'C'mon, Lucas. We've talked about this. It's too important to quit. We can't stop doing what we do because bad things happen. Would it bring back Roddy McAdam? No.'

Jack sniffed contemptuously. Here was a fellow wanting to do the right and honourable thing but his mercenary coach could only thinking about the fame and the money. 'Here's something interesting, Mr Habinski. We've had our experts look into possible scenarios. With McAdam now out of the picture for the Australian Open, the odds of Lucas here claiming the top spot increase by...' Jack plucked an expression out of thin air '...an order of magnitude.'

'Piss orf,' sneered Habinski. 'For one thing, he's got those two blokes in his way...' he pointed at the tunnel '... and Lucas hasn't beaten either of them in two years.'

'Wow,' said Jack, shaking his head. 'If ever I heard negative talk from a coach, this is it. But it doesn't cancel out the fact he *could* beat them. I mean, he's ranked number 5 in the world! So I say he has a great motive to get rid of the bookies' favourite and improve his chances.'

'What I'm trying to say is—'

'Don't tell me what *you're* trying to say.' Jack locked eyes with Habinski as Khumalo continued his muffled blubbering. 'That doesn't interest me.' He turned to the player. 'You tell me, Lucas.'

'Yes,' said Taylor soothingly. 'You tell us...whatever you think we should know.'

Khumalo slowly raised his head, wiped a thin line of snot from under his nose with the back of his wrist and wiped it on his shorts. 'I've been racking my brain, trying to think why someone would want to do this horrible thing.' His pursed lips formed a perfect circle as he shrugged. 'I have no idea. Yes, I admit, my chances of winning the Open, even claiming top ranking, are now better, but I don't care about that. It's irrelevant to me. I earn enough money every year to help feed a small village – the poor village I was born in. I paid for improved sanitation and I subsidise a small medical clinic. That's why I do what I do. God has blessed me with a talent and I use it to serve Him!'

Jack rubbed his temple. The lad was laying it on thick.

'Good for you,' said Taylor. 'But there are others who aren't interested in serving God. People who can kill someone – or pay to have them killed – and still sleep well at night. Are there such people on the tour, do you think?'

Khumalo shook his head. 'Many people disliked Roderick, that is true. But I cannot believe one of my rivals would have anything to do with murder.'

'Are you going to play in the Open or not?' said Jack abruptly.

'My heart is not in it, Detective. And, to be honest, my

coach is right. Even at my most motivated, I am not yet good enough to defeat Stefan or Dragan. As the Australian saying goes, they have the wood on me.' He quickly turned his head towards his coach. 'I'm sorry, Ron, but I'm going to sit this tournament out.'

Jack reached out and shook Khumalo's big right hand. 'OK, you and your coach are free to go.'

Habinski's eyes widened. 'That's it?'

'Yep. But don't leave the country just yet.'

'Why not?' said Khumalo. 'I am not a suspect, am I?'

Jack gave an apologetic tilt of the head. 'Right now, everyone's a suspect.'

---

OCCUPYING the same seats the South African player and his coach had, Stefan Krepper and his coach could have passed for brothers. Ralf Sandberg looked slightly older, but not by much, his blonde hair was a little darker and wavier.

'What did Lucas tell you?' said Krepper, not wasting any time.

'I can't reveal that. You'd have to ask him yourself.' Jack glanced up as a seagull flew across the southern end of the arena, then returned and perched on the edge of the overhanging roof. 'Right now I'm interested in what *you* have to say.'

'Just between us,' said Krepper in a conspiratorial whisper. 'I'd be looking harder at Dragan.'

Jack exchanged a look of surprise with Taylor. So quick to point the finger.

'That comes as a shock to me,' said Taylor, fishing a notebook from her handbag. 'Dragan said...just a 'sec,' she flicked through the pages. *We've already spoken to each other about this. Many times. We haven't got a clue about this murder.*'

'Of course, I'm not going to accuse him to his face. I could be way off the mark, but if you are considering one of us, then it has to be him.'

'Why?' said Jack bluntly.

'The Twitter spat. The two of them didn't hold back with the slurs. Dragan accused him of taking steroids or growth hormone or something like that, can't remember the specifics. Roderick responded even harder, with personal insults.'

'Yes,' Jack rolled up his sleeves. The temperature had jumped at least five degrees in the last half hour. The section of the stadium they were in had enjoyed full shade since they arrived, but it was still warm. He made a note of the time on his watch. 2:45pm. If they could make progress with the players, the detectives were a solid chance to make their flight back to Cairns tonight. 'But that running battle fizzed out to nothing, didn't it?'

'They eventually got sick of their own conversation,' added Taylor. 'I've studied the tweets. You'll have to do better than that. In fact, you've probably got a stronger motive than Dragan. You're on the verge of setting a record that'll beat Federer's. People say it may never be broken if you achieve it.'

The coach decided now was a good time to join the conversation. 'Stefan was confident he could have handled McAdam and broken that record. In fact, nothing would have given Stefan more pleasure than defeating Roddy on his home soil.'

Krepper nodded hard. 'Correct. I value hard-fought battles won honestly. I would rather lose than know I won by cheating. Killing McAdam, apart from being an awful crime, would have been cheating. If you look at my career you'll see I've often conceded points to opponents when the umpires have made mistakes. Even at critical times in matches. Even,' he paused dramatically '...on set point!'

Krepper's claims could be easily verified, so lying was of no benefit to him. 'Perhaps, but now it looks like you *will* get your name in the record books.'

'Not at all! Anyone in the top 10 – hell, even the top 100 – can beat me if I have an off day and they are, what's the expression, on song.'

'We'll take your suggestion to look into Stojanovic on board,' said Jack. 'But know this – we'll be digging deep into all of you.'

Krepper slowly folded his arms across his chest and offered a wry smile. 'I'm an open book, Detective Lisbon. I hope you find the killer soon. The air of suspicion around the players is making everyone uncomfortable. I'm not sure if you've seen it, but there are lots of slanderous memes floating around the Internet.' Krepper unfolded his arms, produced a mobile phone and showed the detectives a Photshopped image of himself standing over a dead McAdam who had been caught in a giant tennis net like a tuna. Krepper was pushing the end of a tennis racquet into the victim's throat. A speech bubble coming from Krepper said *Disqualified once and for all.*

'Oh my God,' said Taylor. 'This is horrible!'

'There's lots more of them,' said Sandberg, brandishing his own mobile. On his phone was the same image, except with Khumalo swapped out for Krepper. He scrolled down his screen and turned it around again. 'And here's one with whatshisname, Clyde Pilmer.'

'Why don't governments crack down on this stuff?' Jack

voiced the question to no one in particular as he looked up to the clear blue sky.

'Impossible to control,' said Krepper. 'But one way to stop this shit from continuing is to find the murderer. And I'd appreciate it if you could do that before the Australian Open starts.'

'Don't worry,' said Jack, nodding slowly. 'It'll happen well before then.' Jack's words didn't match his lack of confidence.

After they'd sent Krepper and his trainer on their way, presumably to resume their hit-out, the scowling Serb stamped up the stairway, his equally angry assistant, Goran Savic close behind. While the other players and coaches chose to sit, these two stood, chests puffed out like roosters.

'Let's get it over with.' Stojanovic tapped his watch. 'I'm behind in my training schedule.'

Again, the entitlement made Jack's skin crawl. 'Be grateful you're still alive, unlike one of your rivals.'

An awkward, uncomfortable silence persisted for about fifteen seconds, a silence the DS wasn't in a hurry to break. Finally, he said, 'People are pointing the finger at you, Dragan.'

'Who is?' Stojanovic inched closer to Jack until the DS could smell onions on the man's breath. 'Tell me!'

Jack reached in his pocket, pulled out a packet of Extra spearmint gum, popped a pellet in his mouth and offered one to the Serb. 'You could do with one of these, your breath stinks.'

Stojanovic exchanged a look of fury with his coach, then directed it towards Jack. 'Who the fuck do you think you are?' He inched even closer, his chest millimetres from Jack's.

'Come on, fellas,' intervened Taylor like a teacher trying

to separate boys fighting in the playground. 'Let's not start an international incident over a little misunderstanding.'

Stojanovic nodded, took a step back from the cocky detective. 'I like her better.'

'Not surprising. She's very likeable.' Jack made a point of slowly chewing the gum. In the bad old days he might have been puffing on a cigarette in this situation, blowing the smoke into a suspect's face. More fun than grinding gum, but you have to move with the times. 'Unfortunately, you're obliged to answer my questions before nice DC Taylor has a turn.'

'First tell me who's accusing me.'

Jack shook his head. 'Sorry. No can do. But that person was very adamant–'

'What does that mean?' Stojanovic hunched his shoulders.

'Sorry, sunshine. You speak English so well for a moment I forgot it wasn't your native language.' Jack was genuine in his praise, even though the arrogant man rubbed him up the wrong way on every other level. 'I meant they were insistent we look into you as someone with a hand in the murder of Roderick McAdam.'

Stojanovic remained silent, perhaps subduing an inner rage. He grabbed the back of his neck, closed his eyes and rolled his head from side to side.

'I'm going to ask you bluntly,' continued Jack. 'And don't take it personally, it's my job to ask these questions, just like it's your job to hit a fuzzy yellow ball back and forth across a net. Did you organise, pay for, or are you any way involved in the murder of Roderick McAdam?'

'No.' The man's face was expressionless, his tone flat.

'That's it? A plain old no?' Jack had expected more histrionics.

'What else do you want me to say?' Stojanovic shrugged.

Jack coughed into his fist, thrown off balance for the moment.

'Who do you think might be involved in the murder?' said Taylor.

'Honestly? I have no idea. Of course, Krepper was about to break the record as longest number one, but the so-called experts said McAdam was going to beat him. You can, what do they say, join the dots.'

'Did *you* think McAdam was going to win the Open?'

'Fuck no! I was – I *am* going to win the Open.'

'And will you become world number one after that?'

'Only if Stefan fails to make it to the quarter finals. But he will, so…'

Jack scratched his head and screwed up his eyes, pretending he was trying to recall a long-lost fact, then raised his finger like he just remembered it. 'A new draw was hastily created after McAdam's death. You and Krepper were originally on opposite sides, now the organisers have put the two of you on the same side. And…' Jack pulled out a folded-up blank piece of paper, pretended to read from it. 'Now, you can potentially meet him in the fourth round. You knock him out, win the next three matches, and suddenly you're the new king of world tennis.'

Stojanovic burst out laughing. 'You know how stupid that sounds?'

Taylor said, 'Sounds like a plausible scenario to me. You've never been number one, have you?'

'No! And guess what, I don't give a shit if I never am. I make more money in a week than you and him,' he stabbed a finger at Jack, 'earn in a year. Besides, I'm younger than Stefan and Khumalo and everyone else in the top ten, so I have plenty of time to become number one. But like I said, it's not the main thing for me. Now I have a question. Why aren't you talking to other seeded players?'

'Because none of them has a realistic motive,' said Jack. 'They haven't earned enough tour points to claim the top spot, even if they win every match at the Australian Open.' He tossed another piece of gum into his mouth, made a move to offer one again to Stojanovic, but pulled the packet away and put it back in his pocket. 'Speaking of motive, McAdam put out a tweet calling you, what was it Taylor?'

'A dirty lying scumbag,' said Taylor. 'Among other things.'

'You've already shown yourself to be a hot-tempered person,' said Jack. 'Getting up in my face, pointing your finger at me. Very rude. You're lucky I didn't headbutt you into next week.'

'Excuse me?' said Stojanovic, eyes wide.

'You heard me. And your behaviour is even more alarming considering we've not called you any nasty names. Just asked you a bunch of harmless questions. In my book, that casts you as someone who treats offensive remarks like invitations to act violently. Maybe to commit murder.' Jack thrust out his chin challengingly.

Stojanovic shook his head as the colour drained from his coach's face. Savic said defensively, 'Dragan and Roderick were using what they call trash talk. It's common among athletes.'

Jack nodded. 'I'm aware of the phenomenon. I've used it myself as a boxer, way back in my youth. Trouble is, when people do this in public forums, things can escalate, get out of hand, lead to some serious animosity.'

'But not in this case, Detective,' said Stojanovic. 'I

started to ignore his rude statements and eventually he stopped provoking me.'

Taylor laughed. 'Provoking *you*? You were the one who started the argument when you accused him of using performance-enhancing drugs.'

The Serb waggled his finger. 'I was careful with my language. I said the ATP should look into it, that it was possible he was cheating. He's the one who chose to insult my honour.'

Time to wind this up, thought Jack. 'I thank you for your time and co-operation. We may not have all the answers yet, but it sure has been informative talking with you, Dragan.'

'In what possible way?' Stojanovic was almost sneering.

'I've learned what an unpleasant man you are.' He gave a nod to the coach Savic. 'Good day to you both.'

As the detectives descended the stairs and turned to make their way through the small tunnel to exit the arena, Jack could feel Stojanovic's eyes burning like lasers into their backs.

---

THE PLANE TRIP back to Cairns was turning out to be uneventful compared to the journey south. No turbulence, no wailing children. The aircraft was half-empty, testifying to the reluctance of Australians from the southern states to visit the Deep North in the height of summer. One stroke of luck – a male flight attendant recognised Jack, made a phone call and got permission from the airline to upgrade him and Taylor to the best seats at the front of the plane.

'The job has its perks at times,' said Jack, flicking open a copy of Melbourne's broadsheet newspaper, *The Age*. The

McAdam case dominated the front page, along with the usual doom and gloom from around the world. In a nutshell, the country was clamouring for someone to be charged with the murder of one of its brightest stars. Jack's gut told him either one of Krepper or Stojanovic could be at the bottom of the killing. Krepper was too cool, Stojanovic – too hot. The only way to nail either of them was to find corroborating proof. But where? He could only pray that something from the pool of physical and digital evidence would tie one of them to the murder.

After they'd finished a delightful meal of garlic prawns for Jack and beef Wellington for Taylor, accompanied by dinner rolls with rich New Zealand butter, finished off by a light and airy chocolate mousse, the conversation turned to the pro tennis players they had interviewed.

'Dragan stands out as the most likely of the two,' said Taylor, stirring a sugar into her Earl Grey. 'But, again, both have a strong motive.'

'Yeah, I'd rank him number one suspect, even if he ain't the number one player.'

Taylor sipped her tea, let out an "aahh" of satisfaction. 'Not a lot to base it on, though, is it? Some online argy-bargy and a theoretical chance to take the title. You'd never get an arrest warrant with that.'

'True. Hey, what about the Cumberland lassie who's meant to have stalked McAdam?'

'We'll find out when we get back home and talk to Steger and Wycombe, I guess.'

'What's this? Not checking your phone or laptop for an update? That's not like you, DC Taylor.'

'Let's just enjoy the flight and forget about work for the next two hours, shall we? You look like you could do with some shut-eye.'

Never had she spoken sweeter words. Jack turned and opened the visor of his window, half expecting to see the ground below. The vastness of the star-studded night-sky outside shocked him back to the reality of the case.

They really had no idea.

As he drifted off to sleep to the accompaniment of softly humming engines, Jack was sure he felt the light touch of Taylor's hand brushing against his.

## Chapter Twenty-Three

THE SCREEN DOOR barely clung to the frame. Its original colour was white, now it was beige and stained with brown spots of rust. Stiff cobwebs entangled with leaves and twigs and dead flies clung to its corners. If the screen was intended for security, it was a fail; a good hard yank would separate it from its hinges. As a barrier against insects, again useless, thanks to a number of gaping holes. The screen door was snibbed shut from the inside, making it impossible to open it and knock on the main entrance door. Detective Steger pressed on a buzzer a number of times only to be greeted by silence. 'Must be broken,' said Detective Tania Wycombe.

'Lots of broken items in this house, I'd say,' said Steger. 'People, too, judging by the state of the place.' To make their arrival known, he grabbed the flimsy screen and gave it a rattle. The noise set off a dog inside the house, its ear-splitting yelping caused a flock of white-crested cockatoos to abandon their perch on a power line and take off for a more peaceful location.

A young woman, late teens, thin build, dark rings under her violet eyes and a cigarette dangling from her slack mouth, shuffled through the gloom and appeared at the door. She wore filthy slippers and a dark blue polyester dressing gown with the logo of the Yorkville Scorpions basketball team above the right breast. 'Yeah, who is it?'

Wycombe held up her ID and introduced herself and her colleague. 'Are you Anne Cumberland?'

'I might be,' she snuffled. 'What's this in regards to?'

'The murder of Roderick McAdam,' said Steger. 'We understand you used to be close to him. May we come in?'

The source of the earlier barking appeared at Cumberland's side. A shaggy brown mixed-breed terrier. It took an instant dislike to the police officers and began jumping about and barking at a volume and frequency that set teeth on edge. But not the owner's, who stared at the officers with a blank expression.

'Sorry, I didn't hear a word of that. I'm very tired. Could you come back later?' She closed the door, leaving the two detectives standing open-mouthed on the rickety deck.

'What now?' said Wycombe.

'We bust in.'

'Are you serious?'

'If this doesn't work, yes.' Steger rattled the screen door as hard as he could, the clamour setting off the dog inside the house again. 'I'm going to keep this up until she lets us in.'

In less than a minute the woman reappeared at the door, the yapping now only half as loud. 'Bloody hell, you're persistent. Come in, let's get this over with.'

'What about that mutt?' said Wycombe, peering into the darkened corridor. 'She looked pretty feisty.'

'Relax. I've tied her up under the house and given her a bone.'

Steger knew they had the right person; he and Wycombe had seen recent photos of her from selfies on Instagram. There was no text with her posts, just morose portraits of an unhappy woman whose appearance had deteriorated over time. The detectives followed her into a small loungeroom blue with cigarette smoke and redolent of dog and cat and three-minute noodles. Cumberland pointed at a hideous brown two-seater couch and gestured for the cops to sit on it. She sagged into a low chair with wooden armrests whose best days were in the late 1970s.

'Why won't you sit?' Cumberland asked. 'Afraid youse'll catch something?' She sucked air through a gap between her front teeth and offered a weak smile. She reached in the deep pockets of her dressing gown and plucked out a packet of budget cigarettes the size of a house brick, extracted a smoke and was soon billowing away like a steam train.

'We would like to sit, as it happens,' said Steger, squeezing his eyelids as the acrid smoke began to sting. 'But not here. We'd like you to accompany us to the Yorkville Police Station.'

'What for?' A nervous edge crept into Cumberland's nasally voice. 'I ain't done nothing.'

'We have reason to believe you never gave up stalking Roderick McAdam. In light of his recent death, we'd like you to answer some questions in a more formal setting.'

'What stalking? What the hell are you talking about? I haven't been near Roddy for a couple of years.' Her hand shook as she tried to flick a collar of ash into a vintage mother-of-pearl ashtray. 'I'm devasted about what happened.'

Wycombe brushed suspicious looking debris from the

couch and cautiously sat down. She leaned forward and said in a maternal tone, 'It's in your best interest to co-operate, Anne. We were told by Peter Gosling that you harassed Mr McAdam for a number of years.' At that moment she felt a vibration in her pocket. 'Excuse me for a moment.' It was a text from Batista, relaying the information gleaned by Taylor. Wycombe felt her face flush as she read the message and realised the Yorkville detective had picked up something she herself had missed. A quick pang of professional jealousy was immediately replaced by gratitude to her colleague. Wycombe was a team-player at heart, not a glory-seeker. 'Why don't you come clean with us, love? We know you tried to call Roderick a couple of times last month, just after it was announced he'd be in town for the Pilmer Challenge.'

'You're lying. I don't even have his number anymore. He's probably changed it after he became such a big shot.'

'Now you know as well as I do he didn't change it. His phone company has provided us with all the activity on his number. Interestingly, they logged several calls made to Roderick from a mobile registered to you.'

'Oops.' She punched out a sharp, maniacal laugh. 'Busted. But I never talked to him, I swear. He didn't answer my calls.'

'Please go and get dressed,' said Steger. 'You can't come to the station looking like that.'

'Like what?' she said challengingly.

'Like you just crawled out of bed after a night of heavy drinking.'

'Ha! No wonder youse are detectives. Cos that's exactly what happened. Up all night downing cheap plonk and watching highlights of Roderick's matches.' She dropped her head into her hands for a second, then looked up again smiling with her mouth but not with her eyes.

Wycombe said, 'You don't seem too upset by what's happened.'

'What? How dare you!' she pouted. 'I told you I was devastated. I cried for hours and hours yesterday and now I haven't got any tears left, especially not for you cops. Believe me, when I heard the news, I couldn't believe it. I still can't believe it! I loved him even if he didn't love me back when he got all rich and famous. I never woulda done anything to hurt him.' She took a deep drag on her cigarette, the end glowing like an oxyacetylene torch. 'Never.'

A shrill voice called out from somewhere in the house, the words distorted.

'Who's that?' said Wycombe. 'Sounded female. Is it your mother?'

'If you'd done your homework you'd know it's just me and mum living here. Dad buggered off to Sydney with some tart.' She turned her head. 'MUM! Come here!'

A woman who didn't look more than ten years older than Anne Cumberland appeared in the doorway to the lounge holding a glass of what looked like white wine. Her hair was messed up, flat on one side from being pressed on a pillow. Her eyes only half open, she peered at the gathering in the room like she was looking through a thick fog. She wore a grease-stained red tank top and navy blue leggings with rips and tears in them, the toenails on her feet were painted an iridescent green. She also wore the haggard expression of someone who'd been up all night on the booze and at some stage passed out. *They've been hammering it together*, thought Steger.

'What's going on?' said the woman in a grating voice conditioned by years of smoking. 'You two don't look like bloody Jehovah's Witnesses. Cops, are you? Took your time about paying us a visit in our humble home. We thought it would have been sooner.'

Wycombe stood and held her open palms to the side of her body as if to say she was not a physical threat. 'Mrs Cumberland, I take it?'

'Call me Sharon.'

'OK, Sharon it is. Would you be amenable to accompanying your daughter down to the station for a preliminary interview?' said Wycombe. 'Just a formality at this stage.'

'What, now? It's Saturday. The cop shop's not open on the weekend.'

Squinting in the smoky haze, Steger said, 'We're open 24/7 when it comes to murder enquiries, madam. In light of information we received regarding your daughter's recent phone calls to the deceased, we'd appreciate–'

'Yeah, yeah, blah, blah,' said the mother. 'Wait a minute while we powder our noses.'

'You can't be serious, mum?' said Anne. 'I'm innocent.'

'Yeah, and refusing to co-operate with the law makes you look guilty, don't it. Now, come with me and no more of your nonsense.'

Wycombe and Steger waited in the car for ten minutes before mother and daughter emerged from the house, hand in hand, heads down, looking slightly more presentable than before, but not by much.

'Jesus, who'd want to be them, hey?' said Steger.

'Better them than McAdam,' said Wycombe. 'At least those two are breathing.'

BATISTA OBSERVED from behind the two-way glass as his visiting detectives worked their magic on the Cumberland women. Such a change to see two good cops instead of nice Taylor and cranky Lisbon. He was doubly glad all interviews are recorded these days; it would be edifying for Jack to see a gentleman interrogator in action. Five minutes in and Anne Cumberland openly admitted to trying to contact Roderick McAdam.

'Why?' said Wycombe. 'You'd been warned off by Adrian McAdam. He applied for a restraining order against you.'

'Yeah, but he pulled it.'

'As a favour to you.'

'Maybe he realised he was overreacting, huh, did ya think about that?'

'I think he didn't want a young lady to have her life ruined by having that kind of a black mark against her in the legal system. Something that would follow her wherever she went, forever judged for her foolish mistakes. You ought to be grateful to Mr McAdam. Others wouldn't have been as kind and generous.'

Anne placed the side of her head on the cold steel table for a moment, like she was listening for a heartbeat. She sat up straight again. 'Listen, I appreciate what old man McAdam did. Even though they never liked me, thought I was beneath them and their la-di-dah ways. But I never–'

'You called Roderick,' interjected Wycombe. 'Several times. Despite you undertaking to leave him alone.'

'Like I said. He never answered. No contact was made.' Anne smiled smugly.

'OK. We're not getting anywhere. I'm going to ask the magistrate to order you to hand over your mobile.'

'Why?' said Sharon Cumberland, suddenly anxious.

'To see if she physically approached Roderick at any time. We can check these things easily. Mobile phones are virtual tracking devices these days.'

'You've got no grounds.'

'We've got plenty. Anne here was clearly anxious to speak to the victim.'

Sharon winced at the term. 'Could you please call him by his name and not "the victim". It's very upsetting to hear.'

'I'll make that small concession, although your level of upset is nothing compared to that of his parents. Now, if young Anne here was prepared to call Roderick despite promising not to, what's to say she didn't try to see him in person? Everyone knew where he was staying.'

Anne pulled out her mobile, let if fall it on the table and fanned her fingers in a "mic drop" gesture. 'Have the fucking phone. Save yourself the bother of getting a court order. You'll see I've spent the last week at home. Only time I went out was to the corner shop to get smokes.'

'That's right,' said Sharon with a rapid nod. 'The girl's been nowhere.'

'We'll be going back further than a week,' said Wycombe. 'As far as we have to.'

Steger scooped up the phone and handed it back. 'I'd rather do things the right way. I don't want to be accused of–'

'You're the ones accusing *me*!' Anne leaned into the spine of her chair, threw her arms back melodramatically. 'When I haven't done nothing! I mean, I heard the sick way Roderick was tied up 'n that. Do I look like I'm strong enough to overpower him? No way…'

'You could have had help,' said Wycombe. 'Did someone help you kill Roderick McAdam?'

'Are you kidding me?' Anne exchanged a look of horror with her mother. 'No! I don't have any friends who would… and…I mean…why would I do that when I loved him?' She burst into tears, her emaciated body trembling as her mother draped her thin arm around Anne's shoulder.

'Now look what you've done to her!' said Sharon.

The detectives remained impassive as the crying reached a crescendo before trailing off.

'Are you going to charge my daughter with something?' Without waiting for an answer she added in a bitter tone. 'Does she need a lawyer? We can't afford one, we're stony broke.'

Steger shook his head. 'Not at this stage. My colleague didn't mean to distress Anne. But we have to consider the scenario of unrequited love leading to murder. *If I can't have him, no one can* kind of thing. More common than you'd think, although it's mainly jilted men who are the perpetrators.'

Sharon folded her arms defiantly across her chest as her daughter mopped up tears with a tissue. 'Anne isn't a perpetrator of anything.'

'We're just exploring possibilities.' Steger stood and paced back and forth for a moment, chewing on the end of a pen. A ticking clock and Anne's snuffling were the only sounds in the interview room. He stopped and addressed Wycombe. 'I think she's had enough now.'

'Yes,' agreed Wycombe. 'I think she's told us all we need to know. For now.'

As the detectives escorted the Cumberlands out the door Steger said, 'You know, Anne, I think I will take you up on that offer of your mobile phone.'

'What?' Her head snapped around. 'Oh, sure.' She handed it over. 'You gonna have it for long?'

'Couple of days.'

She smirked. 'Keep it as long as you need. You ain't gonna find shit.'

---

NEGOTIATING the winding dirt driveway into the Greer family's two-acre property 10 km inland from Yorkville, Detective Steger picked his way carefully. He swerved every now and then to avoid gaping potholes, uncleared fallen branches and random household litter. The rubbish started at the turnoff from the highway and was sprinkled the entire length of the driveway.

'Jack Lisbon said the man was a pig, but I hadn't expected this,' said Steger. 'Looks like my local tip.'

Wycombe shook her head. 'For a so-called businessman, this gives a bad first impression.'

'When you think of the kind of filthy establishment he runs, it's no surprise. A pity the uniforms are still at the crash site; the 4x4 would've handled this driveway better than the Stinger.'

'And they could've grilled the Greers instead of us having to do it.'

Steger gave a chuckle as he struck a large water-filled pothole; both of them grunted.

On a quick radio exchange minutes earlier, Constable Wilson had confirmed the accident was worse than first thought. With an afternoon downpour expected to slow down operations, it was going to take many more hours – perhaps into the night – to clear the overturned goods truck and its spilled load, meaning the Brisbane detectives would have to take on as many of the interviewing jobs as they could manage.

The two-storey wooden house loomed into view as the jungle of trees and red-and-yellow lantana blossoms gave way to an open space covered in kikuyu grass. The litter poking through the longish lawn was diverse and abundant. Cracked plant pots, assorted pieces of packaging cardboard, car engine parts, panels and bumpers, rusty tools and jerry cans, fast-food wrappers and containers, and mound upon mound of dog shit. The producers of the canine manure, two smooth-coated mongrels, set off a belligerent howl when they sighted the cherry-coloured Stinger with its blue-and-white checked trim. Must be like a rag to a bull, Steger thought to himself. Or it may have been the sound of the car approaching that ticked off the beasts. Either way, the snarling and salivating dogs looked anything but friendly. On the plus side, they were attached to star pickets with thick metal chains a safe distance from the steps leading up to the veranda. If they got loose, there was always the defensive capabilities of their Glocks to fall back on.

A quick assessment of the house, with its flaking paint and warped timbers trying to prise themselves free of walls, put Steger in mind of a Queensland version of Bates Motel, with a wraparound veranda but minus the steep-pitched roof. On the veranda, two overweight, heavily tattooed men in overalls with no shirts underneath, swayed back and forth slowly in rocking chairs, each nursing a bright yellow can of a well-known brand of local beer. One raised his can in greeting as the detectives alighted from the vehicle and made their way to the witnesses, sidestepping dog turds as they went.

'Come on up,' called out the bald one with prominent ears, Derrick Greer. 'We've got some beers on ice. Want one?'

At the sound of their owner's voice, the angry hounds magically curled up in balls and shut their eyes.

'No thanks.' Steger brushed a fly from his face. Then another. Each pile of dog poop was covered in a cloud of flies; some of them leaving the mound to annoy any living creatures that got too close.

'Your choice. We ain't got nothing else to offer you 'cept tap water.'

'We'll manage,' said Wycombe, also waving away a couple of flies.

The brother endowed with hair, wiry brown curls that had receded halfway back to the crown of his head, stood unsteadily from his rocking chair. He wobbled slightly as he placed his can on the veranda's handrail and lit a cigarette. The cops had studied the photos and knew this was Garth, the brother more prone to violence. He stared out across his property towards the edge of the forest, almost as if the detectives weren't even there.

Steger and Wycombe reached the top of the stairs. The front door was wide open, the faint stink of something rotten wafted through the doorway. Both officers screwed up their eyes but made no comment. It was an unwritten rule between them not to comment on the living conditions of the general public when you were only at the getting-to-know you stage. After someone revealed they were an arsehole, different story.

'To what do we owe the pleasure?' said Derrick, thick, cracked lips parting in a smile that revealed a couple of missing teeth. 'Never seen youse two before. Where's that English bloke, Jack Lisbon?'

'In Melbourne talking to a bunch of tennis players,' said Wycombe. 'They were expecting to meet up later with a young guy who drew his last breath in your dad's hotel.'

'Right,' said Derrick as if the female detective was talking about the weather.

The officers got out their ID, introduced themselves. Steger explained that the local police were short-staffed and had had to enlist help due to the demands of the murder investigation. 'Is your dad home?'

'Nope,' said Derrick. 'Him and mum are out.'

'Where?'

'Dunno. I never asked.'

'That's fine. It's you two lads we wanted to speak with, as it happens.'

'Yep.' Big Garth gave a heavy sigh, turned around from inspecting his estate. 'We're all horrified by that murder. Problem is, we know nothing about it, so you and the pretty lady may as well get back in your funny little toy car and bugger off.' His words weren't slurred, but another can or two and he'd be on his way.

'My little brother gets a bit tetchy if unexpected guests refuse a beer when it's offered,' said Derrick apologetically. 'Wanna try again?'

'Sure,' said Wycombe. 'One's OK, isn't it Mike?'

Steger extended a hand. 'Hit me up.'

With their backs against the veranda railing and Garth again rocking in his chair, Steger took a sip of beer and decided to go for the jugular. 'Your dad's in a bit of trouble isn't he? I mean, he can't re-open the hotel until Yorkville CIB give him the go ahead. So, if you can supply us information that's helps us solve the crime – even if you think it's not important – he'll be up and trading again a whole lot quicker.'

'Problem is, we don't know anything,' said Garth testily. 'I already told yas.'

'Let's see about that,' said Wycombe, adjusting her glasses. 'Maybe a little prompt will tease it out of you boys.'

'Ooh,' said Derrick. 'Tease me, detective!' He let forth with a belly laugh that shook his barrel of a stomach. 'I like a woman who's a tease.'

Wycombe ignore the remark and pressed on. 'We know guests checked in on Thursday night under false names. One of them could be the killer. Who were these men?'

Silence.

'C'mon,' said Steger, gesturing at Garth with his beer can. 'Surely you know the real identities of, let me think back, Jones, Brown and Citizen.'

Garth hunched his slightly hairy shoulders, stopped the chair rocking. 'Nup. Wouldn't have a clue. Blokes come from all over the place.'

'Surely there are regulars,' ventured Wycombe.

'Wouldn't know. All the guests are strangers to us. They pay their money, do the deed with their dates, then piss off in the morning.'

'What about you, Derrick? Any idea who these mystery guests were?'

He cracked a fresh beer before answering, 'I don't have a clue either. It was a slow night, you know. Me and Garth left pretty early, it was just a bunch of old guys in the bar. They're the only regulars we know. The drinkers. Fritz the German, Larry O'Dea and a couple of others. They cleared off well before 9:00pm. Me and Garth weren't far behind 'em.'

'Did you lock up the bar?'

'Joanna did,' said Derrick. 'She's my girlfriend by the way, lives here with us on the ranch. She locked up at 10:00pm, came straight home.'

'Are you saying the hotel is unattended while there are

guests in the rooms?' Wycombe's voice went up a notch. 'That's a bit irresponsible, isn't it? What if there's a fire?'

'All the guests are given an emergency number to contact if something goes wrong at the hotel.'

'What number is that?'

'Mine.' Derrick took a deep slug of beer. 'But no one's called me on it for ages.'

Steger paused, dug into his memory banks. 'Something I don't get. The housekeeper Valdez told DC Taylor she used to work nights on reception, sometimes delivered alcohol to the rooms. Now you're telling me there is no reception. Who's telling the truth?'

'They both are,' said a sultry female voice from the doorway. 'The guests who want room service, drinks delivered from the bar until dawn, pay extra for that. A set rate of $300. If they do, it's me who gets that job. Until we can find someone else to do it. To tell you the truth, I'm sick of it. Now, if no guests want the extras, no one stays behind.'

'And you are?' said Wycombe, already guessing the answer. The woman was dressed as skimpily as Wycombe imagined the sex workers did who plied their trade at the Gaz.

'Joanna Climpson.' She grabbed a beer from the cooler on the floor, popped it open, went back to standing in the doorway, leaning against the frame with one leg crossed over the other. 'I've been working for this family for eight years.'

Steger locked eyes with her, gave her his best steely glare. 'The lads here haven't been very helpful. Do you know the men who stayed at the hotel on Thursday night?'

'Only one.'

'Who?' said Wycombe, unable to hide the hope in her voice.

Joanna folder her arms across an ample bosom. 'Bloody obvious, isn't it? Roderick McAdam.'

The Greer brothers chuckled. 'Good one, Jo,' said Garth.

'Only,' Joanna continued, 'nobody knew that at the time. Cos no one booked the room they found him in.'

'So how did he get into that room?'

None of them could provide an answer.

As Steger and Wycombe drove out of the property and back to the station, they agreed on one thing: the Greers were hiding something.

## Chapter Twenty-Four

THE PELICAN BAR on the Esplanade was humming with activity, sweaty bodies pressed close, low-level hip-hop music thrumming as a backdrop. No surprise for a Saturday night. It was a little noisier than usual; heavy and persistent rain showers since the early evening had kept many customers inside drinking. People were always looking for excuses to keep partying.

Jack didn't care about the crush. He had Taylor for company.

'Why do you like this place when you don't even drink?' said Taylor, nursing a glass of Merlot. 'You need at least a couple under your belt to tolerate the racket.'

'Was that a tennis pun?' Jack gave her a sideways look.

'No chance,' she blustered, giving the wine a little swirl. 'I'm not into dad jokes.' She saw a feigned look of hurt in his eyes, misread it for real, touched him on the arm and said, 'Oh, I didn't mean…'

A burst of laughter pierced the din of the crowd. 'I'm just kidding you.'

'You arsehole!' She laughed, with slight awkwardness. 'I never know your angle...sunshine.'

This time Jack roared with laughter. 'You're all right, kid.' His own words reminded him of a corny line from an old Humphrey Bogart movie. He raised his glass in salute, she copied.

'A bit early to be "cheersing" isn't it?' she said. 'We're no closer to finding the killer than we were before we flew to Melbourne this morning.' She made a ring out of her thumb and forefinger. 'We got nothin'.'

Jack searched for something pertinent to say, came up empty, took a sip of his Diet Coke. She had agreed to the outing to the Pelican Bar under sufferance. He'd practically begged, said he was overtired and would struggle to sleep since there was so much going on in his brain. A wind-down at the pub would settle the synapses.

Jack glanced up as Wycombe and Steger picked their way through the crowd, drinks in hand. Each favoured a half pint of frothy ale. He looked back to Taylor. 'As they say in the classics, we've got company.'

The detectives abandoned their high stools around an elevated round table, found a booth that was miraculously empty, slid into the seats. The Brisbane duo gave a quick rundown of their interactions with the Cumberland women and the hillbilly clan at the Greer property.

'I found a common thread between the two,' said Wycombe.

'Really?' said Jack, eyebrows arched. 'A link?'

'Yep,' she took a quick slug of beer, wiped a thin line of a foam from her top lip. 'Dogs. Annoying, yapping dogs.'

'Nothing else?'

'I get the feeling the Greers and Joanna Climpson have

a fair idea who stays in the hotel — and who was there on Thursday night besides McAdam, but they aren't saying.'

'They're all in on it, you think?' said Taylor.

'My gut tells me Garth is the one hiding something. His brother Derrick's an oafish clown, but I reckon he'd be the one most likely to be truthful. Garth, though, he's a scary brute.'

'Anything to base your theory on?' said Jack.

Wycombe shook her head. 'Body language, but that's not enough to arrest someone, is it?'

'Nope. What about Anne Cumberland?'

Steger plopped the woman's phone on the table. 'We need to get this to the tech boys and girls and see if Anne tried to approach McAdam.'

'Or,' said Wycombe. 'Perhaps she ventured off to meet someone willing to murder the man at her behest. To be totally honest, I don't suspect Cumberland for this crime. She willingly handed over the phone, she's got her mum as a rock-solid alibi. Besides, I just don't think she'd be motivated to do it. She's barely motivated to get out of bed.'

'I agree,' said Steger, fingering his cleft chin. 'There's more to be uncovered from the strange folks running the Hotel Gasnier than from Anne Cumberland.'

Jack cracked an ice cube between his molars. 'Let's have another chat with the housekeeper tomorrow. I reckon if we lean a bit harder on Valdez she might have a morsel or two to give us.'

'What, all of us?' said Wycombe.

'Of course not. Me and Taylor, innit!' Jack laughed. 'You two have to do whatever Batista asks you to.'

Steger and Wycombe both pouted in tandem then smiled. 'I don't care,' said Wycombe. 'Just don't send me back to the Greers. Although,' she jerked a finger at Steger, 'I'm sure this tough hombre would relish the opportunity.'

'Incorrect,' said Steger. 'I'll settle for staring at computer screens looking for more likely suspects.' He tapped the edge of a beer coaster on the table, looked back and forth between Jack and Taylor. 'So, tell us what happened in Melbourne.'

Taylor took up the cudgels. Again, there was nothing to go on except suspicions based on people's behaviour. They'd be keeping a close eye on what Stefan Krepper and, especially, Dragan Stojanovich, did next. Apart from that, they hadn't learned anything of real value to the investigation.

'Not much else we can do until the full forensics results come in,' said Jack, rolling up his shirt sleeves. 'And I'm betting London to a brick old Margaret Proctor and the lab rats will turn up something that points us straight to the killer.'

'You really think so?' said Wycombe.

'No idea,' said Jack.

---

WITH THE VENUE all but empty, the visiting detectives took their leave just before midnight, keen to get their heads down on soft pillows ahead of a Monday morning of brain-grinding desk work. Taylor wasn't far behind, her eyelids were sagging like a droopy hammock. Jack's body also clamoured for rest. Definitely no gym work tonight – he'd squeeze in a quick weights and heavy-bag routine at the Iron Horse after a run along the waterfront tomorrow morning. Not for the first time, the idea of rescuing a dog from the pound crossed Jack's mind. Good company for running, good company at home. But for that he'd have to get rid of the apartment, buy a house, maybe a couple of acres. *After this case.*

He gathered his keys, wallet and phone, eased on his jacket. *Bloody jacket, why do I even need one in this bloody heat?* He drained the last of a flat coke, leaving an untouched straight rum on the table. Jack gave a two-fingers-to-the-forehead salute to Dave the barman as he headed for the exit. Jack hadn't seen him in a while, partly because Jack had avoided the pub but mainly because the pony-tailed hipster had been on vacation for six weeks. Jack couldn't leave without a word.

'Evening, sunshine. When did you return from your holidays?'

'This morning. Back to work already to save up for the next trip.'

'You enjoyed your time away then?'

'Too right.' Dave grinned, pulled out his phone, showed some happy snaps from his holiday to Thailand. 'First time there. Had a ball.'

'Did you take your girlfriend?'

'I said I had a ball, DS Lisbon.'

Both men laughed.

'Nah, I'm joshing you. I took Liz. See?' Dave showed a photo of his woman lounging by a pool sipping on a margarita.

'I'm jealous,' said Jack. 'My last holiday was a nightmare.'

'At least you caught the bad guys, right?'

'Yeah, I did 'n all. But I'm damned if I know where to go next with this McAdam case.'

Dave bent down, retrieved a tray of glasses from the dishwasher and set them on the bar. 'Yeah, what a drama to happen in little old Yorkville, hey? The owner of this joint reckons he made a mint during the tournament. More tourists than usual for this time of year. But, yeah, everyone's talking about the murder.'

'And what are they saying?'

'All kinds of stuff. Most of it sounds like pure fantasy.'

The DS jangled his keys in his pocket. Sleep was calling but sometimes Dave had proven useful for a lead or two. 'Give me an example.'

'He was hunted down by the Russian mafia.'

'If you said Serbian mafia, I'd be more inclined to believe you.'

'What? Is Dragan Stojanovic a suspect?'

'I can neither confirm nor deny, blah, blah, blah.' Jack slapped the counter. 'Anyway, I gotta be off.' As the hydraulically hinged door hissed closed behind him, Jack remembered something he'd been meaning to ask Dave but had forgotten in the excitement of the Melbourne trip. He went back inside, managed to catch the barman as he was locking up the till. 'One more question.'

'Yeah?'

'You hear of anyone selling roofies around the place?'

Dave hadn't, but he brought up the name of a local drug dealer who'd also been an informant for Jack three years ago. He'd been pretty useless as far as informants go, but he was prone to ratting out others to save his own skin.

Jack looked at his watch. 00:15, bucketing rain, and he could barely keep his eyes open.

Still, he'd be paying Evan Zane a surprise visit in about 20 minutes' time.

## Chapter Twenty-Five

FOR A WASTE-OF-SPACE DRIFTER, Evan Zane seemed to have finally set down solid roots. Three years ago he lived in a rented dump at 49 Tallis Street in the down-at-heel suburb of Lockyer. And here he was, still at the same address. Wonders will never cease, thought Jack.

'Nice to see you, Evan.' Jack beamed his most congenial smile. 'Lemme in, I'm getting soaked under your leaking eaves.'

Yes, Evan Zane may have managed to bring some stability to his life. He'd kept the rented house, even his woman and kid, who were probably asleep somewhere in the house. But one habit hadn't changed. Zane's pupils were huge black circles under the porch light. A tell-tale sign the man had been smoking dope. Another sign was the stink of the drug's by-products coming from inside the house.

Zane blinked hard a couple of times. 'Is that you DS Lisbon? What the hell are you doing here at this time of night?'

Jack grabbed Zane by the collar of his shirt and dragged

him, uttering feeble protests and feet flailing, down the hallway and plonked him on a plastic chair in the kitchen.

'What's going on?' Zane's breathing was laboured. 'I've done nothin!'

'I'm not here to cause trouble for you, mate. You and I are going to have a little chat, that's all. Mind sparing me a few minutes of your time?'

'Ah, no, course not.' Zane pushed strands of lank, greasy hair from his face. 'Want a cuppa?'

Jack glanced at the nightmare of dirty dishes in the sink. He saw a couple of fat cockroaches scurrying underneath an old, humming refrigerator. 'I'll skip that, but thanks for the offer.'

Zane's hands shook like an old man's as he fumbled to retrieve a cigarette from a squashed packet of Winfield Blue. 'I've been clean for ages, you know. I'm only smoking ciggies and pot these days. No other shit, I swear. And I definitely stopped selling.'

'Not been tempted to go back to your old ways?'

Zane shook his head vigorously, flakes of dandruff flew from his scalp. 'Nah, I even got meself a job packing mangoes at a warehouse. Driving forklifts, you name it.'

'To be honest, I really don't care about your lifestyle habits or your career moves. What interests me is your knowledge of what's going on in this town. In particular, Rohypnol.'

Zane sparked up a match, drew the smoke in deeply. 'Nup. Don't know nothing about it. Who's he?'

Jack reached for the cigarette and pulled it from Zane's mouth, crushed it out in a glass ashtray. 'You're gonna have to do better than that.'

'Hey, you didn't have to do that. I'm co-operating, aren't I?'

'Are you aware of the murder committed in the Hotel Gasnier on Thursday night?'

'Yeees,' said Zane slowly. 'Surely you aren't looking to fit me up for that, are ya?'

'We're desperate for leads, I'm not gonna lie. But we believe the victim was sedated, most likely with roofies.'

'Like I said…'

'The man who died was born in Yorkville, went to high school up the highway in Cairns. He was kind of a hero in these parts. You could potentially benefit financially by helping us out.'

A flash of interest appeared in the man's eyes. 'What do you mean?'

'Well, his parents are super rich, thanks to their son.'

'Are they?'

'Yeah. Rolling in cash. They might be inclined to push a little something your way as a sign of gratitude if you were to…' Jack showed open palms.

'To what?'

Jack winked. 'You know, point us in the right direction.'

'Look,' Zane whispered unnecessarily. 'I may have heard something on the grapevine about a guy trying to offload, whatcha call 'em? Roopies?'

'Roofies.'

'Yeah, them. I don't know much about 'em.'

*Sure, you lying little shit, thought Jack. Pretending you don't know the street name.*

'Anyway, who's this bloke?'

'Look, *I'm* not saying he's doing anything wrong, but there's whispers he's not playing by the rules. Treading on a few toes in territory where he shouldn't, know what I mean?'

Jack smashed his fist down on the kitchen table,

upending the ashtray and sending a glass to the tiled floor where it broke into tiny pieces. Zane's hand went to his chest.

'Give me the name, you toe-rag!'

Zane's face went white. 'Hunt. Lindsay. No…wait a minute…Linford, yeah that's it.'

'Where does he live?'

'Fuck me, DS Lisbon. You can't expect me to know everything.'

It didn't matter. The name was enough to make a start. Something in Jack's lizard brain told him the answer to the riddles lay here in Yorkville, not Melbourne. 'Cheers, mate,' said Jack as he stood to leave. 'Keep your nose clean.'

'What about that financial benefit you mentioned?'

'Simple.' Jack gently prodded Zane in the chest. 'Work hard and save your money.'

'But…'

Jack yelled out over his shoulder as he grasped the doorhandle, gave a backwards wave. 'Ciao, sunshine.'

*Hilux. Highway. Homework.*

## Chapter Twenty-Six

FOR THE SECOND time in less than a week, Jack arrived first at the station. He'd resolved to push through the sleep-deprivation barrier after leaving Zane's house at 01:45am, drop into the station and research Linford Hunt. Reality hit home when he started nodding off behind the wheel and narrowly avoided collecting a power pole. After the close call he made a left at the next set of lights instead of a right and drove straight to his apartment.

Jack switched on his computer and logged onto the QPS database, searched for Linford Hunt. Jack grinned; Zane had provided a lead to a real person.

'Morning,' came a cheery voice attached to a face Jack rated one his favourites in the world. 'I got your text this morning. You were up late.'

'Yeah, it was way past my bedtime.' He quickly explained how he'd followed up a hunch with his old informer, which had provided a tenuous lead.

'You reckon Zane was on the level about this bloke?'

'Only one way to find out. Oh, thanks.' Jack reached out

to grab a double shot espresso Taylor had brought in from the Good Bean. He blew steam off the top, savoured the first hit of caffeine for the day. 'Let's have a look at this Linford Hunt.'

'Is that rhyming slang?'

Jack burst out laughing. 'No, but I may use it in future.'

The two detectives hunched around Jack's computer monitor. Taylor's proximity was again working its tricks on Jack's physiology. Her hair smelled deliciously of pina colada. He did his best to ignore his body's reactions and concentrate on the screen, but as usual it wasn't easy.

'Here's his address,' said Taylor, pointing with a pen. 'I know that apartment block. Some pretty unsavoury types have lived there.'

'That's perfect,' said Jack. 'I'm a sweets man myself, as it happens.' He scooped up his car keys. 'Let's go ruffle some feathers, shall we?'

---

THE SUN HAD BEEN UP for just over an hour, and already the heat and humidity were causing dampness under Jack's clothes. A shimmer of steam rose from the black asphalt. Cawing crows a couple of streets away were the only sound on this peaceful Sunday morning.

There were four units in the complex at the end of the cul-de-sac. Two up, two down, the top ones accessed by external steel stairs that looked like fire escapes. The overall impression was of a small prison: a squat, square edifice, red tin roof, white rendered breeze blocks. The place was crying out for a fresh lick of paint. In this welfare-dependent demographic, aesthetics would never be a priority.

A sleek orange cat guarded the balcony of Hunt's flat. It

mewled then slalomed, tail in the air, between Jack's legs as he readied himself to knock. 'Looks like you made a friend,' said Taylor.

'Yeah, and I'm about to make myself a new enemy.'

Jack pounded on the door relentlessly until it was opened two minutes later by a tall, squinting man with a faint black moustache. 'You Linford Hunt?'

'Who wants to know?'

'I do.' Jack shouldered the door with all his weight. Although the man on the other side was heavier than Jack, he was unable to prevent the DS from shoving him out of the way and sprawling on the floor. *You can never underestimate the power of the element of surprise.* Jack heard Taylor muttering behind him as he barged his way into the two-bedroom apartment, but he couldn't make out the words. No doubt criticism of his methodology.

'Hey, hey, hey!' Hunt had regained his feet, waved both hands in the air. 'Calm the fuck down, will yas!' Stocky and dark complexioned, he wore nothing but a pair of jockey shorts. Profuse acne on his face and body, as well as a pair of perky bitch tits, indicated a bodybuilder's steroid habit.

Jack and Taylor whipped out their IDs. Jack barked for Hunt to take a seat on the couch, and be quick about it.

'Can I at least put some clothes on first?' said Hunt.

Jack pointed at a laundry basket on the floor. 'Good idea. See if you can find something in that.'

Hunt grabbed a pair of running shorts and a singlet and wriggled them on.

'We apologise for the lack of prior notice,' said Taylor. 'But there was little choice due to the urgency of the matter.'

Jack smiled inwardly. She was playing the quintessential good cop, but being firmer than usual. He liked it. A lot.

'And what matter is that?' Hunt rubbed sleep from his eyes. His attempt at nonchalance was belied by his heaving chest.

'Show me where you keep the roofies,' demanded Jack. 'I know from a reliable source that you've been selling them on the black market.'

'Whoa. I'm just going to call my solicitor.' Hunt stood and made to walk to a small dresser by the door. Jack spied the man's cell phone on it. He grabbed it and tossed it to Hunt, who fumbled the device and it fell on the carpeted floor.

'Go ahead,' said Jack. 'I'm sure he'd love to hear about your breach of parole conditions.'

'I never breached my parole.' Hunt picked up the phone, hefted it in his hands, tapped the back of it with a fingernail.

'I don't see you calling that lawyer of yours.' Jack folded his arms across his chest. 'If you even have one.'

Hunt didn't rise to the bait. Instead, he said, 'You haven't told me why you're here, disturbing my peace and quiet. I have a right to know what's going on.'

'It's to do with the murder of tennis player Roderick McAdam. Heard of him?'

The colour drained from Hunt's face, a large vein in his thick neck began to throb. 'And how does that concern me, exactly?'

Jack turned to Taylor. 'Make everyone a cup of tea, Claudia. I'd like to ask the gentleman some man-to-man questions.'

Taylor wordlessly retreated behind a screening wall. From the lounge Jack could hear her fussing about with cups, filling a kettle and switching it on. Jack stood over the top of a sweating Hunt. 'My partner doesn't operate like me. She's too nice for the police force, if I'm gonna be totally honest with you. Should be a nurse or a librarian. Now, I'll ask again. Where are the effin' roofies?'

'I don't–'

Jack's backhand slap sounded like a whip cracking. He held back on the blow, the effect more acoustic than pain-delivering. Hunt's hand instinctively darted to his cheek and gave it a rub. He glowered and gritted his teeth, clearly battling the urge to fight back. Jack wouldn't have minded the challenge; Hunt was all muscle and probably too slow to handle Jack's speed and agility. Instead of goading him further, though, Jack retreated one stride, opened his jacket slightly to reveal the dark mass of his Glock nestled in the holster.

'Everything alright in there?' came Taylor's voice.

'All under control.' Jack turned back to Hunt. 'We've checked your criminal record. One breach, even a minor one, will see you sent back to Copperhead Jail for a number of years.'

Hunt's nostrils flared like a racehorse at the end of a gallop.

'Hey, DS Lisbon!' Taylor called from the kitchen. 'I've found something interesting in here.' She returned to the living room carrying a tray upon which sat three china cups, teabags, spoons, sugar, milk, and a Ziploc bag bulging with white pills.

Hunt's eyes widened like the ripples of a stone thrown into water.

'I ain't got time to listen to protests,' said Jack softly. 'DC Taylor did *not* fit you up by planting evidence. Other coppers might do that, she would never even think of it. So I know beyond a doubt this is your property. You follow me so far?'

Hunt nodded.

'What's in the bag?'

'Rohypnol tablets. One milligram dosage.'

'This doesn't have to end badly for you,' said Taylor. 'In fact, your co-operation could earn you a reduction in your sentence.'

'Listen to the nice lady, Linford,' said Jack with the empathy of a grief counsellor. 'I'll put in a good word for you with the magistrate when your case goes to court. You'll only be in for another six-months. If Saint Barbara Nunez gets your case, hell, you might even walk.'

Hunt wore the expression of a crushed man for whom telling the truth would be a burden lifted. 'A bloke approached me at the gym a couple of weeks ago.'

'What gym?'

'Bakers on Oliphant Street.'

Pity it wasn't Jack's haunt, The Iron Horse, which had excellent CCTV. As far as he recalled, Bakers was a nuts-and-bolts garage gym light on mod cons. 'Go on, son.'

'I've never seen him before. *Got any roofies?* he says. *Sure*, I say. He only wanted a couple of tabs, but he was prepared to pay well over the odds for them.'

'How much?'

'Two hundred bucks apiece. He didn't even haggle, handed over cash.'

Jack whistled. 'What the hell? They only cost about $20 on the street.'

'Yeah, but there's been a drought lately. Something to do with logistics and distribution through legitimate channels. I've been trying to shift that lot for months, but no one's been interested until this bloke rocked up out of the blue.' Hunt shrugged. 'All I can say is he was dead keen to get his hands on 'em.'

'Can you describe him?'

'Sure. He was about—'

'Actually. Let's do the rest of this down at the station. I want to make everything official, no loopholes.' Jack cracked his knuckles before making himself a tea from the items on the tray. 'Go and have a shower and tidy yourself up. We'll hit the road in ten. And feel free to ask your lawyer to pop in for moral support.'

Hunt nodded.

'Before you do that, I need to know something else.'

'What?'

'If we take a peak in your bedroom, are we going to find any more gear?'

'Phials of steroids under the bed. Couple of boxes of syringes.'

'That's all?'

'Yep.'

'For your personal use only?'

'Yep.'

As Hunt headed for the bathroom Jack pulled him up. 'One last question.'

'What?'

'You got any sweet biscuits to go with this tea?'

## Chapter Twenty-Seven

JACK WALKED behind a tripod with a camera mounted on top. He looked down the lens, gave the apparatus a jiggle, uttered a grunt of satisfaction and turned the camera on. Taylor waited patiently in her chair, offering Hunt a wan smile. The witness had declined to call a lawyer or any other form of representation.

'You ready, Linford?' said Jack, resuming his seat next to Taylor.

'Yes,' he nodded slowly. 'Let's get this over with.'

Jack recited the obligatory spiel, gave the time and asked those attending to confirm their presence. 'I won't muck about, Linford. Please tell me the name of the person you sold the tabs to.'

'He didn't give a name.'

'Did you ask?'

'No. That's not how this kind of business is conducted.'

'Fair enough.' Jack sighed. 'And how many did you sell this mystery man and what was the amount of money he paid you?'

Linford repeated what he had told the officers at his flat.

'Excellent. Now, can you describe him for us please.'

'It's not gonna be easy. I only met him twice and I honestly didn't pay much attention. Let's see. Rather tall, average build. Blue eyes. Or maybe they were green. Shit, I can't remember.'

'You'd better start remembering a bit more detail,' said Taylor, scribbling in a notepad. 'Or we won't be able to intercede on your behalf with the DPP.'

'I'm trying.' Linford scratched his close-shaved head. The action must have made him think of hair. 'He's got, ah, mousey coloured hair, I guess. Styled a bit like yours. Detective Lisbon's I mean.'

'So,' said Jack. 'Brown hair, short back and sides. Better. Any outstanding facial features?'

Hunt puckered his lips. 'His ears are a bit bigger than normal, but not that you'd really notice. Nose slightly pointed up at the end. Ordinary mouth, same for the teeth.' Beads of sweat formed on his brow, which he wiped away with the back of his hand.

Jack exchanged a whisper with Taylor. They weren't getting much to go on from Hunt. They may have to arrange a meeting between him and the facial composite expert from Brisbane.

'What about clothes?'

Hunt shook his head. 'Plain t-shirt and jeans. I can't tell you what colour the shirts were.'

'Long sleeves or short?'

'Short.'

'Tattoos on the arms?' prompted Taylor.

'None that I could see.'

Jack stood and paced for a moment. 'Linford. Where did the sale take place? At your gym? Your flat?'

'No. A park two blocks from my place.'

'What car did he drive?'

'That's the funny thing. No car or bike. He came in a taxi. He paid me, grabbed the gear and jumped back in the cab. Fucken weird, hey!'

'Not an Uber?'

'Nah, Yorkville Cabs. One of their new ones with the bright green-and-yellow logo on it.'

'What's the name of the park?'

'Beetson Recreation Ground.'

'You remember the date of the transaction?'

'It's in my phone. One second.' A quick scroll. 'Yep. 28 December.'

Jack turned off the camera. 'OK, Linford. You're free to go.'

'What?'

'Do you recall either of us saying you were under arrest?'

'Ah, no. Do you mean…?' His eyes lit up like the sun.

Taylor closed her notebook, looked up at Hunt with cold eyes. 'We believe the roofies you sold to this person may have been used to sedate Roderick McAdam before he was killed. Now, you'd have no way of knowing that, but if we catch the perpetrator, you will be called on to testify. When the details of your unwitting contribution come out in court, it will be up to the DPP and the parole board whether or not to take another look at your bail conditions. On the plus side, your co-operation this morning will stand you in good stead.'

'That's right,' said Jack. 'I'm in no mind to arrest you for selling Schedule 8 drugs. If we can prove your pills were used to sedate the victim, blaming you for that would be like blaming the guy in the liquor store who sold booze to a driver who got drunk and killed someone. But,' he opened the door to the interview room. 'I have been known to change my mind. Now, beat it.'

## Chapter Twenty-Eight

JACK WASTED no time ringing the taxi company. All he could get was a busy tone. 'Dammit!' He slammed down the phone.

'Be fair,' said Taylor. 'It's only 08:45 on a Sunday morning. This is Yorkville, not New York.'

'Putting things in perspective. You're good at that.' Jack took a walk outside and sucked in some fresh air, grabbed take-away coffees for him and Taylor. Back in the office, Batista had arrived, in civvies for a change. He informed Jack that uniforms were out on patrol, although Wilson was due in at 10:00am to write up a report on yesterday's traffic accident.

'If I knew you were coming in I'd have grabbed you a brew,' Jack said.

'DC Taylor's brought me up to speed on your activities this morning. Sounds like a promising lead.'

'Don't get too excited yet. The toxicology report could put the kybosh on it. What if McAdam was drugged with ketamine or something else?'

'True. But I'm calling it excellent progress until proven otherwise.' Batista unbuttoned the cuffs of a long-sleeved shirt, rolled them up as he spoke. 'I've got an inbox full of emails again, from all around the bloody world. Demanding information. Ask Claudia to write a vague media release to the effect that we are making headway. Something to go out Monday morning.'

'Sir.'

The Inspector rubbed his hands like he was keen to get stuck into some task or other. His next words confirmed it. 'Another thing. Veronica McAdam rang me late last night. They're talking about hiring a private investigator. I want to talk to her again about it.'

'What?' Jack couldn't believe his ears. 'I hope you're going to put them straight.'

'You scared of a little competition?'

'Of course not. But the investigation's barely a couple of days old. Don't they have faith in us?'

'I think she's been watching too much CSI on the telly.' Batista adjusted his unruly glasses. 'She kept saying over and over that most crimes are solved within 48 hours and every day that goes by means there's less chance of catching the perp.'

'I hope you put that into perspective for her, sir. Statistically, I mean.' Jack knew the stats well. Most murders were easy-to-wrap-up crimes of passion committed in the heat of the moment, not by criminal geniuses. And when the killer *did* do their homework and planned the crime meticulously, it generally took longer to track down the killer.

'I did. But if they take that step, I'd like whoever they hire to work with us, not against us.'

'Good call, sir. Speaking of calls, I'm going to try that cab company again.'

Batista wished him luck and retreated to his office.

Heading back to his desk, Jack saw Taylor talking animatedly on the phone. She thanked someone, hung up and jotted a few words down in a notepad.

'What was that about?'

'I rang Yorkville Cabs while you were chatting to the boss. I got hold of a shift manager. Gave her the time, date and Beetson Recreation Ground as a drop-off point for our drug buyer.'

'Well done. Did you ask if we could get a copy of the taxi's security camera footage for that day?'

'Yes, but there's a problem.'

'Lemme guess, no camera installed.'

'Wrong, there is. But the camera in that particular cab is a new one. The old one was faulty. It was in the workshop on the day we're interested in.'

'I should have bleedin' guessed. Did you at least get the phone number of the passenger who ordered the ride? That should have been recorded in their system.'

'Payphone with a curb-side pickup.'

'Christ!' Jack realised they were dealing with a person who crossed all the t's and dotted the i's. 'I guess we could track down which phone booth, door-knock the area. More bleedin' hard slog.'

'Not necessarily. I got the cab driver's personal details and…'

'You genius!' Jack placed both hands on Taylor's cheeks, leaned in and kissed her on the lips. A quick peck, but the deed was done. He immediately let go and took a step back, shocked at his boldness. Her eyes were bigger than golf balls. *God, what is she thinking?* 'I…ah…you aren't going to…I mean…'

'For heaven's sake, Jack. Get over yourself.'

The heat rose in his face, he figured his complexion would have turned beetroot red. A quick glance around confirmed no one else had seen what he did. It was only the two detectives and Batista in his fish bowl, engrossed on the call to Mrs McAdam. Jack cleared his throat. 'Claudia, there's something I've been wanting to…'

The phone on Claudia's desk erupted. 'Hello? Yes, I'll meet her at the front door in five minutes.' She hung up the phone. 'Bingo!'

'What?'

'The cab driver's been ordered to drive to the station and help us with our enquiries.'

'You've got the Midas touch, DC Taylor, no doubt about it.'

'Why, thanks. Anyway, what was it you wanted to tell me?'

'Ah, sorry.' Jack could barely look at her. 'It's gone now.'

'Perhaps you'll remember what it was later.'

All he could think of to say was a lame, 'Sure.'

---

THE CAFÉ ROUND the corner was as good a place to chat to taxi driver Maree Vesko as anywhere. The large-set, jovial woman in her late 40's gratefully accepted the offer of brunch at the expense of the Queensland Police Service. She addressed her jam-and-cream donut with relish after knocking over a steak-and-kidney pie.

'You didn't have a problem driving around town with no camera operating in the cab?' said Jack. 'You know, technically it's a government requirement to have a working camera installed, right?'

The woman guffawed. 'Deary me. I've been at this job

for eight years, I reckon. Never had an incident. Maybe I'm lucky. But, no, it doesn't bother me. I actually hate them. I'm one of those drivers who sticks a finger up their nose at traffic lights.' She burst out laughing again. 'You think I want that stuff recorded?' A throaty chuckle. Jack assessed her as one of those people who are at once endearing and annoying, laughing at every opportunity.

'I'll start with the obvious,' said Taylor. 'Can you describe him?'

'Young man, I'd say early 20's. He wore a dark cap down over his eyes, like he didn't want me to look at him.'

'Clothes?'

'Yes, he was wearing clothes,' she ripped another guffaw, blowing icing sugar from the top of her donut. 'But again, I can only remember dark jeans and a black t-shirt.'

'Any logos or patterns on it?'

'Can't recall.'

Jack's patience with the woman, nice as she was, was running out. 'I'd just like to remind you we're investigating a murder, not an unpaid fare. You got me?'

The woman gave an apologetic nod. 'I'm sorry.'

'Did he behave in any odd way? A twitch or a nervous habit?'

'None of that. But he did take a quick phone call while I was driving him back from the park. Spoke to a woman, what was her name again…that's it, Lily.'

A waiter stopped to ask if they wanted anything else. Jack ordered another donut to reward Maree, whose information was improving in quality.

'And do you remember what he said on the phone?'

'Matter of fact I do, 'cos he got all snippy with me. He said "I'll pick up the stockings for you on the way home, Lily". I made one of my usual off-hand remarks, something like, "Stockings, hey? You on a promise?" Something like that. He said, still kinda hiding his face, that I was a disgusting perve and the person he was talking to was an elderly lady. The stockings were to stake up a tomato plant. After that I just kept my eyes on the road.'

'One last question,' said Jack, his pulse quickening as the pieces of the puzzle were coming together. *Rohypnol, stockings, hiding his face.* 'One I should've asked at the beginning. Where did you drop the guy off?'

'Same place I picked him up. At the Salvation Army charity shop downtown in Strudwick Avenue.'

Jack paid the bill inside the café while Taylor made small talk with Maree. On his return the officers thanked the woman profusely for her assistance, told her she'd have to testify in court if her information led to the perpetrator. 'So don't go planning any holidays in the near future, OK?' said Jack with a wink.

'If it was a holiday with you, Detective Lisbon, I'd be applying for leave in a heartbeat.'

This time it was Taylor's turn to roar with laughter.

---

BACK AT THEIR DESKS, Jack had his head down, hunting for names associated with the Salvation Army thrift shop. He reasoned the person of interest may have ducked in there, maybe even to purchase a pair of used stockings – maybe even the fishnets used to asphyxiate Roderick McAdam. So far, all his calls were going unanswered. They were the Salvos after all, and today was Sunday, so everyone was probably at church services. Catching a glimpse of Jack's eyes darting across a printout, Taylor wondered what went through her partner's brain sometimes. Was he still thinking about that spontaneous kiss? She certainly was. Did she want more? She wasn't sure, although the attraction to the brute was getting stronger if anything.

But there was something more pressing to think about now.

She pulled up the online electoral roll to see how many Lilys there were in Yorkville. Two hits on the old-fashioned name. The first one, Lily Jackson.

'This first one lives in an apartment judging by the address format.' She turned her neck to see Jack cradling his head in his hands as he stared at one of his two monitors. 'Should I rule her out?'

'Why?'

'No garden for veggies.' The statement carried a rising inflection at the end that turned it into a question.

'You can grow tomatoes in pots. On balconies.'

'Right.' She made a note of the address. She then looked up the surname Jackson on a phone number database, filtered for address. She rang the mobile number, a man answered. She asked for Lily Jackson and he called someone to the phone. Taylor introduced herself, then asked the woman if she grew tomatoes.

'That's a weird question for a police officer to ask. What radio station is this? Is this a prank?'

'I assure you it's not a prank.'

'I'm allergic to tomatoes, as it happens. But seriously, who is this?'

Taylor thanked the woman for her valuable time and hung up, repeated the process for Lily Sullivan. A sweet, creaky voice answered from a landline number. Despite the temptation to use subterfuge, Taylor couldn't bring herself to do it. It was bad form to trick pensioners; you probably went to hell for it. Instead, she played it straighter than a carpenter's ruler. 'Yorkville CIB would like to ask you a couple of questions.'

'What about? Am I in trouble? I'm sure my council rates are paid up.'

'No, nothing like that.' Taylor gave a reassuring laugh. 'You aren't in any trouble. But it's a really important matter and we think you might be able to help us.'

'I can't think how.'

Taylor's hand fiddled with her scrunchie. 'Are you going to be home for the next few hours?'

'Yes. Although I'm expecting the young man from next door to pop over after lunch to help me put up new curtains. He's so helpful, is Keith, always going to the shops for me, running errands.'

'That's wonderful.' Taylor's heart galloped. She put her hand over the mouthpiece, said to Jack. 'I think we might have him.'

'What?'

She placed the call on loudspeaker. 'You still there Lily?'

'Yes, I thought I'd lost you for a second.'

Taylor stood and waved frantically at Batista, who caught the display in the corner of his eye, came out of his lair to see what all the fuss was about.

'I just wanted to have a quick word to you about Keith,' said Taylor in a conversational tone.

'What do you want to know about him?'

She took a deep breath. What *did* she want to know about him that wouldn't tip the old dear off. 'Nothing, really. I wanted to say how fortunate you are. It's refreshing to hear of young people doing nice things for their neighbours.'

'Oh, yes. Just the other day he spent hours in the garden

with me, helped me prune and stake up this big tomato bush that was getting right out of hand.'

Jack and Batista had their palms pressed firmly on the edge of Taylor's desk.

'This is it,' Batista whispered to Jack. 'This is the breakthrough.'

---

TAYLOR RAN the addresses of the houses either side of Lily Sullivan through the electoral roll. And there he was, Keith Fishwick, hiding in plain sight at 67 Ella Road. A reverse search of the address showed two females with different family names were currently registered there. A share house. She found a house plan of the property on a real estate site, hit the print button and ran off five copies, kept one and handed the others to Jack, the Inspector, Wilson and Steger.

'Fishwick. That name was definitely on Wycombe's list.' Steger's memory was like nothing Jack had ever encountered. Another Rain Man, he was. If they could wrap this up quickly he might invite Steger to Cairns Reef Casino for a spot of card counting. 'Not flagged for any reason, though.' Steger rubbed a pencil behind his ear.

'Who is he to McAdam, I wonder,' said Jack to the hastily assembled crew.

Steger showed he was human. 'I'd have to double check. Either they went to primary school together or he's a distant relation or… One second.' He popped open the briefcase he liked to lug around and retrieved the list, licked a finger and flicked through to the sixth page. 'No, I was right the first time. They were in the same class in Year 7 before the McAdams moved to Cairns. All his schoolmates going back to kindergarten are here. Nothing to ring any alarm bells.'

'I aim to make him tell us all about it.' Jack looked at his watch. 'It's just gone 10:45.' He addressed Batista. 'Shall we make a plan, sir?'

Batista immediately called Wycombe, dispatched her to Ella street to keep an eye on things from a safe distance. For the next fifteen minutes the team got busy. They carefully studied the house plan, Batista allocating each officer an access point. Extreme caution was to be exercised – Fishwick was an unknown quantity. Each officer checked their firearms and comms, strapped on bulletproof vests and bodycams. 'There can be no fuck-ups on this one. The press will slaughter us if McAdam's killer gets away because of our sloppiness. Understood?'

A silent choir of nodding heads.

Steger's mobile bleeped. 'I just got a text from Wycombe. She spotted a young man in a blue singlet moving about on a veranda at No. 67.' The phone started ringing. 'Hello? Right, we're on our way.'

'What is it?' said Batista.

'He's jumped on a bike and starting pedalling up the street. He could be onto us.'

'No chance,' said Jack. Despite his words, he was already donning his jacket and patting his Glock. He turned at the exit to the street. 'Well, what are you all waiting for? Let's go make an arrest!'

## Chapter Twenty-Nine

ELLA ROAD WAS LOCATED a good spit from the Yorkville CBD, around 1.2 km from the General Post Office as the crow flies. Older-style dwellings with a touch of colonial elegance lined the lush, leafy thoroughfare. Jack parked his Toyota Hilux six houses away from the target's residence on a slight dogleg bend, additionally screened by a neat hibiscus hedge dotted with red flowers. 'Worth a mint, some of these joints,' he said with appreciation. 'You get a much nicer class of criminal the closer you get to town.'

'If you say so,' replied Taylor. 'You Brits are so hung up on class, aren't you?'

The remark went ignored as Jack turned his head to speak to Steger, sitting next to Constable Wilson in the rear seat. He didn't get a chance to say anything as Steger's phone rang. Steger activated loudspeaker. 'Yes, Tania?'

'Good news. Fishwick's back. He's inside right now. Looks like he took a trip to the bakery. He was carrying a package with baguettes poking out the top. Looked quite cheery.'

'Thanks, we'll be making a move shortly,' said Jack. 'Let us know if anything changes. Stand by.'

'Actually...wait... two young women have come out onto the veranda. Dressed in pyjamas, towels on their heads, giggling. Maybe you'd like to wait, see what they do?'

'Agreed,' said Jack.

Twenty-three long minutes passed, to the soft accompaniment of Mozart's *Marriage of Figaro* pouring through the car's four-speaker sound system, before Wycombe called again. 'The women have left the premises together in a red Mazda 3. Heading your way.'

Jack rubbed his brow as the car zipped past, all officers except the DS ducked their heads. 'Let's get this over with before those flatmates come back. Geez, the old lady next door's going to be devastated.'

'Tell me about it,' said Taylor, sitting up straight again. 'Just as well we've got Ben with us.'

'Yep...hey, what do you mean?' said Wilson.

'After we've arrested Fishwick, you and I are going to do a spot of community liaison. Meaning I'll console Mrs Sullivan and you can put up her curtains. Deal?'

Wilson had no chance to respond as Jack leapt on the accelerator and zoomed the short distance to the front gate of Fishwick's brick-and-tile bungalow. Ripping the handbrake he said, 'I'm curious to know what motivated a 19-year-old kid to do what he did.'

Steger said, 'Aren't we all?'

Jack radioed Batista, Steger called Wycombe via mobile, advised them the arresting party was good to go. All officers made a final check of their gear.

'One last thing,' said Jack. 'He's shown he's got a warped mind,' said Jack. 'So expect anything.'

The three detectives and one uniform closed their doors

gently, jogged across the quiet, empty street in a semi-crouch.

Jack strode up a short flight of concrete steps to the front door; Steger slunk down a side path to the back door; Taylor and Wilson took up positions under the largest windows on the left and right side of the sprawling one-storey dwelling. Jack took a deep breath and with the heel of his fist pounded on the door with all his might. 'Open up, Keith! It's the police!'

He waited twenty seconds, pounded and yelled again. Nothing.

He radioed his partners. 'I'm using force to get inside. Steger, do the same. Taylor and Wilson, stand by.'

Several solid lunge kicks splintered the doorframe. He braced his right shoulder before bashing his body against the door. It moved a fraction. More force was required. *Again.* More wobble, but no access. The door was heavy and thick and solid, but the third shoulder charge flung it open. Jack staggered inside under his own momentum before regaining balance. He extracted his .40 calibre Glock 22, raised it with one hand, radioed his colleagues. 'I'm in.'

'Me too,' came Steger's voice through faint static. 'Proceeding from the laundry.'

Jack held the gun in a two-handed grip, swept it from side to side as he checked two bedrooms off the hallway. 'Clear!'

He heard the same word booming from the other end of the house. Bathroom and toilet, both empty. At last he emerged into a large, open kitchen. And there was Keith Fishwick, calmly reading a paperback as if nothing was happening.

'It's over, Keith,' said Jack. 'Put your hands behind your

head. I'm placing you under arrest for the murder of Roderick McAdam.'

The lad, every bit as average in appearance as described by Linford Hunt and Maree Vesko, calmly placed a bookmark between the pages of the book and closed it, then slowly interlaced his fingers behind his head. 'You're making a big mistake, you know that, right? You're going to look like fools.'

'We'll see about that,' said Jack as he pushed the man's hands behind his back and applied zip-tie handcuffs. Steger appeared and helped Jack haul Fishwick to his feet. The man offered no resistance as he was led out of the house, Jack continuing to read him his rights as they walked.

'Yes we shall,' said Fishwick, cool as ice. 'I never laid a finger on McAdam.'

As they descended the front steps, the two housemates pulled up in the driveway, Taylor and Wilson standing at the front gate. Seconds later Wycombe arrived in the Brisbane officers' rental vehicle.

'Hey! What the hell's going on?' yelled out one of the women, fear in her eyes. Fear for the fate of her friend, Jack thought. Not imaginings of what Fishwick may have done that got himself arrested.

'It's all good,' said Fishwick. 'Just a misunderstanding. I'll be back soon, don't worry.'

'Sorry ladies,' said Jack. 'But I'll have to ask the two of you to remain outside the house while my colleagues conduct a search.'

'A search for what?' said the other woman, not as distraught but still clearly rattled. 'And what are we supposed to do while that's happening? I don't want you touching my things!'

'I can't tell you what we're searching for because we

won't know until we find it,' said Jack. 'We'll be as quick as we can but it could take hours. Constable Wilson here will grab your details and ask you a few questions. It'd be best if you made alternate arrangements for the rest of the day. We'll call you when it's OK to return.'

Jack ignored another barrage of questions from the women, hustled the suspect towards the Hilux. He instructed Wycombe to coordinate a search with Taylor and Wilson, seizing anything and everything they thought could help a prosecution. Pay special attention to electronic devices, notebooks and the like. All on board, Jack buckled up, turned on his classical compilation USB. Mozart again. *Eine kleine Nachtmusik*. With Steger in the back next to Fishwick and the violins merrily humming, the Hilux sped to the end of Ella Road, turned right and tore through the city streets to Yorkville Police Station.

## Chapter Thirty

'YOU SURE YOU don't want a lawyer?' said Batista at the reception desk as Constable Wells entered the details of the arrest into the system. 'A relative?'

'Not at this stage,' Fishwick replied with a thin smile. 'I don't want to be wasting anyone's time when all you're going to do is let me go.'

'I like your confidence,' said Jack. 'But I know you're lying to us.'

'Do your best,' said Fishwick. 'You got nothin' on me.'

'I've got another piece of bad news for you,' said Taylor, arriving with a briefcase tucked under her arm. 'You'll be spending the night in a cell. You picked the wrong day to be arrested. The courts are shut on the weekend, so no chance of bail.'

'You can't do that.' A shakiness crept into his voice. 'You have to charge me.'

'I fully intend to do that after our little chat,' said Jack.

INSIDE THE STARK, white-walls of Interview Room 1, Fishwick's defiance suddenly wavered. 'I've changed my mind. I want a lawyer. I'm not saying anything until one arrives.'

'Not a problem,' said Jack. 'We'll reconvene once we can arrange that for you.'

The sun was just about to set when the brief arrived. A shambolic, pear-shaped man in his mid 30's wearing jeans too big and a polo shirt too small. Jasper Winehouse, known around town as Amy. A last-resort type for desperate crims requiring legal aid. He was no less talented than many other lawyers in Far North Queensland, he simply couldn't say no to anyone who sought his services.

The CIB team had been thrilled with the delay. Vital questions remained unanswered, but at least they had their man in custody. Taylor prepared a press release to go out at 7:00pm, then researched the present and past of one Keith Richard Fishwick; Jack, exhausted from a lack of shuteye over the last 48 hours, took a power nap on the lunchroom sofa; Steger and Wycombe managed to sneak onto a flight back to Brisbane; Wilson visited Mrs Sullivan and helped her put up her curtains.

Most productive of all was the Inspector. Once Fishwick was secured, Batista got on the phone to the McAdam family, who were horrified when they heard the name of the arrested man. Did they remember him? Very well. He and Roddy played tennis together before they reached their teens. Keith adored Roderick, looked up to him. The McAdams had hoped the two boys would become big stars together one day, maybe form a powerful doubles combination. But not to be, little Keith wasn't chosen for a scholarship and the boys never saw each other again after the McAdams moved to Cairns.

# Drop Shot

When the interrogation of the suspect recommenced, the revelations discovered by Batista informed the direction of questioning.

'Why did you hate Roderick McAdam enough to kill him?' said Jack, standing behind his chair and gripping its backrest. 'Was it because he became an international tennis star and left you behind as the unchosen one? A nobody, destined for obscurity.'

Winehouse leaned his bulk across to offer some advice, but Fishwick didn't need it. He stared straight ahead and said, 'No comment.'

'Well, Mr Fishwick,' said Jack with gravitas. 'You won't be a nobody for too much longer. Everyone will know your name. As early as 7:00pm tonight when the press release goes out.'

Fishwick held his head in his hands, uttered the words through his fingers, 'Piss off.'

'You must have despised McAdam. His parents were shocked to hear we'd nabbed you, sunshine. Such a nice little boy you were, they said. What happened?'

'No comment.'

'You could save everyone a lot of time by confessing. We're waiting for DNA and other forensics to come back that will nail you to the wall, but it could take a month or more. Evidence from the boating accident in Cairns is clogging up the laboratories, meaning this case could be delayed for some time. You'll be held in remand until we get those results back, maybe longer. Can you imagine? General population at Copperhead Jail. A sweet young bloke like you would be a hot commodity in there.'

'I don't like your tone, Detective' said Winehouse. 'I'd ask you to refrain from that kind of talk.'

'I do apologise.'

'Moreover,' he continued. 'You need to stop scaremongering. A magistrate will likely grant bail on Monday when the courts are open.'

Taylor shook her head. 'Your lawyer's being very optimistic. The crime is a heinous one, it's high profile. In short, Keith, you'd better start co-operating for real or things will only get worse.'

'No comment.'

Jack placed a mobile phone on the desk.

'Hey,' said Fishwick. 'I wondered where that had got to.'

'We found this in your bedroom. Any chance you could tell me the password?'

'Nope. It's my private property.' The defiance was returning. Jack had to hand it to the lad, he wasn't easily intimidated.

'Again, it's just delaying the inevitable. We've got tech nerds in the QPS who could crack that phone faster than I can solve a Rubik's cube. And that's pretty fast. We've got your laptop too.' Jack finally took a seat next to Taylor. 'So, how's about you give us all the passwords, huh?'

Fishwick reached for the water jug, poured himself a glass, drank it down in one gulp. He smacked his lips. 'Look,' he said to Jack. 'How about this…fuck you!' He flipped Jack the bird, then shared the gesture with Taylor.

With the suspect remaining incalcitrant and no corroborating evidence on hand, the questioning was suspended until 9:00am the following day.

## Chapter Thirty-One

THE SHORT EMAIL had given Jack palpitations. They now had probable cause to charge Keith Fishwick with murder. Somehow, Margaret Proctor had called in a favour with the Head of Forensics Services. It wasn't a full report of all the evidence – nothing on the stockings or the handwritten note or the items at the murder scene or in Room 2003 – but the toxicology was enough.

Rohypnol had been detected in Roderick McAdam's body.

With testimony from Hunt and Vesko, they had enough to begin to make the case. Probably to convict. But there was too much left unanswered. Only Fishwick himself could show them the fastest route to the truth.

This morning Winehouse was dressed formally. A stained light-grey suit, crumpled white tie and the traditional oversized pants. Fishwick wore a fresh t-shirt brought in by flatmate Mallory, who flat out refused to believe the bullshit she heard on the news about her friend Keith. She'd given Damon Wells a gobful of abuse, as if the constable himself had conspired to frame her roomie.

'Good news!' said Jack after he'd turned on the recording equipment.

'Really?' said Fishwick.

'For us,' Jack chuckled. 'Not you, I'm afraid.' He relayed the contents of this morning's emails from the pathologist.

'Big fucken deal.' Fishwick folded his arms across his chest. For the first time, Jack noted numerous faint scars on his forearms. Cutting. Self harm. 'Nothing to do with me.'

'We've spoken to the man who sold them to you.'

'He's lying, whoever he is. I've never bought whatever you called that stuff. His word against mine.'

Taylor whispered in Jack's ear. 'He's got a point. Hunt's got a record. And he's on parole. Could be viewed as an unreliable witness.'

'Bloody hell, Claudia.' His early enthusiasm faded. Taylor was right. Even a second-rate lawyer like Winehouse could destroy Hunt's testimony in court.

Taylor's phone buzzed. 'One moment, please.' She silently read a long text message, leaned across to Jack and whispered again. 'This might make him squirm.' She then addressed Fishwick.

'Your neighbour Lily's a lovely old dear, isn't she, Keith?'

'Uh, yeah. Why are you hassling my neighbours?' He exchanged a look with his lawyer, who nodded as if to say, *this is a soft ball coming, you'll be OK.*

'It's standard procedure to speak with neighbours. To get more of an idea about what kind of person you are. Actually, when we go to court, you could do worse than call on her as a character witness. She absolutely adores you.'

Fishwick smiled warmly. Lily meant a great deal to him, too, that was obvious.

'Pity you weren't able to help her put up those curtains.'

'I'll do that when I'm released.'

'No need. My colleague Constable Ben Wilson gave her a hand this morning. He's like you, loves to help people. Of course, she was bragging about you. Ben asked her about the stockings we learned of from the taxi driver who drove you to the park where you did the deal with Linford Hunt.'

'Alleged deal,' said Winehouse. 'And you've no proof of the taxi ride, you admitted that yesterday. All unsubstantiated hearsay.'

'Still, a nice little chain of circumstantial evidence is building,' said Jack, absently fiddling with his watch.

'Jack!' Taylor snapped. 'Please don't interrupt.'

'Sorry.' He made a contrite frown that made the tendons in his neck stick out.

'So, Lily mentioned *you'd* bought her the stockings.'

Fishwick gritted his teeth. Jack wondered whether the kid was suddenly regretting his relationship with an all-trusting old lady.

'She told Ben you got them at the Salvos, and that you often bought her things from there. Well, after he'd got those curtains up for Lily, Ben paid a visit to the thrift shop. Showed the saleswoman a photo of you. And guess what? She remembered you also bought three pairs of black fishnets. What did you do with them?'

Fishwick stared at Taylor like he was looking right through her.

'Keith, did you hear me? Roderick McAdam was strangled with black fishnets. Once the forensics come in, are you confident none of your DNA will be on them? Or on the items recovered from the Hotel Gasnier and Room 2003 from the Grand Hotel? I reckon you're cooked.'

'All right, enough!' he snapped. ' Fuck it, I'll tell you everything. But I want a deal first.'

Jack laughed. 'You must be kidding!'

Fishwick shook his head. 'I can give you other names. One of them a big one.'

'Let's take a break,' said Jack. 'I want to have a word with the Inspector.

## Chapter Thirty-Two

'WHEN DID you get the idea to murder Roderick McAdam?' said Jack, keeping his tone as neutral as possible. The time for games was over, now it was simply a matter of putting the pieces of the puzzle together with a broken confessor.

'Did Inspector Batista agree to a deal?' said Fishwick.

'Not exactly. Decisions like that are made by the Department of Public Prosecutions in consultation with your defence, not us. Police don't have the power to engage in plea bargaining. However, we can and do make recommendations. Confessions are looked on very favourably, especially if you can give us other names. The Inspector agrees we should aim to have your co-operation factored into sentencing.'

'Nah.'

'Listen, sunshine. We've got your fingerprints now. We're going to find them everywhere you've left a trail. Like Hansel and bleedin' Gretel.'

Fishwick pouted and stared at the ceiling, but his hands were twitching.

'You've not worn gloves because you aren't in the system and you thought you'd get away with it. Didn't you?'

Fishwick took a deep breath, blew out all the air he'd inhaled. 'Alright. But you'll do all you can to get me a better deal with the judge, right?'

'Of course.'

And then, the flood gates opened.

The idea to kill McAdam formulated in his mind when he heard about the Pilmer Challenge.

'But why?' said Taylor. 'Surely nothing he did to you when you were children could warrant killing him?'

'He was an evil kid. Pure evil. What people see today, the on-court brat, that's a watered-down version of his real self.' He pointed at the scars on his forearm. 'See these cuts?'

Jack nodded. 'Nothing to be ashamed of. You did that to yourself because he bullied you.'

'Fuck no! *He* did it with a fucking razor blade. Held me down and cut me. When we were little kids!'

A hush fell over the room. Jack, for once, was lost for words.

'Does anyone else know about what he did to you?' said Taylor after a while.

'Only me and him. I told anyone who asked that I got caught up in barbed wire. He warned me to keep my mouth shut. He said,' Fishwick's face trembled, 'if I told anyone he'd hunt me down and kill me.'

'Did he do anything else to you?'

'Oh yeah. He was always putting me down, calling me useless, said everyone hated me. That my parents hated me.' Fishwick was blinking like a strobe light. 'And so, when he came back to town like the conquering hero, it was all too much.'

'Who helped you?' said Jack.

'Garth Greer.' Fishwick spat the name out without hesitation. 'It was no more bother to him than rearranging furniture.'

'And getting Roderick to go to the Gaz? How on earth did you convince him to do that? He must've known it was a filthy dive.'

Fishwick smiled broadly. 'That was easy. All I had to do was appeal to his ego.' He explained how he'd gate-crashed the party at the Grand Hotel and made his move. 'I told him there'd be a couple of hot women there who would do anything he wanted. Crazy local fans who wanted to score with Big Rod. I told him I could get these wicked drugs that would help him party all night but be right as rain the next day. The bastard peeled off a couple of grand and handed me the money to buy whatever I needed. Can you believe it? The idiot paying me money? He was so full of himself he'd completely forgotten the hell he put me through. To him, I was nothing!'

The detectives and Winehouse listened in stunned silence as Fishwick told his story. Jack could imagine Batista's eyebrows going up and down behind the one-way glass. He was sure the Inspector had never heard the like of this. None of them had.

'But before I got the cash from Rod, I got a shitload of money from someone else. I can show you my bank account. Ten thousand it was. I used five grand of it to pay Greer to rent out all the rooms in the hotel and help me get the stockings rigged up once Rod was unconscious. I showed him the diagram from the Internet. I thought it was tricky, but he figured it out quick. He used to be a long-distance truck driver; they're the best at tying knots.'

'You rented all the rooms?' said Taylor. 'The register had entries for three other guests that night.'

'Nope. Garth reckoned we should at least pretend some of the rooms were booked and that it was a slow night. His father was suspicious as hell when he found out there was so few bookings. Anyway, it worked out fine. We had free run of the joint. I think I fucked up with the keys when I left, though.'

Jack nodded. 'Yeah, you did 'n all.'

'But believe me,' Fishwick said. 'There was no one else there.'

Jack held up a hand. 'Let's back this up a wee bit. Who paid you the other money? Was it Stefan Krepper or Dragan Stojanovic?'

'No, not them. Someone else.'

## Chapter Thirty-Three

TWO TRIPS to Melbourne in four days. He'd never even been to the southern capital of the state of Victoria before, and now he was becoming a regular visitor. Once again, he had career-man cop Toby Horner for company.

'You didn't bring that lovely partner of yours this time?' said Horner, wheezing slightly as they strode towards one of the restaurants dotting the Melbourne Park complex. The crowd around them was thick and slow moving, the Australian Open having started the day before.

'The QPS budget only stretches so far,' said Jack. 'Besides, she's been seconded to assist in the investigation of the boating accident in Cairns.'

'I heard about that.'

'There's a theory floating around that the captain, who was also the owner of the charter business, was losing money hand over fist. It's likely the whole episode was an insurance job gone wrong. The bloke started the fire and planned for his paying customers to jump overboard into a waiting dingy. Problem was, he tripped and knocked himself out. Panic ensued. He died and so did two others.'

Horner tut-tutted. 'Best laid plans, hey?'

The men entered the trendy restaurant, alive with men and women in bright apparel. 'The tennis crowd looks like a box of colouring pencils, these days,' Jack observed.

'Yeah,' agreed Horner. 'I remember a time when they all wore nothing but white. You could hardly separate them from cricketers.'

'I spy someone I'd like a word with over there,' Jack extended his arm towards a mountain of a man in a grey flannel business suit. He was sitting with two other men in suits, three tables back from the open-view kitchen where chefs in big hats, bodies a blur, pumped out the gourmet goodies at breakneck speed. Seafood baskets, piled high with fried morsels, sat before each of the men. Side orders of green salad and puffy little bread rolls jostled for space on the table. The neck of a bottle of white wine stuck out of an ice-filled bucket.

'Mr Pilmer?'

'Yes? Oh, it's you DS Lisbon. What a nice surprise.'

Jack introduced the Victorian detective to Pilmer and they acknowledged each other with nods.

'I thought you were still working on the McAdam case?' The billionaire took a sip of wine, said "aah" and wiped his mouth with a napkin.

'And I thought you needed to fly to Adelaide to talk with your, who was it again? Brazilian partners.'

'This is them here. Bruno and his interpreter Jose.' He turned to one of them. 'No need to interpret this conversation. You and Bruno relax for a moment, OK?'

The interpreter gave a toothy smile, said something in

Portuguese to the other man, who nodded understandingly, and they fell into their own conversation.

'Didn't you give me an undertaking not to leave Yorkville for 72 hours?'

'Ah, yes. But since you charged that young man with the murder, I figured it'd be OK to leave. Actually, would you gentleman like to join us? We're about to start eating, but I'm sure the maître d' could rustle something up for you quickly.'

'No thanks,' said Jack. 'I'm not here for long. I have to fly back later today.'

'Right,' said Pilmer slowly, a slight quaver in his baritone voice. 'So…'

'I'm here to make an arrest.'

---

PILMER SWEATED PROFUSELY. Jack figured him for a heart-attack victim within the next five years. Maybe sooner. Horner wouldn't be far behind.

'What court did you say he was practising on?' said Jack, having to slow his pace so the bigger men could keep up. Pilmer's recent sponsorship of the player Jack was about to arrest would soon be cancelled. For a moment, when Jack revealed who it was, it looked like that predicted coronary would be of the immediate and lethal variety.

'Not much further. I can't remember the number, just how to get there.' He stopped, bent double, sucked in a couple of litres of air.

Three more minutes of negotiating the intricately designed complex and they arrived at the court where the man was enjoying a leisurely hit-out with another player, the coach watching on from a blue plastic chair.

'Mind if I return to my partners?' said Pilmer. 'I'm not keen on witnessing this.'

Jack waved him away, and the magnate lumbered off back to his calorie-rich lunch.

Jack and Horner walked through a narrow gate, unnoticed by the players and the coach. They skirted the doubles lanes until they reached the man preparing to serve.

'Yes?'

'Lucas Khumalo,' said Jack.

'Yes?' His eyes darted towards his coach, who shrugged as if to say, *Damned if I know what's going on?*

'Please accompany me and Detective Horner.'

'What…what…what's going on? I've got a match this evening. I can't go anywhere.'

'No more matches for you, Lucas, I'm afraid. I'm arresting you for conspiring to murder Roderick McAdam.'

## Chapter Thirty-Four

'THE PROBLEM you've got is this, sunshine.' said Jack. 'Keith Fishwick's shown us all the online chit-chat between the two of you. Here, look.' Jack placed on the table printouts of the text conversations between Khumalo and Fishwick via the online platform Telegram. Fishwick had been the one to approach Khumalo, both members of a group called Tennis Global. Although the main group had public visibility, members could chat to each other with encrypted privacy. 'It's all the proof we need.'

'But I never thought he would kill McAdam!' Khumalo wouldn't look at the piece of paper. Instead, he shook his head so hard Jack thought his neck would snap. 'It wasn't supposed to be like that!'

'You paid him $10,000 dollars, Lucas.'

'To *inconvenience* Roderick! That was the word Fishwick himself used. Look at the texts.' He pointed a shaky finger.

Jack picked up the paper, cleared his throat and read aloud:

Fishwick: If you pay me 10K I will make sure Rod doesn't play
Khumalo: I agree. If I can win the Open, I can use the extra prizemoney to help my poor village
Fishwick: My a/c number is **********
Khumalo: You will only inconvenience him, correct?
Fishwick: You can count on me.

'You're lying to me,' said Jack, putting down the script. He reached right across the table and tapped his finger on it inches from Khumalo's arms, resting on the table. Khumalo pulled his arms away, folded them across his chest. 'It was *you* who used that word. Not your only lie, is it? You said you were going to sit out the Open. And here you are, into Round 2 after a crushing victory in Round 1 yesterday.'

Coach Ron Habinski raised a tentative hand, asking permission to speak.

'Wot?' Jack barked.

'I convinced him to stay. His chances of winning had increased, even if it was in tragic circumstances. Why should he not take advantage of the opportunity? But I swear, I had no knowledge of this...conspiracy.'

Khumalo shot his coach a look of disgust that said, *Traitor!* Jack clocked the coach for an arrogant coward at their first encounter. This statement cemented the opinion.

'Nevertheless, it was Lucas who financed this murder. In addition to Fishwick, we have in custody the man who assisted him to carry out this horrible, horrible crime.' Jack pushed his seat back, stood and began pacing. 'I'm of the belief that you really didn't care what happened to McAdam. If he died, too bad.'

'No! Not true!'

'My diligent partner DC Taylor had a good hard look

into your affairs. Turns out you've been buying up property all over the world. Expensive property. Villas in Tuscany, condos in Florida. For yourself and members of your family. But this little village of yours, it's as poor today as it's ever been.'

'That's because of drought…and…flood…and…'

'Enough of the lies, Lucas, please.' Jack then looked at Toby Horner, who had said nothing for the entire interview. 'Shall we take him downstairs and process him?'

'What do you mean, process me?' The man's whole body was shaking.

Horner said, 'You'll be officially charged with conspiracy to commit murder and held in custody until we can get you before a court. You'll likely get bail, but I reckon you'll have to surrender your passport.'

'What the…?'

'You'll be required to attend court in Far North Queensland.' Jack sighed under his breath. 'I'm not sure how the public prosecutor's gonna play this one. One murder trial with three defendants or separate trials with the charges split up. Either way, you'll be facing the conspiracy charge together with Fishwick. Quite an adventure coming up for you.'

The room went quiet except for the gentle sobs of Lucas Khumalo.

'One piece of advice,' said Jack as he cupped his hand under Khumalo's armpit and helped him to his feet.

'What?'

'You've got plenty of money. Get yourself a good lawyer.'

## Chapter Thirty-Five

THE MORNING FUNERAL UNDER DRIPPING, leaden skies reminded Jack of one he'd attended for another murder victim in Yorkville. Low-key and sombre. Another young person's life snuffed out prematurely.

But he couldn't grieve alongside the McAdams for their son. For the simple reason Roderick had been a bad person. Perhaps he may have reformed his ways had he lived. People do mellow with age. Jack himself had done so. Nothing was impossible. Unfortunately, Roderick had not had the opportunity for redemption.

The person he felt sorriest for in this case wasn't anyone in the McAdam family, not Fishwick, not Khumalo, not Anne Cumberland, and certainly none of the Greers.

It was Lily Sullivan.

He'd go and pay her a visit this afternoon. Jack had an eye on a rundown acreage just outside of town. Enough of living in an apartment in this huge country blessed with wide open spaces! He only lived in a flat because that was what he was used to. The property he had his eye on had an orchard full of tropical fruit trees and established vegetable gardens. He hadn't a clue about where to begin with that. Perhaps Lily could offer him some basic tips on growing tomatoes.

When the last sod of earth had been tossed onto the coffin, Jack took Taylor by the arm and walked her out of the cemetery.

———

JACK JUMPED out of the shower, wrapped himself in his dressing gown, tore down the corridor and grabbed the phone. The ring tone, "Never Gonna Give You Up", told him it was his daughter calling from London.

'Skye!' he yelled, as if the physical distance separating them required extra volume to communicate effectively. 'How are you, sweetie?'

'Great, dad.' Her girlish South London accent made his heart ache. 'I saw all about that tennis player getting arrested. And the other guys. Well done, daddy!'

He took a seat on the couch. 'That was a terrible case, sunshine. I don't want you reading up on all the gory details.'

'Too late. I know all about the stockings and the drugs. I mean, how am I ever going to become a police officer if I can't handle that stuff?'

Jack rubbed his forehead. *Geez, she's only thirteen years old.* Change the subject, quick.

'Hey, listen. I'm going to buy a house. It'll be perfect for when you come to visit. Right in the middle of the jungle.'

'You serious?'

'Absolutely.'

'When can I come?'

'I guess whenever your mother says you can.'

Skye let out a deep sigh. 'Great. That'll be, like, never.'

'She'll say yes when she sees how cool it is. You could almost call it a farm!'

'Really?'

'Yes. And I'm going to need a dog to keep me company on such a big property. I saw this really cute one at the pound. I think I'll go and rescue her. Not sure what kind she is, a mixed breed I reckon. Big black and white spots on her. Looks like a cow more than a dog.' He poked his head in the fridge, hoping for leftovers but then remembering he ate them yesterday. Home-delivered pizza it would be. 'What do you think I should call her?'

'How about Daisy? That's a great name for a cow. I mean a dog.' Skye burst out laughing.

'You like your own lame jokes, don't you?' said Jack.

'Remind you of someone you know?'

'Who?'

'You, silly!'

Jack drew back the curtains to reveal another beautiful day in Yorkville. 'You got that right, sunshine.'

After the call to Skye, Jack revisited the real estate website and had another look at the listing for the acreage. Later today he'd ring and make an offer.

## Next in The Fighting Detective Series

vinci-books.com/point-blank

**A peaceful morning at the country club erupts into violence. One man lies dead, another critically wounded, and a woman's screams pierce the air.**

Keep turning the pages for a free preview…

A free prequel novella...

vinci-books.com/takedown-free

**Get the explosive prequel to The Fighting Detective series, absolutely free.**

# Point Blank: Chapter One

THE LIE of the golf ball was perfect for the next shot. Never mind it took seven strokes to get here from the tee. Detective Sergeant Jack Lisbon of the Yorkville Police Central Investigation Bureau was sure he could put all the preceding muffed shots behind him and nail this next one. He was as rusty as an old barbed-wire fence when it came to golf, but at least he was doing better than his partner. Constable Aden Trevarthen had needed ten strokes to make it onto the green, where his ball sat tantalisingly close to the pin.

Jack cast a quick look back to the tee, about 300 metres distant in a straight line. A quartet of golfers were waiting for the two cops to finish the first hole and move to the second. Jack didn't need a degree in body language to know their rocking from side to side, pacing and foot tapping meant the other players were running out of patience. But he wouldn't let that rattle him. He and Trevarthen had paid their green fees and were entitled to take the time they needed to complete the hole.

The DS rubbed his craggy nose thoughtfully as he re-examined the ball in its little nest of kikuyu. The tuft of grass was the ideal launching pad – a bit of length, spongy and soft and easy to swing through. A gentle stroke with a pitching wedge to the lip of the green and the ball should slowly roll down the slight incline and pull up somewhere near the flag. Perhaps even in the hole. Only one problem. Jack didn't have a pitching wedge in his bare-bones hired golf bag. His request to borrow one from Constable Aden Trevarthen was met with a blank stare.

'Which one's that?' The large-framed officer leaned over the bag, eyes darting from the head of one club to another. 'I haven't played in that long I can't remember much about the equipment.'

'Not sure either,' said Jack. 'I think it's got the letter P imprinted on the top, innit.'

'Wouldn't that be the putter?'

Jack wiped a runnel of sweat from his brow. Even autumn in tropical Far North Queensland generated enough heat to make a body warm. 'Nah. The putter doesn't have a letter on it. Even a novice like you should be able to tell which one's the putter.'

Trevarthen, ten kilos lighter since Christmas thanks to regular running and gym work with Jack, as well as disavowing his favourite sugary snacks, placed his hands on his new slimline hips and gave a lopsided smile. He then reached into the bag, handed Jack a long club with a bulging black head on it. 'Like this?'

'No, you pillock. That's a five wood.'

'But it's made of plastic.'

'Still called a wood. Tradition 'n that.'

Trevarthen blew out a breath of exasperation. 'Then I can't help you.'

A hand darted out and snatched the club from

Trevarthen's grip. 'Tell you what, I think I remember using one of these around the green before.' Jack hadn't played the game in at least fifteen years, so his memory was fuzzy. 'It's got a bit of loft on the face of the club so you can use it like a wedge.' Jack paused. 'Probably.'

'Well, make up your mind. That group up there,' Trevarthen pointed towards the first tee, 'don't look very happy.'

'Tough luck,' said Jack. 'The more they carry on, the longer I'm gonna take. I espouse the same philosophy when it comes to tailgaters. The closer they get, the slower I go. But it don't matter. I'm taking the shot.'

After rehearsing the shot in his mind, "visualising" like the professional coaches advise, Jack was sure he'd figured out how hard to hit the ball. A deep breath, eyes focused on the small white object on the ground, a swing…and the ball sailed over the top of the flag before disappearing into a bunker on the other side of the green. Chattering green parrots in bushy trees that lined the fairway seemed to be mocking his poor play. 'An effin' sand trap on the first damn hole!' Jack flung the club towards the electric buggy they had rented, then shook a fist at the avian spectators. 'Who designs these courses? The Marquis de bleedin' Sade?'

'Careful, Jack!' Trevarthen blurted. 'I paid for that buggy with my credit card, if you damage it by throwing…'

But Jack wasn't listening. He reefed a sand wedge from his bag and stomped around the side of the elevated green. He wasn't sure if he could hear Trevarthen chuckling or if it was the birds again. Then the noise got louder. A buzzing sound like a thousand mosquitoes heading straight towards him. He squinted into the sun as the object skimmed over his head. The thing stopped, hovered in the air two metres or so directly over the brim of Jack's baseball cap. He heard

Trevarthen yelling out garbled words, then sensed the vibrations of his approaching footsteps as he ran towards his boss.

'What on Earth is it?' Trevarthen extended an arm towards the levitating object.

'A drone. But I've not seen one like this before.' The flying machine was an elongated H-shape with four arms bearing whizzing rotors. Black struts, visible red and green wires, with a stumpy, angular object crudely attached at the front end with what appeared to be grey gaffer tape. 'I reckon that's a jerry-rigged camera hanging there, look.'

'Yep. I'd say so.' Trevarthen squinted. 'Actually, no, I think that's an inbuilt camera under it. I can see a flashing light.'

'What's that then?' Jack pointed at the L-shaped blackness.

'Not sure, could be some kind of data logger,' Trevarthen replied. The machine's buzzing noise increased, now loud enough to make the two men wince and put fingers to their ears. The volume then dropped by half, rose again, before the device elevated to a height of about five metres. It waggled from side to side a few times, then zoomed off. It followed the path from the right of the green that led to the next tee and disappeared behind a stand of pandanus palm trees.

'That's a bit intrusive, don't you think?' said Jack.

Trevarthen shook his head. 'I reckon some kids are having a laugh. Frightening golfers and filming them. We'll probably end up being YouTube sensations by tonight.'

Jack pursed his lips. 'It's an effin' menace, that's what it is. I'm going to investigate this and kick up a stink.'

Trevarthen chuckled under his breath and returned to the far side of the green. Jack glanced up, mentally calculating the distance to the pin. He wriggled his feet into the soft sand to get purchase. This shot was going to be a Hail Mary. He had no idea how far behind the sand he was supposed to hit the ball. Should he give it a full swing or a stiff-armed jab? No, the "golden middle" in between was what was required.

He paused a moment to curl his bottom lip and blow an annoying fly away from his nose. A deep breath and a couple of practice swings beside the ball. Yes, Jack was pretty sure he'd get this one in the sweet spot and the ball would land a metre or so past the pin and then, with the gentle backspin he'd impart, it would roll back towards the hole. Too easy.

Then, all hell broke loose.

## Point Blank: Chapter Two

THE IMAGES on the 10-inch first-person-view monitor shook about annoyingly. Sweat beaded on the skin between his nose and top lip. The pads of his thumbs worked on the thin black control sticks as he guided the device onward. The slightest touch impacted on the drone's flightpath. Nudge the left joystick for up and down and rotating side-to-side, the right one for forward and back. But there'd be very little back movement – just ploughing relentlessly forward to reach the target.

More sweat formed, trickled down the back of his neck. Eyes narrowed as he focused on the job. His heart raced like a freight train. Swirling sounds of blood rushing inside his head. Like the sound of the sea when you hold a shell to your ear. Except it was in both ears at once.

He blinked a droplet away, closed his eye and quickly wiped the lid with his upper arm, never letting go of the controller. Then, eyes quickly back to the FPV monitor. The tricky terrain of the golf course, plus the five kilometres separating him from the target, didn't make a hard job easier. On the plus side, he was safely tucked away. His location was comfortable, remote and secure, with practically zero likelihood of being disturbed. The signal to the drone was strong – the communications facilities in the area perfect for maintaining a steady flight path without the signal dropping out and derailing the mission.

Six months of intense training had gone into this plan. Practise, practise and practise some more, until it became a matter of muscle memory. Like driving a back-hoe or a ride-on-mower or a forklift, until you could make all the right moves without even thinking about it. Most people had no idea of the technical skill required to manoeuvre a complex machine in three dimensions. It was damned difficult and he was proud of the hard work he'd put in – hours and hours of boring drills, recharging batteries countless times, the odd crash. No one had a clue what he was up to. Once this task was completed, he'd drop the hobby with more enthusiasm than a kid freed from after-school piano practice. He'd carried out all his training in a supremely clandestine fashion, away from curious eyes. And ears – this bad boy made more noise than he would have liked. But hey, that was the current state of technology and, as he was fond of repeating to himself – *it is what it is*.

And that was just the flying part of the operation.

There was also the gun part to nail down. A video he'd found on YouTube proved the set-up was not only possible, but functional and effective. Mount a semi-automatic pistol on a drone and fire it remotely. He'd had to practice long hours, hovering and shooting at tin cans on a fence, working out how to keep firing after the flight path was altered by vicious recoil. At last, after three months of practice, he was satisfied. His skill levels were good enough to execute the plan and bring the fucker down.

The cream on the cake was the addition of a megaphone, attached with Velcro and activated via a dedicated transmitter unit. That sucker could blast sound a distance of 1200 metres, had three hours of talk time and 24 hours stand-by. Not that anything like that would be required for this mission; this would be an in-your-face announcement followed by a clean execution from a distance of less than two metres. In total, the modified quadcopter capable of carrying the required payload, including the semi-automatic pistol – nearly a kilogram with a full clip – and the loudspeaker, had cost over a grand. But the result was going to make it all worth while.

At first, when he watched the online video, it all sounded and looked easy. But that was a two-minute long news report, not a step-by-step guide. So he had to figure it out himself. And to be extra careful, his research had been carried out at a library, logging onto the Internet anonymously, even reading old-fashioned printed books. And not a local library either; he made several trips to Cairns to gather the information he needed to buy the right drone and turn it into a killing machine. A lot of slog, sure. But it would all be worth it once the target was neutralised.

Despite the practice and drills, though, the danger of a collision or a mechanical failure was ever-present. A bird could swoop on the drone, a wayward golf ball could knock it out of the sky. Or he could do what humans often do in stressful situations – simply fuck up. If the craft crashed, the chances of him being discovered increased by an order of magnitude.

And so, at this most critical moment, his concentration was at peak level.

He hunched his shoulders, one more left turn at the back of the $18^{th}$ hole and he'd be on the way to the first tee.

Exactly where the trio would be hitting off at – he checked the convenient digital clock in the corner of the screen – 09:30. And if people filmed it all, so what! The drone would be ditched out to sea where it would sink to the bottom, never to be found again.

The drone cruised at a height of fifteen metres to clear the tallest trees on the course. He piloted the machine to a position vertically above the first tee, panned the camera down. And there they...wait, what?

*Shit! It's not them.* Instead of the expected party, it was a quartet of pensioners. He knew the prime target was a stickler for punctuality – could they have cancelled the round? Maybe they weren't even on the course at all... Or, maybe they'd gotten off to an early start. Yes, that must be it!

A mental recalculation, a toggle of the sensitive controls, and he was – virtually – down at the first hole putting green, levitating above two guys mucking about in a bunker.

*Again, not the target!* The man with the weather-beaten face and craggy nose, shielding his eyes as he stared directly into the camera, was annoyingly familiar. It was the face of a violent man best not to mess with. He might view the footage later and try to ID him. No time to waste, though. The hunt was becoming desperate.

One more hole. If the target wasn't there, he'd abort the mission. If the course managers got wind of an unauthorised drone buzzing about...anything could happen.

He flew to the second hole tee block. Vacant. And then the camera picked them up, standing in a bunch halfway up the fairway. *The plan would be carried out to completion.*

Under a cloudless, clear blue sky, the drone and its deadly cargo raced up the middle of the neatly mown fairway. Three pairs of curious eyes turned up to observe. Smiles of wonder on their faces.

He took a deep breath as he set the device to hover, aligned the camera's cross hairs to a point exactly above the target's head. He pressed a button to turn on the megaphone. His voice would be scrambled by software – none of the party would recognise who was speaking. *This is it, no turning back now.*

'Come a step closer please, sir. We're taking photos of our favourite members for the Country Club yearbook.'

Oh my God. The egotistical prick's doing it. He's actually doing it. He's grinning like an idiot, saying something to the two people with him. The drone only carried a loudspeaker, not a microphone. Sadly, his last words won't be recorded for posterity. What a shame. Now he's laying his five iron on the turf. The vain bastard's even taking off his cap and smoothing his mane of black hair. A beaming smile. The drone dropped to be level with the man's forehead, inched forward towards the beaming fool.

'Say cheese!'

A press of another button and the gun jerked the drone backwards with the recoil. BANG! Right on target. A split second to realign. Another shot to finish him off. BANG!

Now, time for the old man...

**Grab your copy...
vinci-books.com/point-blank**

## About the Author

Blair Denholm is a born-and-bred Australian crime fiction writer whose previous jobs have been as varied as translator, debt collector, technology researcher, banking and insurance consultant, and even car-wash attendant. Over the years he has lived and worked in New York, Moscow, Munich, Abu Dhabi and Australia. His life-long love of sports is reflected in the plots of The Fighting Detective series.

Denholm's flagship series, The Fighting Detective, stars ex-boxer Detective Sergeant Jack Lisbon and is set in the steamy tropics of North Queensland, Australia. The series features heavy doses of noir crime with a vigilante justice twist. So far there are eight novels and one prequel novella in the series, with more in the pipeline.

Denholm's debut novel, *SOLD*, is the first in a noir trilogy featuring the detestable yet lovable one-man wrecking ball Gary Braswell. The book was long-listed for movie adaptation by Screen Queensland in 2019. The other books in this series are *Sold to the Devil* and *Sold Dirt Cheap*.

Denholm has also written two thriller novels set in Russia. Captain Viktor Voloshin is a hard-boiled investigator who has to fight the establishment in order for justice to be served in his own special way. The first in this series, *Revolution Day*, was published in 2021, with the follow-up, *The Defector*, released in 2024. One more book will round off this series.

In 2024, Denholm signed on with UK-based publisher Vinci Books.

Blair Denholm grew up in suburban Brisbane, Queensland. After two lengthy stints in Tasmania, he now resides in the relatively cooler climes of the Southern Downs region of Queensland with his partner, Sandra, and faithful dog, Bruno.

## Acknowledgments

This one is for all my hard-core loyal readers who support me through thick and thin. You guys are what keeps me going when things aren't going according to plan. And, as always, to Sandra.

www.ingramcontent.com/pod-product-compliance
Ingram Content Group UK Ltd.
Pitfield, Milton Keynes, MK11 3LW, UK
UKHW040230220126
467235UK00004B/65